SILVER MAGIC

BRUCE DAVIS

Brick Cave Media
brickcavebooks.com

Silver Magic

Cover Illustration Artist: Thitipon Decruen
www.xric7.com

Brick Cave Media
brickcavebooks.com
2022

Dedication:

To those who value excellence above ease, truth above fiction, and fiction as a way of revealing truth.

Silver Magic

BRUCE DAVIS

Brick Cave Media
brickcavebooks.com

CHAPTER ONE

By the third night, the death count was rising so fast that several senior teams were pulled off the front lines of riot control and put into emergency investigative rotations in the central Hollows, east of Canal and south of Knacker. Lieutenant Simon Buckley, the newly promoted head of the Magic Enforcement division, was temporarily teamed with Corina Sterling, a day-watch Civil Patrol Lieutenant. They were assigned to a roving sled with two gunners from Civil Patrol for protection and were dispatched anywhere they were needed, anywhere a new body turned up.

The four-Keeper team moved in a black patrol sled, jumping from crime scene to crime scene, never standing still for long. It wasn't the proper way to investigate a killing, not even close, but it was the best that could be done by a Peacekeeper Force stretched to the breaking point in a city that had come apart at the seams.

The Hollows were a war zone. Fires burned everywhere. Looters moved in packs from storefront to storefront, all semblance of dignity and moral code gone in the smoke that rose over Cymbeline, reaching in dense clouds as far as the posh shopping districts of the North Side. The Orc gangs of the Hollows stepped in to control the darkness, even calling for a truce in their own turf war to create a united front against the King's Peacekeepers.

More than one hundred people, mostly Orcs, but also Dwarves, Humans and a few Elves, had died already. Shopkeepers had killed looters, Peacekeepers had killed looters, and looters had killed looters all in varying combinations of self-righteous defense of property, perceived protection of innocents, and disputes over the spoils of a burning shop or warehouse. Then there were the others—killers who used the camouflage of chaos and riot to settle old scores that had nothing to do with the frustrations of the moment or the emotions of the streets.

The black sled raced through the acrid smell of burning garbage and the smoldering dreams of a thousand Orcs. Flames from hundreds of fires flickered like demons dancing in the dark sky. Shouts of rage and of pain and of fear echoed nonstop in the wake of the patrol sled. But the four Keepers in Sled 6-King-18 did not stop for any of these. They stopped only for murder.

They were on B-Watch, the emergency mobilization designation for night watch, a twelve-hour shift from eighteenth hour, through midnight to sixth hour in the morning. Buckley and Sterling had the back seat while Keepers Steelhelm and Delwyn from Civil Patrol had the front. Delwyn drove. Steelhelm, in the passenger seat, held his D'Stang repeating bolt thrower across his lap, its muzzle poking through the open window.

They were rolling to a dead body found in an alley

off Canal Street. This was 6-King-18's third call of the night and it was still ten minutes shy of twenty-first hour. The last one had been both easy and hard—a looter shot through the head with a pneumatic bolt fired by a shop owner. Both were Orcs, but the looter was only sixteen years old, and the bolt pistol was an unregistered Gowron the shopkeeper had bought from a low-level gang soldier the day before. On any other day there would have been serious charges pending. Maybe there still would be once things calmed down. But Simon doubted it. He and Corina had recorded the shop owner's statement including his frank admission of the illegal purchase of the weapon, while Steelhelm and Delwyn stood guard in full riot gear, D'Stang's at the ready. The body would be picked up by an ordinary cargo sled driven by Keeper auxiliaries. The Coroner's Office was too overwhelmed to send a team for a dead looter.

Orc on Orc crime was low priority on a quiet day. Simon knew this would be written off and buried in the chaos. Not the right way, but the mission was simply to get in and get out. And do it safely. Any real investigation would come later. Maybe.

They drove south on Canal, passing occasional crowds of Orcs, mostly young males gathered on corners or in roving packs. At Canal and Hob, a group wearing Loblolly colors jeered as the sled raced by at high speed, without lights or siren. A hail of cobblestones and bottles followed, but the sled moved too fast and most fell harmlessly behind. A Fire spell exploded in an already burning shop off to their right, but the sled skated easily past the sudden rush of flame.

"We'll be back," Steelhelm bellowed through the open window, his Dwarfish burr carrying above the fading shouts of the Loblollies.

Simon smiled grimly. The young Keeper's threat

was as hollow as Simon's own promise to protect the King from blowback from his daughter's abdication. Six weeks ago, he'd helped Princess Rebeka and one of his own team, Fire mage Liam Aster, get out of the Commonwealth to the Free States. The story had initially been one of a foolish young woman abdicating her title to run off with a commoner. What Simon and only a few others knew was that the Princess was a latent Fire mage who could barely control her magic and who had set several fires in the Hollows. She had thought she was burning only drug stashes, but the last fire had also killed the Chieftain of the Canal Street Scalpers and three of his top enforcers.

Simon thought that secret was safe and secure, but somehow word had leaked out that Farsk Kronska and his top boyos had been killed by an unregistered Human mage. At first it was only a rumor, but then one of the scandal sheets had picked up the story and run it with pictures of the burned warehouse and a statement from an "anonymous source" within the Peacekeeper Force that the crime was being covered up to protect "important people."

That had been enough to rupture the fragile racial, social and economic fractures that ran under the city with seismic intensity. Crowds of angry Orcs had gathered on the streets to decry the injustice. Never mind that Kronska had been a predator who had preyed on his own people. He'd been an Orc, killed by a Human mage linked to the seats of power. Before long, things turned violent and the ever-vigilant media went high and live from the air, broadcasting images into every home in the city, and then to much of the world.

Delwyn steered the sled at high speed around barriers of burning trash, the skeletons of wrecked sleds and acres of shattered glass, never slowing until they reached a blockade of armored personnel sledges athwart Canal Street and manned by a Peacekeeper Special Response Team. The current strategy was to seize control of several main thoroughfares and then move outward, containing trouble spots and driving organized resistance into isolated pockets.

As he pulled up to the barricade, Delwyn lowered his window. A SpRT Keeper with a Sergeant's badge on his tactical vest approached and leaned down to look at the sled's occupants.

"Sergeant Burstin, Fifth Squad. What can I do for you fellows?" he asked.

"Murder Squad." Delwyn hooked a thumb toward Simon and Sterling.

Burstin straightened and made a wide circular motion with his arm. A path was cleared so they could go through.

"Right," Burstin said. "She's in the alley between Canal and Claridge. We found her about ten minutes after we got in position here as we were setting up a perimeter. Go on through and my guys will show you where."

Delwyn put his window back up as they drove through.

"My guys," he said, mimicking Burstin's Dundarian accent. "That guy's probably never been south of King's Road. I heard most of the Spurt teams were brought in from Dundaria and Fallonvale. From anywhere but Cymbeline, as if the local guys couldn't be trusted. Probably couldn't find the Hollows on a map."

"Two years ago, neither could you," Steelhelm said.

"That's different," protested Delwyn. "And it don't give him the right to be all take charge high and mighty. Like we couldn't handle things."

Sterling spoke up. "I've got news for you, Delwyn. We couldn't handle it. This caught us with our pants down and we've played catch up ever since. Now shut it and do your job so Simon and I can do ours."

Delwyn muttered something under his breath but said nothing more out loud. He brought the sled to a stop at the head of the alley and canceled the Air spell that kept it aloft. He was out before it settled to the pavement. Steelhelm joined him without a word and the two of them took up sentry positions on either end of the grounded sled.

One of Burstin's 'guys,' a Keeper named Dorcas with a strong Northwestern accent, led them into the dark alley. Simon pulled a torch from its sheath on his uniform belt and muttered the incantation to turn it on. The Fire spell sent a small tingle down his spine as it activated and a blue ball of light kindled in the torch's reflective globe. He twisted the handle and focused the harsh light into a tight beam that he swept across the ground. Corina followed close behind, activating her own torch.

"She be just back here," Dorcas pointed into the dark. "'Bout half to the next street." He slowed as if reluctant to go farther.

The alley floor was clotted with debris, mostly old but some new. Looters had passed through, discarding packaging and bags, unwanted small items, and empty liquor bottles. Simon didn't see a body as he played his light back and forth. With a rustle of paper and a clank of bottles striking the ground, a large rat dashed out through the beam of his light, startling him. He stepped back a pace.

Corina moved ahead; her torch set to a tight beam and held shoulder level as she searched the ground in front of them, searching where the rat had been a second before. The blue-white beam reflected off salt white flesh, part of an arm and hand stretched out on the ground as if reaching for the torch.

Simon stepped up, adding his own light to hers. Corina knelt next to the body. Simon could see the shape of a woman lying prone on the trash strewn paving stones, her head turned sideways so that her face was seen in profile. She had the finely pointed ears of a high Elf but her hair was dark brown and curly, like the Free People of the far Northwest, or the Free States. He couldn't make out much else in the focused beam of Corina's light.

"Get some more light down here," he shouted to Dorcas. "We need to do an exam and take some images."

"Right," said the young Keeper who turned and started shouting for his Sergeant.

"Look how pale she is, Simon," Corina said. "She's one of the Free People. They're usually darker skinned than the Havens Elves. She's pale as new snow."

Corina lifted the woman's hand. "Her nail beds are white. So are her lips." She gently lifted the woman's head to look at the side of her face that had been pressed into the pavement. "There's no lividity, no bruising. It's like all her blood has been drained. But I don't see a wound, or a blood trail. Was she moved and dumped here?"

Simon didn't answer. He swept his light slowly along the length of the body. She wore a quilted vest over a long-sleeved silk shirt. The vest was sky blue embroidered with stylized fish in darker blue thread. The shirt was a plain crème color. Dark blue canvas trousers covered her hips and legs and were bloused over lightweight ankle length boots. Her clothes were clean, unstained; the soles of her boots were covered with a sticky black substance, like pitch, to which stuck a few pebbles and shards of glass. Simon saw no bloodstains.

Simon played his light around the area beyond the body. It swept briefly across the wall of a building that made up the Canal Street side of the alley. Simon gasped and swung the torch back, illuminating the wall. Gang signs and other graffiti covered most of the space within easy reach. The multiple layers of paint had built up over time and had been indifferently covered with whitewash as well. But what caught Simon's eyes and held them was the red outline of a person, as if a stencil had been applied over the layers of paint and whitewash. The color was uneven, thick and dark in some spots, lighter and fuzzy in others. A broad streak ran down the center of the image and fed into a puddle of red where the wall met the pavement.

"I think I know where the blood went," Simon said.

CHAPTER TWO

Dorcas returned with a light stand. Simon and Corina helped him set it up across the alley from the strange blood silhouette. Simon muttered the incantation and three powerful glowglobes atop the stand flared to life, illuminating the dark space. Under the harsh artificial light of the globes the alley looked less sinister and more forlorn. At least a century of city grime had stained the paving stones black. Random piles of trash, mostly paper and desiccated garbage, lined the angle between the wall and the pavement.

The dead Elf lay prone, one leg bent at the knee as if stepping up a curb, her right arm outstretched, her left bent under her body. Her skin looked even paler in the blue-white light of the glowglobes. Simon knelt and examined the left side of her face, the side he could see in profile. Her skin was unmarked by scar or blemish. Her ear pattern formed what the forensic mages called a reverse whorl, the ridge of cartilage swirling back and down before sweeping up to the fine point at the tip. He made a note of it because it was uncommon. Unlike Humans, Orcs, and Dwarves, Elves had no fingerprints. But the exact pattern of whorls and curves in an Elf's ears was as unique as Human fingerprints.

His eyes swept down the back of her embroidered vest and trousers. With better light, he noticed that the back of her clothes was slightly darker than the front. He reached out and brushed the vest with the back of his hand, feeling the slight residual dampness. He looked at his hand but there was no obvious blood transfer. He sniffed. The slightly metallic, raw meat smell of blood on the back of his hand almost overwhelmed the damp rot odor of the alley itself.

Simon stood and approached the wall. Meanwhile, Corina had retrieved the image recorder from the boot of the sled and was systematically sweeping it over the scene. Simon stared for a moment at the red outline on the wall, like some bizarre splatter painting. He noticed that the outline matched the position of the body—one hand outstretched and a little off to the side, as if reaching for something; the other not visible, lost in the thicker redness marking the torso. Again, he followed the thick splash of blood in the center down to the ground where it pooled and ran between the paving stones.

Off to the left, about a foot from the wall and even with the dead Elf's left foot he noticed a lump of leather, half concealed by ragged packing paper torn from some looted magic mirror. He bent down and pushed the paper to one side. The lump proved to be a small leather knapsack, half open, with the right shoulder strap ripped away from the back.

"Corina, would you get an image of this before I move it? It might contain some ID or information about who she is."

Corina stepped over and took several images from

different angles. She stopped and stared at the red splash on the wall.

"Gods, Simon. What happened here?"

Simon glanced up at the wall. "Dark magic," he said. "Water spell. It pushes all the blood in the body out through the pores. I've read about it, but never seen it actually used." He stood, lifting the small leather knapsack and looking inside. "And I've never heard of a Water mage powerful enough to cast it."

"I thought Water mages were only good for digging wells and putting out fires." Corina shivered. "Fiendish way to kill someone."

"I've seen worse," said Simon as he rummaged in the knapsack. "At least we know who she was." He held up a laminated badge attached to a string lanyard. "Her name was Anika Sommerstag. She's a reporter for a Free States news outlet, the Associated Reporters Guild. ARG's a minor player here, but pretty well known in Fredonia. Was she covering the riots, do you think?"

Corina frowned. "Fredonia's one of the coastal States. A long way from here. I doubt she'd have had time to travel to Cymbeline from there. More likely she was here for some other reason and saw an opportunity to get a jump on her competitors."

Simon pulled a wallet and an Astral 8 handheld mirror out of the knapsack. He checked the wallet. "Nearly 200 crowns in here," he said. "This wasn't a robbery, and it wasn't random violence. This was a murder. We need a full forensics team down here."

Corina laughed. "Good luck with that."

Simon tucked the knapsack under his arm. "Gotta try. I'll get the crime scene kit from the sled and call it in."

He walked back to the sled. Delwyn and Steelhelm hadn't moved. Steelhelm glanced at Simon and nodded, then resumed scanning the street. Delwyn looked bored. He ignored Simon and fiddled with the magazine of his D'Stang.

Simon reached into the back seat and lifted out the crime scene kit in its worn leather case. The kits were standard issue for Coroners, CSA mages, and Homicide detectives. Simon and his team rarely used them, relying instead on the forensics mages to handle the crime scene.

He dropped the knapsack on the floor of the sled before walking around to the driver side door. He reached in and lifted the Farspeaker stone from its cradle next to the steering yoke. He activated the spell and spoke into the now glowing stone.

"Dispatch, 6-King-18," he said. "We need a forensics team at..." he glanced at the building to his right. "6621 South Canal, in the alley. DB is a foreign national."

"6-King-18, wait one." The dispatcher sounded tired.

Simon waited a full minute as the Farspeaker cracked with the half-heard conversations of other sleds.

"6-King-18, that's a negative on the forensics team. Higher Authority requests you process the scene expeditiously and then report to new crime scene at Knacker and Chandler. Two DB's near that location."

"Dispatch, this victim was killed by an illegal Water spell. Evidence is time critical. Let me speak with B-watch Actual."

"Negative, 6-King-18." The dispatcher's voice had taken on a hard, cold edge. "Actual is Captain Axhart. He's in conference with the King's Prosecutor at the moment. It's not worth my job to disturb him again. Your orders came directly from him. Dispatch out."

Simon slammed the Farspeaker stone back into its cradle with a curse. Off to his left, Delwyn smirked but had enough smarts to say nothing. Simon glared at him before picking up the crime scene kit and stalking back to Corina.

"Any joy on the forensics team?" she asked.

"No," Simon grumbled. "You called it right. The Ax wants us to process this scene 'expeditiously' whatever the hells that means." He set the case on the ground and opened it. "I'll get some blood samples as well as hair and a tissue sample for aural analysis. Do you want to process her clothes or keep recording?"

"I'll record, you get the samples. That way it's easier to certify the chain of custody."

"You got it," said Simon. He took a small scissor and a glass vial out of the kit. He snipped a few inches of hair from the back of Anika's head and put them in the vial, sealing the top. He took out another vial and moved over to the blood spatter on the wall. He noticed that even where the color was thickest, there was little or no clot, just a thick liquid, about the consistency of heavy cream. With the back of his pocketknife, he scraped some of the bloody fluid into the vial, sealing it as well.

Simon returned the vials to the leather case and drew out a metal tube with a sharp beveled tip, like a large needle. He turned to Corina. "Ready?" he asked.

She nodded. "I hate this part."

Together, they rolled Anika onto her back. Corina carefully recorded images of her chest and abdomen. She nodded to Simon.

He knelt and lifted Anika's silk shirt, exposing her right flank and ribcage. He quickly thrust the metal rod into her side, between her lower ribs and deep into her liver. He twisted the handle of the device and heard a muted click as the spring-loaded blade inside it cut a core sample from the liver. He drew it out and placed the entire assembly into the kit.

"That's all we can do right now," said Corina, lowering the image recorder.

Simon snorted. "Gods damned little as it is. This isn't the way to process a crime scene and you know it."

"What do you expect, Simon? In case you hadn't noticed, there are a couple of hundred crime scenes down here in the Hollows. Why do you think this one is different?" Corina turned to face him, hands making a sweeping gesture to the surrounding streets. "What about them?"

Simon stood and snatched up the crime scene kit. "Don't tell me you can't see the difference. This wasn't a looter shot in the heat of the moment. This was murder. Murder by Dark magic, not Orcs killing Orcs over a handful of cheap jewelry."

Corina glared at him. "What is it that bothers you, Simon? That this was illegal magic? Or is it that she's an Elf?"

"Come on, Corina," said Simon. "You know how I feel about Orcs, especially the Orcs down here. This is about the magic. It's my job, Corina."

"And ordinary murder is mine. You think it doesn't gall me that we had to leave that sixteen-year-old kid lying in the middle of the floor? That we couldn't talk to the shopkeeper and find out who sold him the Gowron? Or haul him in for reckless behavior?" She started toward the sled, still holding his eye. "Gods, Simon, get off your high horse and let's just get through this night."

Simon stood for a moment, looking at her back as she walked away. *No, damn me, it isn't because she was an Elf,* he told himself, even as an image of Sylvie Graystorm formed in his mind. *"It's about the magic. It's about someone using this chaos to cover a crime.* He glanced back at Anika Sommerstag. *I will find out who did this. I promise you that.*

He turned and walked quickly after Corina, to offer an apology, or at least say something to mollify her.

CHAPTER THREE

Back at the sled, Delwyn remained insolent, Corina ignored Simon's clumsy attempts to apologize, and Steelhelm looked confused as he shifted his gaze from one to the other. Delwyn drove again, Steelhelm next to him in the front. Simon and Corina settled into an uneasy silence. Simon had set the knapsack from the scene on the seat between them where it formed a sort of barrier.

Simon stared out the window at the flickering light of the fires along Canal Street. Delwyn drove north to Knacker, then turned east toward Chandler, some twenty blocks away.

Knacker Street was quiet for the moment, mainly because the entire south side of the street had been burned out on the first night of the riots. With nothing left to loot or burn, the rioters had moved south and west. The north side of Knacker was residential; dilapidated single-story homes and low-rise tenements, now boarded up as fortification against the violence of the streets. An occasional light glowed in an upper window, but the rest of the houses were dark, as if looking unoccupied might offer some protection.

The sled reached Chandler a few minutes later. Delwyn slowed and pulled in behind another black sled with its orange and green roof lights flashing. Two other sleds blocked access to Chandler Street as four civil patrol Keepers stood in cluster nearby.

Simon jumped out of the back seat almost as soon as Delwyn came to a stop, eager to be doing something. Anything was better than the strained silence with Corina.

One of the Keepers standing near the grounded sleds looked up as Simon approached. He was Human and wore riot gear with a sergeant's badge hanging from the lanyard at his right shoulder.

"You the murder team?" he asked. "Name's Corwin, Night Watch out of Westport."

"Lieutenant Buckley, Magic Enforcement." Simon glanced over his shoulder as Corina stepped around the front of their sled. "This is my partner, Lieutenant Sterling, Day Watch Civil out of Wycliffe House."

Corina's frown softened at Simon's introduction as his partner. "What have you got for us, Sergeant Corwin," she asked.

"Two dead, both Orcs, down on one of the docks off of Chandler." Corwin's voice was matter of fact, a veteran stating the facts. "Looks like drowning, but they weren't in the water. Clothes are dry, so they must have been pulled out some time ago and just left there on the dock."

"Why do you think they drowned?" asked Corina.

"I've been at Westport station near on ten years, Lieutenant. I've seen my share of drownings. They've got the blue lips and pink foam around the mouth that's the mark of that kind of death. Funny thing is, their hair and clothes aren't wet and they're not stiff.

If they were dead long enough to be dry, they should be stiff with rigor. That takes only about four hours for Orcs, and in this weather, they should still be damp at least."

"Any wounds? Any sign of assault or other injury?" asked Corina.

Corwin scratched his chin. "No, but it seemed queer, them laid out on the dock and no sign as to where they went in the water or how they got out. This wasn't an ordinary drowning, Lieutenant." Corwin pointed at Simon. "Something more along the lines of his job is my bet."

Simon said nothing as Corina shot him a glance. *Thanks a lot, Corwin,* he thought.

"Lead on, Sergeant," was all Simon said.

Simon and Corina followed Corwin down the darkened street. The streetlamps were out, and the overcast sky glowed with reflected light from the fires farther east. There was enough light to find their way but not to see any details. The east side of the street fronted the Great Cut, one of the largest canals in the city. Farther north, Tanner Road crossed the Cut over the Haverford iron bridge, once the tallest single span bridge in the world. Here, a mile or more south, the Cut was almost a half mile wide and still affected by the slight tides of the Finnegan River estuary.

Chandler Street was lined with the ships' supply yards from which it took its name as well as fish processing factories and commercial warehouses. Every hundred feet a jetty or wooden pier jutted into the Cut from a gap between buildings that provided access to the main thoroughfare.

Corwin led them into the third gap and out onto a sturdy wooden pier. Orange crime scene rope had been strung across the foot of the pier and two more Civil patrol Keepers stood near its far end under the glow of a portable light stand.

Simon took in the scene. The pier itself was longer than most on this stretch of the Cut and had feeder branches to the left and right that connected to smaller jetties on either side. There was no other access to the water within several hundred feet. The pier and jetties were in good repair, obviously still in use, although empty at this time of night.

Corina looked about as well. "No good access other than this pier, and the water, of course."

Simon nodded. "Not much light, though. Even though it's exposed, not too much to see in the dark, unless you're right on top of it."

They reached the edge and the two Patrol Keepers stepped aside. At their feet lay two Orcs, heads toward the water, feet toward the shore. The Orcs lay side-by-side, face up. They both wore grease spattered tan coveralls bearing some sort of sigil on their breast pockets. The one on the right had on a tool belt with cold iron and brass chisels and a broad headed hammer strung through loops along the left side and a pair of heavy tongs strapped to the right. The second Orc wore a harness strapped to his chest that held a welding torch. The glowing aquamarine gem in the torch's handle showed that its Fire spell was fully charged.

Simon crouched down and touched the back of his hand to the clothing of both Orcs. It was bone dry, not even damp. He examined their features. Both of their faces were mottled and pale with blue discoloration of the lips and ears. Pinkish foam had dried on their lips and their open staring eyes were already clouded. All signs of drowning.

He checked for rigidity by lifting the hand of the Orc on the right. The skin was cold and firm, but the muscles had only started to stiffen. Simon estimated he'd been dead for at least two hours, but less than four.

He stood, glanced at Corina, and walked back to the branch to the left-hand jetty. There was a layer of sand across its surface, undisturbed. He turned back to look at Corina again.

She was just rising from a crouch, having completed her own examination of the bodies. She cocked her head at him, a look of resignation on her face.

"Go ahead, Simon. Make your case," she said.

"First, like Corwin said, their clothes are dry, but there's little to no rigor. Second, they're laid out side by side with their heads toward the water. There's no ladder or hoist at the end of the pier. The only access to the water is the ladder at the end of this jetty. But the sand here hasn't been disturbed. If they'd been dragged there, there'd be traces. And it would have been hard to get their heads that close to the edge and not fall in. Finally, I could see the torch the Orc on the left carries not drifting off, but the chisels and hammer the other fellow has on his belt aren't strapped in, they'd have fallen out if he went in the water." He looked her in the eye, and she looked away.

"You're right," she sighed.

He walked back to her. "This was the same mage at work here. This is Dark magic, Water magic. We need to investigate this properly."

"Let's say you're right," she answered. "What can we do? Dispatch has already denied us a forensics team, and I don't want to be the one to call the Ax out over something like this when he's trying to keep the whole city from burning down."

Simon nodded. "You're right there. Compared to all this," he waved an arm around to take in the flame lit skyline. "Even if it was Dark magic, three deaths against hundreds aren't going to seem very important to Command. But there may be another way."

Corina's eyes narrowed. "What have you got in mind?"

Simon didn't answer but pulled out his mirror instead. He entered a locus.

Kyle Evarts, head forensic mage at Wycliffe House, answered after a few seconds. "Make it fast," he said without greeting. "We're swamped down here."

"Any chance you can break away with a couple of your boys, Kyle?" Simon turned the mirror so Evarts could see the dead Orcs. "I've got a situation here and need your help."

Evarts laughed, a harsh cracked sound. The half-Elven mage looked pale and drained. "No way, Simon. I've got Dead Bodies piled up on the loading dock. More DB's than we have slabs to hold them. I've got my Water mages maintaining cold spells on half the holding cells down in Booking so we can get them off the street. I can't go haring off to the waterfront for a couple of dead Orcs."

"One mage can keep them cold for a couple of hours. This is Dark magic, Kyle. I've got these two drowned without getting their clothing wet and a dead Elf halfway across the Hollows with all of her blood splattered against a wall and not a mark on her. I need you."

Evarts face seemed to light up. "Dry drowning?" He tugged at an earlobe. "A simple precipitation spell could do that. But transdermal exsanguination? That's Master level casting." He looked around and lowered his voice. "Where are you?"

"On the docks down by the Cut, Chandler Street, near Knacker."

"And the Elf?" Evart's's voice was almost a whisper.

"6621 South Canal, in the alley behind the furniture shop. Scene commander there is a SpRT Sergeant named Burstin, a Dundarian fellow who seems like a cool head."

Evarts tugged at his earlobe again then seemed to come to a decision. "Call him. Tell him to keep the scene intact. Don't let them move the body. It'll take me a half hour to get out of here with a couple of my guys who can keep quiet about this. I'll go to Canal and send them around to you to start processing the Orcs."

"Thanks, Kyle," said Simon, but the mage had already broken the connection.

Simon spoke to the two Keepers nearby. "Keep this scene secure. There's a team on the way. Lieutenant Sterling and I need to get back to our sled and coordinate a few things."

Corina followed him back to the street. "Did you just go around the Ax to get a forensics team down here?"

Simon smiled. "No. I just told Wycliffe's chief forensics mage what was going on out here. How he allocates his department's resources is entirely up to him."

"Right," scoffed Sterling. She grew thoughtful. "If you're right, though, someone is using the riots to cover their tracks. But what do a couple of Orc tradesmen have to do with a reporter from the Free States. It doesn't track."

Simon shrugged. "I don't know. But I promised Anika I'd find out."

Sterling gave him a sidelong glance but said nothing.

They reached the sled and Simon lifted the FS stone from its cradle. "Give us a second, fellows," he said to Delwyn and Steelhelm. He handed the stone to Corina.

"You make the call," he said. "I'm already on record as asking for a team and FS calls can be monitored. If you ask for Burstin, it's less likely Dispatch will notice."

Sterling looked doubtful, but she took the stone. "Dispatch, this is 6-King-18. I need a patch."

"6-King-18, Dispatch, state your patch request," the operators voice may have been someone different, but Simon couldn't be sure.

"Dispatch, patch requested to SpRT Squad 5, Sergeant Burstin."

"6-King-18, wait one."

There was a burst of static and then a Dundarian accented voice said, "SpRT 5, Burstin."

Simon took the stone. "Sergeant Burstin, this is Lieutenant Buckley. Is our Elf still in the alley?"

"Aye, and she ain't going anywhere soon. Pickup is at least an hour out."

"Good." Simon breathed a sigh of relief. "Keep the scene secure until a forensics mage by the name of Evarts shows up. Don't let them take the body without his say-so."

"Aye, Lieutenant. Can do. You pull some strings for this?"

"Just tweaked a mage's interest, that's all."

"Right. Burstin out."

Simon replaced the stone and said, "Thanks, Corina. Let's start imaging the scene and get the preliminaries done before Evarts's boys show up."

No sooner had he said it, than the FS speaker squawked. "6-King-18, Dispatch. Status report."

Simon lifted the stone again. "Dispatch, 6-King-18. On scene at Chandler south of Knacker."

"6-King-18 be advised, new assignment, 618 West Knacker, second floor. Command requests you expedite current scene and proceed to new location."

"Dispatch, 6-King-18, acknowledged." Simon replaced the stone. "No rest," he said to Corina.

"Gods, I hope this stunt doesn't blow back on us, Simon. I like being a Lieutenant."

He smiled. "Have a little faith. We're a high-profile murder team. What could go wrong?"

She shook her head with a bitter laugh. "You may

be able to get away with this shit. You're the Ax's golden boy. Me? I'm just a hard-working Keeper trying to get through my twenty and retire."

Simon didn't answer. He looked instead at the sticky black residue on the bottom of his shoes.

CHAPTER FOUR

They dragged into Wycliffe House just before seventh hour, tired and irritable. They'd fielded over ten calls during the shift, finally slowing down around fourth hour as even the rioters seemed to tire of the violence.

They'd caught one last call at half past fifth that had kept them overtime. Nothing special, what looked like an ordinary domestic violence situation that had gotten out of hand because of the general violence all around. The woman, a Human married to an Orc, had stabbed her husband with a pair of scissors because he'd come home drunk and had smacked her around. Simon felt some sympathy for her when he'd seen the bruises on her cheek and her swollen eye. But he'd had no choice but to put her in shackles and call for a sledge to take her away. The whole time they'd waited for the pick-up, the woman had sobbed uncontrollably and apologized over and over to her dead husband.

Simon held on to Anika Sommerstag's small

knapsack as they climbed out of the sled. Corina went to check in with the stablemaster. Simon turned in his duty sidearm to the armorer. He kept the Czech and Hawley needler in his concealed shoulder holster as a personal weapon and climbed the two flights of stairs to the squad room. The day watch was at work, although most were already out on the streets. It gave the normally bustling space an eerily empty feeling. Simon left Corina at her desk near the staircase and headed toward his office on the command level. They had completed most of their reports during the lull between fourth and fifth hours and Sterling had volunteered to finish the report on the last call.

Simon cast a glance toward the frosted glass and wood cubicle at the far corner of the room. His old office, now the domain of Haldron Stonebender, his Dwarfish foster father and new Sergeant in charge of Simon's old team. Hal and the team were likely out on riot control duty and he wouldn't be able to ask the old Dwarf for advice until the end of shift.

He climbed the stairs to the third level and made his way to his own office. As usual, his secretary, Lessa Greenwater, was at her desk looking fresh and organized. He nodded as he entered and dragged himself across the small anteroom and into his office. He slumped behind his desk and closed his eyes.

He opened them a few minutes later as Lessa entered and set a steaming mug of coffee in front of him with her right hand and a stack of message flimsies and papers with her left.

He picked up the mug and sipped gratefully. "Thank you, Lessa."

"You're welcome, sir," she answered. "I've arranged the messages in order of priority, and there's a report from the Forensics lab on the bottom."

Simon waved a hand tiredly. "Thanks," he said. "And call me Simon, or LT or Lieutenant, if you must.

I'm too young to be 'sir'."

"Yes, sir," she answered with a smile. It was a discussion they'd had many times in the few weeks Simon had been in the job. He still had a hard time with the whole concept of an office and a secretary.

In truth, Lessa was perfect for him; organized, personable and efficient, but distant enough that he felt comfortable giving her orders without explanation. She was an Orc, but that mattered little to Simon. He knew that some at the House saw this as proof that he was a hopeless Progressive, but he cared little about that either. Lessa had learned her duties from Elvira Cairns, Gelbard Axhart's legendary Dwarfish secretary who could reduce even Hal Stonebender to stammering silence with a single withering glare. That was good enough for Simon.

"Will there be anything else, sir...uh, LT?" Lessa asked.

"No thank you, Lessa."

She closed the door as she left, and Simon took another sip of the coffee. He flipped through the messages but saw nothing that needed his immediate attention. There were brief status reports from his three Sergeants about the activities of their teams, again nothing of consequence since they were all on riot control duty. There was a note from Hal asking him to meet sometime during the day shift. Simon thought about that for a second and decided he'd stop down at Hal's office before he went home to sleep.

The bottom sheaf of papers was Kyle Evarts's preliminary forensics report. Simon pushed the rest of the reports aside and started reading. The first page was just a description of the scene, of the position of Anika's body, and an aural analysis that placed the time of death within ten minutes either side of twentieth hour. That tallied with Simon's initial impressions.

She had died as a result of a Water spell—transcutaneous exsanguination. A powerful mage had accelerated all the liquid in her blood vessels in the same direction, forcing it out through the pores of her skin. What Simon had seen as blood was actually the water and protein and heme that had once been contained in her red blood cells. It explained why the stain on the wall had not clotted and why there was so little residual on her clothes.

The second paper was a report on the two Orcs found on the dock. The aural analysis put their time of death at just before 18:30, so within ninety minutes of Anika. The two had not yet been identified, but they carried tools that were suspicious for less than legal purposes. Many of the loose tools were made of brass which canceled certain Air and Fire spells, mostly those used in Warding alarms. Then there were the lead shims and dowels found in a concealed pouch, proof against nearly any door or window Ward. Even the torch that one of them had carried was modified to conceal any residue from its use.

Both Orcs had been killed by the same condensation spell. The spell had caused the water vapor in their lungs to instantly condense. Each breath they drew in filled their lungs with more water, drowning them as they struggled to breathe.

Aural readings showed that the same mage had cast both spells, but the pattern was not recorded in any commercial or criminal registry. A handwritten notation from Evarts indicated he was checking military registries and had reached out to colleagues in the Free States.

A final notation indicated the black residue on Anika's boots was marine pitch, used to seal the wooden hulls of canal barges. Simon jotted a quick note to have one of the teams check for break-ins in the warehouse district near the crime scene.

He drained the last of his coffee, set the mug to one side and began emptying the contents of the small knapsack that had belonged to Anika Sommerstag. He arranged the items on his desktop.

First the reporter identification card with Anika's image and press agency printed on one side, and the official seal of the Communication Ministry on the back. The card was laminated in clear resin and attached to a black cord lanyard. Next, her passport from the city-state of Fredonia, one of the loose confederation of cities and small states known as the Free States. The date of entry stamped on the last page showed that she had entered the Commonwealth through the West Faring port of entry two weeks earlier.

Simon set the passport next to the identification card and removed Anika's wallet from the bag. It contained one hundred eighty Crowns in twenty Crown notes as well as four gold Henriks, so named for the Crown Prince's likeness on the five-crown coins. Two hundred total. Not an unusual amount, but more than Simon usually walked around with. He made a mental note to check with one of his contacts in the news corps to see if that would be common for a foreign reporter traveling light in the Commonwealth. The sum pretty much ruled out robbery as a motive. It was more than enough to tempt any cutpurse from the Hollows.

He groped in the small knapsack, hoping to find a room key or receipt that might tell him where Anika had been staying during her time in the capital. He drew out a small leather-bound notebook with a short stylus on a strap attached to the binding. He opened the book. The pages were filled with closely spaced notes in an elegant hand. Unfortunately, they were written in some sort of code or shorthand notation that Simon was unable to read. Wedged between the binding and the last page of the notebook was a flat rectangle of ebony, about the thickness and width of his thumbnail and half as long as his forefinger. It was inlaid with a strip of aquamarine on one flat surface. Simon recognized it as the summoning wood from a handheld mirror. If he or the forensics team could activate it, the wood might contain a record of the loci it had called and any images the mirror might have saved

The rest of the contents of the knapsack were personal clothing, underwear, and a pair of hose. Simon wondered if this was the whole of Anika's travel kit, or if she had other luggage stored somewhere. He looked through the forensics report again, but the inventory of her clothing contained no mention of a hotel or room key. There was no other personal information in her clothing or pockets.

So, what were you doing in Cymbeline? Simon thought. *And why would you go alone into a riot zone?*

Simon returned all the items to the knapsack, filled out a short form attesting that he had removed and examined the contents and that nothing had been diverted or separated from the lot. He signed the form and included it in the bag. He'd drop it off with the forensics lab before he left the House.

He leaned back in his chair. It had belonged to his former boss, a Lieutenant named Gulbrandsen who had lost his badge and his freedom in a scandal involving Orc terrorists and an Elf nobleman from the Gray Havens. Gulbrandsen had come from money and liked fine things. It was a very comfortable chair.

Simon must have dozed off, for he jerked upright at Lessa's soft knock on the door. He glanced at the timepiece on the wall. It was near on tenth hour.

"Come in," Simon called as he rubbed his eyes.

"Sorry to disturb you, s...LT, but Sergeant Stonebender is here. He'd like to see you."

Simon smiled. "Send him in."

Before Lessa could turn, Hal Stonebender swept into the room. He was dressed in his regular uniform, not riot gear. His chest-length beard was trimmed, and he looked far better rested than Simon felt.

Simon stood and stepped around the desk to embrace his foster father.

"Good to see you, Hal," he said.

"And you, lad," Hal answered in his thick Dwarfish burr. "I guess now that you're a high and mighty Lieutenant you can get away with napping on the job."

Simon grinned at Hal's ribbing. "Aye, and I guess your senior status has gotten you off riot detail." Simon laid heavy emphasis on the word senior.

"Just a poor old Street Keeper, trying to get by. But as to that, the teams have been returned to regular duty as of ninth hour this morning. You should have gotten a message on it." Simon glanced at the stack of message flimsies he'd hastily reviewed.

"Sorry, it was a tough night and I haven't properly looked over the latest news."

Hal nodded. "I heard about your little caper with Evarts. Better hope the Ax doesn't get wind of it."

"So, what's the latest on the street," Simon asked, changing the subject.

"Looks like we're finally getting the upper hand. SpRT teams control all the major bridges and intersections, and Civil Patrol is on the street in regular uniforms. Riot teams are standing down as a gesture of goodwill. Most of the serious devilment seems to have burned itself out. Command has released most of the special details back to normal duties."

"Thank the gods," sighed Simon. "How did it come to this, Hal? I know it was bad down in the Hollows, but I always thought it was about the poverty, not about the race."

Hal grunted. "You always were the idealist. Might have been, one day, the world would have come around to your point of view. Ask me, that day's been pushed back a good bit over the past week."

"You may be right," Simon agreed. "What's on our plate now that we're back to business?"

"Aside from your rogue Water mage, you mean?" asked Hal.

"What have you heard about that?"

"Nothing much," Hal shrugged. "I heard you called for a forensics team to look into the dead Elf but got turned down. Then when a couple of dead Orcs turned up, you did a side dig around dispatch and called out Evarts on your own hook."

Simon leaned against his desk. "It wasn't quite like that, Hal. I just called Evarts informally and told him what we'd found. He decided to come to the scene with a couple of his boys."

"You stick to that story, lad. Especially when the Ax calls you on the green carpet."

"It was the right thing to do, Hal."

The old Dwarf waved a hand at him and sat down heavily in the chair in front of Simon's desk. "Since when did that cut any shale with Command? I don't doubt you, lad. Some mage is out there using the riots as cover for foul murder. I understand. But you need to tread lightly for a while."

Simon frowned and walked back around his desk. He sat down and leaned his elbows on the desktop. "What's going on, Hal? What have you heard?"

Hal had been a Peacekeeper for longer than most of the rest of the force had been alive. He had wide reaching contacts and seemed to know everything that happened in the Force almost as soon as it happened.

Hal scratched at his beard. "Nothing specific. Just that the Inspector General is looking into the circumstances of the Crown Princess's abdication."

Simon felt a chill. "What do they know?"

"Know?" scoffed Hal. "Nothing. Just rumors and

innuendo. The Weasel Squad thinks it's 'interesting' that the Princess left to marry her Fire mage lover just after the arson that killed Farsk Kronska and his top boyos. They're wondering if there was any collusion between Magic Enforcement and the arsonist to keep the nature of the fire under the sod and spare important people in the Peacekeepers any 'embarrassment'."

"They're looking at Liam for that?" Simon asked.

"No, Liam's out of their reach. They're looking at you for helping him escape the country and covering up the identity of the real arsonist."

"No," Simon whispered. "They can't be looking at the Princess. I gave the King my word. I committed Captain Axhart, and George Latham, and Stenson Harold to a conspiracy to keep her secret. We can't let it get out that she set the fire."

Hal made a calming gesture with his hand. "Rein in, lad. There's no talk of the Princess. They seem to think you and Aster hatched the plot and that the Ax may have known about it. The Princess is being cast as a naïve victim here. They'll make a run at you to try to get to Axhart."

"Who tipped them off, Hal? Was it Frank Killian?"

Hal barked a sharp laugh. "No, Killian doesn't know dreck about this. Besides, he's too afraid of the Cabal to talk to anyone, much less the Weasel Squad." Hal paused and stroked his beard. "My guess would be someone who has a gripe with Axhart and is high enough to have contacts in the Royal House. How well do you know Harold? He's the head of Palace Security and can't be too popular with their Majesties for letting their daughter consort with a commoner."

Simon shook his head. He wasn't so sure about Hal's dismissal of Killian, but he knew where Stenson Harold's loyalty lay. "Stenson loves the Princess like one of his own daughters. He'd die to protect her. And the King met Liam. He may not approve of his daughter 'consorting' with a commoner, but he blessed the idea once it was clear that she'd have to abdicate anyway. The Commonwealth Accords are strict on the point of Royalty wielding magic. If word got out that she was a Fire mage, it could spark a revolution that would make these riots look like a rowdy block party."

"So, not likely the Royal House. That leaves it in our laps." Hal pursed his lips. "I'll check around, see what rocks I can turn over."

CHAPTER FIVE

Simon and Hal spent a few more minutes going over the open cases the teams were working. There wasn't much of note, just the usual magic-based swindles and insurance fraud cases, one murder by immolation that was awaiting extradition from the Ironlands where the killer had fled to seek asylum with some distant relatives, and a case of illegal golem animation that had resulted in the death of the mage who had done it without the proper obedience spell.

"Who's up next in the rotation?" asked Simon.

Hal frowned. "Gervis Birchfield. But if it's all the same to you, I'd like to give him the Ironlands case and take this one on my team."

Simon thought for a moment before shaking his head. "No. I know Gervis is a bit green, but we all have to learn to run with the big dogs at some point. Besides, I need you on the Ironlands case. We may need to invoke the Stonebender name to get the extradition warrant, and I want you to be the one to make the pickup there."

Hal looked like he was going to protest, but then nodded in understanding. The Ironlander Dwarves were a suspicious lot, and Stonebender was an old and noble name. Having a patriarch of House Stonebender as the Commonwealth representative in the detention of a criminal in the Ironlands might be helpful in getting the extradition approved.

"Birchfield won't ask for help," said Hal. "He's got a problem with that."

"I know, Hal," Simon answered. "But he's a damned good investigator and a solid team leader. He's a bit too sure of himself, I know, but I'll be looking over his shoulder. This one feels personal."

Hal frowned again. "Don't let her being an Elf get you at crossed tunnels. Work the case, not the victim."

Simon waved a hand. "I will, Hal. This isn't my first dance."

Hal gave him a dubious look, but nodded, nevertheless. "Right then. Go home and rest. Molly will expect you tomorrow night for dinner, so be on time."

Simon nodded. Over the years, they had developed a tradition of Weeksend dinner at the Stonebender house in suburban Glenharrow. Usually it was just Simon, Hal, and Molly, Hal's formidable wife and Simon's foster mother. Not infrequently, one of Simon's foster brothers would come and would bring his family. And whenever Sylvie Graystorm was in the capital, she would make a point of being there. A little over a year earlier, Molly had granted Sylvie Rights of the Hall, making her practically family. Simon knew his foster mother dreamed of the day she would celebrate Simon and Sylvie's wedding. He just wasn't in a hurry to make her dream come true.

"I'll be there," Simon said.

Hal stood and took his leave. Simon rechecked the

stack of messages and found the update returning his teams to normal duties. He stacked the forensic reports and his notes from both crime scenes and placed them in a folder noting the time and date. He'd turn what he had over to Birchfield along with Anika's knapsack.

He found Gervis Birchfield in his cubicle near the back of the squad room. In size it was the same as Hal's office, Simon's old place. But instead of the battered couch and government issue desk that Hal still used, Birchfield had brought in or requisitioned a new desk of modern design. It was chrome steel and blond wood and looked like it belonged in a real estate office rather than a Peacekeeper station. A pair of matching chairs faced the desk and a polished wooden file cabinet stood behind it.

Birchfield looked up when Simon knocked on the doorframe. The young Sergeant jumped to his feet when he saw who was at the door.

"LT," he said. "What can I do for you?"

"As you were, Gervis." Simon waved a hand. "I have a case for you. Actually, a couple of them, but they're linked, so find the answer to one and it'll likely lead to the other." He held out the forensics reports, and Corina Sterling's write up of the crime scenes.

Birchfield flipped through the pages, skimming the reports. He sat down with a low whistle. He looked up at Simon. "Heavy magic, LT."

Simon nodded and sat down in the nearest chair. He set the knapsack on the desk. "This was Anika Sommerstag's. Her reporter's credentials and wallet are inside. She was working for a news outfit from the Free States."

"Entry visa?" Birchfield asked.

"Not in her possession. And she either travels light, or she has a room or base somewhere. There's nothing much else in the sack."

Birchfield set the knapsack aside. "I'll send it down to forensics, and I'll get one of the guys on a canvass of the hotels and inns that cater to the out of town newsies. Maybe we can come up with something." He paused and flipped through Corina's report of the dockside crime scene. "These two Orcs, LT. They were carrying burglar tools. I think I should get the rest of the team working the docks along Chandler, checking for break-ins."

Simon smiled. Gervis was sharp. "Sounds like a good start. Keep me informed. And make sure you check with Evarts tomorrow. He's working on identifying the two Orcs."

"Aye, LT," Gervis said. He looked at Simon. "Thanks for this."

Simon stood, ready to leave. "Don't thank me yet. This could turn out to be a blind tunnel. Work it hard for a few days, but don't lose sight of your other open cases."

"Will do, LT."

Simon made his way across the squad room to the stairs. The large room bustled with the controlled chaos of a normal day watch, a welcome change after days of riot control. He knew the real work would start later as the Peacekeepers restored order and safety to the shattered streets of the Hollows. But for now, the sounds of routine were comforting.

He found his Oxley in the underground stables. He unclipped the scabbard holding his saber from his belt and slid in behind the steering yoke, setting the sheathed blade on the passenger seat next to him. He slid the Czech and Hawley needler out of the shoulder holster under his left arm and set it on the seat as well. He lifted the steering yoke and muttered the incantation to activate the Air spell that lifted the sled.

The black Tornado sports sled was sleek and fast, but not terribly practical for navigating the crowded streets of Cymbeline. Simon drove with exaggerated caution, the fatigue of several stressful nights catching up with him. He caught himself dozing at the intersection a block south of the converted mews where he had his flat. He jerked upright at the blare of a horn behind him and shook himself awake. A few minutes later he slid into the courtyard of the mews. He canceled the Air spell and the sled settled to the ground, but he made no move to get out.

He leaned his head back and sighed. *Just five minutes. I need five minutes.*

He opened his eyes a few moments later and climbed out of the sled. He slid the needler into its holster but held the scabbarded saber in his hand. He glanced at it and smiled. It was a Gallinberg Reaper, a fast and elegant weapon. Far too fast and elegant for his barely passable sword skills. He was improving under Sylvie's tutelage, which was why he had smiled. She was an expert swordswoman but had nearly a hundred years of training in the art. Being rated as 'passable' by her was high praise.

He swayed slightly with fatigue. His flat was only fifty feet away and it had a shower and proper bed. They became his only focus as he crossed the courtyard.

He made it to his door and unlocked it. He rubbed his badge to cancel the Warding spells on the threshold and stepped inside. The curtains were still drawn tightly across the front window keeping the main room dim, if not completely dark. His bedroom in the back was completely blacked out for sleeping in the daytime.

Simon felt rather than saw the other presence in the room. Adrenaline surged, wiping away his fatigue. A shadow moved and before he thought about it, the Reaper was in his hand, the tip at the throat of the man in front of him.

"Peace, Simon," a familiar voice said. "Peace!" The

man spoke an incantation and the glowglobe in the ceiling flared to life.

Simon blinked in the light. He lowered the sword. "Kermal? Gods above and below, man. I almost skewered you. How the hells did you get in here?"

The Half-Orc smiled. "You really should update your Warding spells now and then."

Kermal Brackenville had the height and lean build of his Human mother and the sharp features and almond shaped eyes of his Azeri Orc father. The former armorer for Simon's old Magic Enforcement team now wore a well cut black business suit, white cravat, and black hose. Simon noted the slight bulge under his old teammate's left armpit that even the obvious custom tailoring of the suit couldn't quite conceal.

Kermal noticed the direction of Simon's glance and held his hands out from his sides, palms outward, the Orc signal for peace. "No harm here, Simon. I'm not working. I need to talk to you."

Simon frowned but sheathed the saber. "Are you here for the Old Men, or is this a social call?"

Kermal didn't answer but gestured toward the overstuffed chairs in Simon's front room. "Why don't we sit down. You look knackered."

Simon hung his uniform jacket and the sheathed Reaper on pegs by the door and followed Kermal deeper into the room. They sat across from one another in the big chairs, a low table between them.

"What's this all about Kermal?" Simon asked.

"Last night you found a couple of dead Orcs on the docks down by the Cut," Kermal said without preamble. "So far, Evarts hasn't come up with an identification."

"How do you know that?"

Kermal cocked his head. "Am I wrong?"

"No. Just wondering who your source is.

"Not important. What's important is that I can give

you their names."

Simon sat back in his chair. "All good, but why? Why do the Old Men want to help our investigation?"

The Old Men to whom Simon referred was the Cabal of Clans, a shadowy group of Orcs who controlled gang and criminal activity in the Hollows. Simon had not even believed they existed until six weeks earlier when he'd been summoned to a meeting with them. At the meeting he'd learned that he'd been set up by a fellow Keeper named Francis Killian. Killian had plotted with Farsk Kronska to take over the drug trade in the Hollows by assassinating a rival gang chieftain and pinning the blame on Simon. Thanks to Simon's reputation and Kermal's intervention, the Cabal had provided Simon with proof of Killian's plot. The price had been high, however. Kermal had left the Peacekeeper force to take up his late father's duties as Enforcer for the Cabal.

Kermal leaned forward. "The Cabal is worried. They were caught napping by the riots and most of their *kharo's* couldn't control their own territories. Rumors of a rogue mage in the mix aren't sitting well on the streets."

Simon wasn't surprised that Kermal knew about the Water mage. Little that happened on the streets of the Hollows escaped the Cabal's notice. Every neighborhood had its *kharo,* more or less a watch captain who got things done and made sure the Cabal maintained control. The riots must have shaken them to their core.

"So, who were they?" Simon asked.

"Brothers, Lasko and Fortis Harsaka. They are... were originally from Rathskellig, out east near the Azeri border. Both of them born in the Commonwealth, but Serpent Clan to the core. They were plumbers, handymen by day, but the best jimmy heisters in the city by night."

Simon nodded. It explained the burglar tools they'd had in their possession when they died. "They were on a job last night."

Kermal spread his hands. "Don't know for sure, but we do know they were working on something big. They'd cleared it in a general sort of way with the Dockside *kharo.* Not the specifics, just making sure there was nothing else going on during a three-day window starting the day before yesterday."

Simon considered his next question carefully. "Why did the Cabal send you, Kermal? You could have called me on the mirror, or even left an anonymous tip. I get why you didn't come to Wycliffe House, but why the face-to-face?"

Kermal looked uncomfortable. "Look, Simon. I'm just the messenger here. I don't want to presume on our past relationship."

"What's the message, Kermal?"

"The Cabal is requesting, requesting Simon, that you give these deaths your personal attention. Make sure they're completely investigated and not just left in the ashes."

"You know I wouldn't give them any less attention than any other murder, Kermal. This was Dark Magic, using the riots to try to cover someone's special dig."

"I know that, Simon," said Kermal. "But the Old Men want to make sure it's you looking into this, not some rookie. They're asking as a favor to them and to the Harsaka family."

Simon's laugh was harsh. "Why would I do those Old Men a favor? A personal request from you maybe. Do you have some connection to these brothers?"

Kermal looked away. "No, nothing personal. But it wouldn't hurt to have them in your debt. They don't forget favors." He looked back at Simon. "Or slights. I told them that with you, everyone is important, even Orcs."

Simon cocked his head at that. He didn't think he'd ever told Kermal about his own father, about the motto he'd always quoted when Simon asked him why he treated Orcs, Humans, and Dwarves all the same in his chandlery shop.

"Everyone is important," his father had said. "Or no one is. If an Orc is less than a man, then any man can be less than any other."

"Everyone is a person," Simon murmured, realizing that for years, he'd lived by his father's motto without ever giving voice to it.

Kermal gave him an odd look, but simply nodded.

"Tell the Cabal that you delivered the message, Kermal." Simon said. Kermal nodded and rose to leave. Simon grabbed his arm. "Tell them this is not a favor. I'll work this case the way I would any other. No special access for them, no behind the scenes updates. Understood?"

Kermal smiled. "I told them you'd say that, too. Good parting, Simon."

Simon let go of his arm. "Good parting, Kermal."

Only after Kermal had gone did Simon realize the importance of the comment about a rookie working the case. How had the Cabal known he'd given the case to Gervis Birchfield?

CHAPTER SIX

Simon slept for a little over four hours before the message tone on his mirror awakened him in his darkened room. He dragged himself out of bed and into the bathroom for another shower and change of clothes. Technically he was on a 96-hour stand-down in order to readjust to a day watch schedule. Practically speaking, as a Lieutenant in a high-profile unit, he was on call all the time.

He checked his mirror. There were three messages waiting. Two were from his teams with routine updates. Birchfield sent that he'd gotten a report from Evarts with the names of the dead Orcs. It agreed with what Kermal had told Simon.

The third message was from Sylvie Graystorm. She was leaving the Borderlands for Cymbeline early and expected to be in the city by late afternoon tomorrow. *See you in Glenharrow for dinner. Love you!* she ended the message. Simon thought about calling her but decided against it. He'd see her soon enough and didn't want to call if she was on duty.

He sent a quick message to Birchfield asking him to check the criminal histories of the Harsaka brothers. Even if they were the best break and enter artists in the city now, they had to get their start somewhere. Chances were, they'd been pinched sometime in the past.

Simon lifted his jacket from the peg by the door, intending to head into Wycliffe House to try to get some paperwork done before Weeksend. The summoning tone on his handheld mirror interrupted him. He looked at the mirror but didn't recognize the locus.

"Buckley," he said after swiping a hand across it.

He didn't recognize the woman in the crisp business suit who regarded him through the mirror.

"Lieutenant Simon Buckley?" she asked.

"Yes, speaking," said Simon.

"Please hold for the Lord Mayor."

A second later the woman's face was replaced by that of Rondel Aspenwald, Lord Mayor of Cymbeline. Simon had never met the Elf who had won election just a year before but knew his face well from news reports and campaign ads. Rondel had ridden a wave of law and order sentiment in the wealthy North Side to a narrow victory over the incumbent Roger Grimsby. Rondel's subtle and sometimes not-so-subtle anti-Orc statements bothered Simon. He didn't like Aspenwald, and the smug face now in his mirror did little to change that.

"Good meeting, Mr. Mayor," said Simon, intentionally using the less formal form of address rather than the formal *My Lord*. "What can I do for you?"

If the slight bothered Aspenwald, he didn't show it. "Good meeting, Lt. Buckley. I've heard good things about you. I'm sorry we aren't meeting under happier circumstances."

It was Simon's turn to conceal his surprise. "I'm

not sure what you mean, sir. I'm just finishing a night tour and haven't caught up with my teams yet. Is there some new turn of events?"

"No, Lieutenant," said Aspenwald. "I'm referring to the death of Anika Sommerstag."

"Did you know Anika Sommerstag, sir?"

"She was my daughter, Lieutenant." Aspenwald's face was grave but his voice was steady and betrayed no emotion. Simon's look of shock must have been obvious because Aspenwald hurried to explain. "She took her mother's name when my marriage contract ended over forty years ago. To be honest, Lieutenant, my daughter and I have had little contact since she reached her majority, and none in the past ten years. I wasn't even aware she was in the Commonwealth until I was informed of her death this morning."

Simon knew that marriages between Elves were 50-year contracts, not lifetime commitments. When both parties were essentially immortal, a lifetime could be very long indeed. He also knew that Elven parents could be rather indifferent once their children reached their majority at age thirty and became responsible for their own lives. What troubled Simon was the fact that Aspenwald had information about Sommerstag this soon after her death.

"If I may ask, sir, how did you learn about Anika?" he asked.

"I noticed her name on the list of deaths in the Hollows that Captain Axhart forwards to my office each day. My staff did some checking and confirmed her identity. I knew she was living in the Free States but didn't know about her professional life or why she was in the Commonwealth."

Simon considered that. He hadn't known that the Ax was providing daily updates to the Mayor's Office, but it made sense that he would. It surprised him that the Mayor personally reviewed the lists. He may have misjudged the man.

"So, what can I do for you, sir," Simon repeated.

"I'd like you to look into Anika's death."

"I'm already doing that, sir," said Simon. "She was killed by an illegal spell, which puts the investigation in my division."

"No, Lieutenant," Aspenwald said as if explaining something to a child. "I want you to take personal responsibility for the investigation and provide my office with regular updates on your progress. Anika and I may not have been close, but she was my daughter and I have a duty to see that the investigation is thorough and complete."

Simon felt his face reddening, both at the Mayor's tone and the inappropriate request. He managed to control his voice. "It is a longstanding policy not to discuss ongoing investigations outside of the Peacekeeper Force or the Office of the King's Prosecutor."

Aspenwald smiled indulgently. "Quite so. But this has already been approved by your Captain Axhart at the request of the King's Prosecutor. I'm surprised he hasn't informed you about this."

Simon opened his mouth to speak, then closed it again. Now he understood. High brass jingle, Keeper code for cases where politicians had a vested interest in the outcomes. Never a good omen for the poor Peacekeeper trying to run a clean investigation.

"I see, Mr. Mayor. I'm currently off duty after a string of nights on riot control. I'll be taking charge of the case as soon as I resume my duties. I will inform the team leader of the need for the updates immediately."

"Thank you, Lieutenant," said Aspenwald. "And I want you to know how much I appreciate your efforts on the front lines of these unfortunate disturbances. I hope we can all learn from this and find a way to alleviate the suffering in places like the Hollows."

The Mayor's words were smooth, his tone appropriately concerned, but his eyes were hard. Simon had little confidence that he planned anything other than reprisals and heavy-handed street justice. It's what his wealthy North Side constituency would appreciate.

"As you say, sir. Will that be all?"

"Yes, Lieutenant Buckley. Thank you for your time." Aspenwald's smile was cold and lifeless and Simon felt a chill as the connection was broken.

He summoned Birchfield next. His team Sergeant looked a bit confused when he saw who was on the mirror.

"LT?" asked Birchfield. "Is something wrong? I have Claggert checking with records about the Harsaka brothers and we've found a couple of warehouse break-ins near enough to the crime scene that they could have been involved. I figured you'd go back to sleep seeing as you're off duty."

"I had planned on it, but I just got off the mirror with Rondel Aspenwald. This case just got a dose of high brass jingle."

Birchfield's eyes widened. "The Lord Mayor himself? What the hells is going on LT?"

"It seems our dead Elf newsie was the Mayor's daughter." Simon went on to detail the rest of his conversation with Aspenwald. "So, I'll need to be more involved in this one than usual. No reflection on you or your team, but this has the potential to bury us all under a rockslide and better I should take the load than you."

"All due respect, LT, but I can take the heat. I'd just as soon continue as lead here."

Simon smiled. "You will, Gervis. I have two other teams to manage, a diplomatic situation with the Ironlands, and a difficult conversation to have with Captain Axhart. I'll be too busy to look over your shoulder every minute. What I would like is a daily brief, either in person or by mirror. I'll pass it on to the Mayor so that you don't have to get tangled in the politics. His lordship has a logical reason for following this dig, but my gut tells me there's rot in the shoring, and he has something else in mind here."

"Aye, LT," said Birchfield. "Is there anything I need to do right away?"

"Write up your findings so far and shoot a copy to my message scroll. I'll forward it with some brass polish to the Mayor. Leave out the Harsakas for now. That's technically a different case and I want something in reserve if I need to jingle a bit myself."

"Aye, sir." Birchfield broke the connection.

Simon's next summoning was to the Command offices at Wycliffe House. The mirror was answered by Elvira Cairns, Axhart's secretary.

"Good meeting, Lieutenant Buckley," she said in her usual gruff Dwarfish burr. "To what do we owe the pleasure?"

"Good meeting, Mistress Cairns. Is the Captain in? I know he was night watch actual last night, but I have a matter that I need to discuss with him."

"I wouldn't disturb him if I were you, Simon Buckley. He's none too happy about the stunt you pulled with the CSA team last evening." Cairns's tone was gruff, but the concern in her eyes was genuine.

"I know," said Simon. "But there's more going on than just that backdoor maneuver. I have information that he may need to hear, and I need him to clarify something before I can move forward with an investigation."

Elvira frowned but nodded. "He told me you'd likely be looking to see him today. Come to the office at end of watch. He'll give you ten minutes." With that she broke the connection.

CHAPTER SEVEN

Simon arrived at the command office at Wycliffe House at sixteenth hour, just as the day watch was ending. Elvira Cairns was still seated at her desk in the outer office, but the battered carpet bag she carried as a purse was on the desktop.

"Go on in." She indicated the inner door to Axhart's office. "They're waiting for you."

"They?" Simon asked in alarm. He wanted a private interview with Axhart, especially when he meant to tell him about Hal's warning about the Inspector General.

"Sergeant Stonebender summoned me with the same request not five minutes after I spoke to you." She stuffed a few papers into her carpet bag and stood. "It looks like your foster father is watching out for you. Good parting, Lieutenant."

"Thank you, Mistress Cairns." Simon turned to let her pass as she walked toward the outer door. Her only reply was a grunt and a slight smile.

He opened the inner door and entered Axhart's

office, coming to attention as the door closed behind him. The office had a large window overlooking the greenbelt along King's Road. Axhart's desk faced the door across a strip of dark green carpet that was flanked by a pair of couches and a couple of leather covered chairs.

The Captain and Hal sat facing each other on the short couches that formed the sitting area in the center of the office. They looked relaxed. Axhart didn't smile as he looked at Simon, but he didn't frown either.

"At ease, Lieutenant," said Axhart. His voice held none of the Dwarfish accent that tended to creep in when he was truly angry. "Come sit next to your foster father. It seems we have a few things to discuss."

"Aye, sir." Simon crossed the green carpet between the couches and sat next to Hal. He received a slight nod in reply to his inquiring glance.

"Sergeant Stonebender has already told me about the IG and the rumors of an investigation." He held up a hand as Hal shifted in his seat and appeared about to say something. "Just rumors so far, Hal. I trust your sources, but my own have heard nothing. I believe you; it tallies with other events that I believe Simon wishes to confront me about."

Both Hal and Axhart looked at Simon. "Aye, sir." Simon took a deep breath and began. "This afternoon I had a mirror summons from the office of the Lord Mayor. I spoke to the Mayor himself who told me that Anika Sommerstag, the Elf newswoman we found dead in an alley last night, was actually his daughter. He wanted me to assume personal responsibility for the investigation into her death and to provide him with daily updates on my progress. When I told him that it was against Peacekeeper policy to discuss an ongoing investigation outside the Force or the KP's office, he told me that you had authorized it." Simon tried to keep the accusatory tone out of his voice, but it crept in at the last second.

Axhart made a sour face. "Authorized, yes. But only under extreme protest. And the order didn't come from the Mayor, it came directly from the Justice Minister."

"Minister Kershaw?" asked Simon.

Axhart nodded. "Kershaw is Lord Alorton's brother-in-law. He wasn't implicated in the Flandyrs affair and was able to stay on as Justice Minister when Alorton was forced to resign from Foreign Affairs. But the two of them have always been as thick as tailing mud. You can bet Alorton has his hand in this."

The previous winter, Simon and his team had uncovered a plot by a Gray Havens diplomat named Flandyrs and elements in the Peacekeeper command and Justice Ministry to supply arms to the Azeri Liberation Brigade terrorists. They had hoped to incite a war between the Commonwealth and the Azeri Empire. The Havens would benefit from a weakening of the Commonwealth economy and the Commonwealth plotters would get rich from war profiteering. The scandal had resulted in the arrest of Simon's immediate predecessor and the resignation of several high-ranking Keepers and Foreign Ministry officials. Flandyrs had escaped and had not yet been found.

"This meshes with Hal's information," Axhart continued. "Aspenwald's law and order campaign has made him the darling of Minister Kershaw. I'm betting he sees this as a way to take me down, and likely you as well, to avenge his brother-in-law. Whether the Mayor is just a pawn, or a willing participant, I don't yet know. But for now, it's all high brass jingle and we have to play along."

"Tell the Mayor to pound sand," said Hal. "He doesn't have any steel with the Keeper Force. We report to the King."

Axhart laughed. "No, we report to the Minister

as the King's representative. Like I said, this came directly from Kershaw. I don't know how tight he is with the Lord Mayor. Maybe they belong to the same club. Maybe they share the same mistress on the side. I don't know and that's one of the things I need to find out. For now, nothing leaves this room. If the IG is making a move on me, an illegal investigation into the Lord Mayor of Cymbeline would be blood in the water."

Simon nodded. "So how much do I tell His Lordship, and how much can I hold back?"

Axhart considered that for a moment. "Use your judgement, Lieutenant. You know how this game is played and your instinct for the politics of Princess Rebeka's situation was accurate." He paused for a moment. "Speaking of which, who knows about her Fire talent? That seems to be a focus of this IG charade even if they haven't been explicit about it."

"The three of us, their Majesties, Stenson Harold, George Latham, and Ranger Sylvie Graystorm," said Simon.

"No one who'd gain from revealing it," put in Hal. "We certainly didn't, nor did the King or Queen. Latham is bound by his advocate's oath, and Sylvie is practically family. I'd trust her with any secret."

"What about Harold? He can't be too happy that she fled the country on his watch," said Axhart.

Simon shook his head. "Stenson loves her like one of his own daughters. He was ready to follow her into exile. He's not the leak."

"Well, something leaked," Axhart replied. "The IG inquiry is too specific and these riots were sparked by the mere rumor of a mage with royal connections burning that warehouse."

"There's another possibility," said Simon thoughtfully. "Maybe two."

"What do you mean, lad," asked Hal.

"Think about it, Hal. Hiramis Silverlake. He didn't know for sure, but the Princess almost incinerated him at the Palace when Liam and I interviewed him. He may be smart enough to know what she was and why he felt what he did."

"Aye, I can see that." Hal scratched his beard. "But he's still in lockup awaiting trial. I can't see him talking to the newsies, even if they thought he had something to say. Who else?"

"Frank Killian," said Simon.

Hal scoffed audibly, but Axhart just furrowed his brow. "How so? I know you don't like the man, but why do you think he knows about the Princess? From your report, it's clear he was working for the Old Men, and even they didn't know."

"He knew about the earlier fires." Simon glanced at Hal and ticked the point off on his finger. "He knew they weren't started by the Loblollies as Kronska suspected." Another finger. "He knew the Princess was significantly involved with Lily Ponsaka and her people." A third finger. "And the timing of Kronska's death and Princess Rebeka's sudden departure may have filled in the picture for him. Despite being dirty, he was still a sharp investigator. Even if it was only a suspicion, he could have leaked it to the newsies if only to get back at the Peacekeeper Force, and at me in particular."

Axhart looked at Hal. "Where is Killian?"

Simon looked at Hal as well, surprised.

Hal squirmed in his seat. "We lost track of him about a week ago. Last known address was a third-class hotel in Westport. His wife is divorcing him and has the kids in the house down Bowater way. She hasn't heard from him in near a month."

"What the hells, Hal," said Simon. "You've been watching Killian? Why wasn't I told about this?"

"Because I ordered him to keep this in his pocket,"

Axhart said before Hal could speak. "Killian resigned rather than face charges because the Ministry didn't want another scandal after the Flandyrs debacle. That didn't mean he wasn't dirty, and I won't let any Keeper from this House walk away if he's on the cuff to gangsters." He favored Hal with a cold stare. "Hal was assigned to keep Killian on a loose surveillance until he slipped up and did something we could use to pinch him."

"Aye," Hal bristled. "And I did. Would have run him to ground again, too, if I hadn't been busy busting heads down on Canal Street."

Axhart held up his hands in a placating gesture. "I know, I'm just frustrated. These riots caught everyone wrong footed and we're only now regaining some control. But if Killian is our leak, we need to find him. If we can't control who he talks to, we can at least find out what he's saying."

"Where do you think the IG will start, Captain," Simon asked.

"Well, without a formal complaint, or actual charges, they'll likely start with you and Hal. Liam is in the Free States with the Princess and off the Force in any event. Brackenville is out as well. Unless he gets detained or indicted, they have no leverage over him."

Simon elected not to mention his conversation with Kermal earlier in the day. He'd discuss it with Hal later. "So, what will be their approach with us?"

Axhart's face softened. "Sorry, Simon, but it looks like you're going to be the one they'll lean on. As team leader, they'll set you up as the one who planned to kill Kronska and Liam for the actual arsonist. They can't get to him, so they'll try to build a case around you, then offer you a deal to weasel on me as the puppeteer pulling your strings."

"But none of that's true," protested Simon.

"Since when did truth matter when the brass starts jingling?" said Axhart. "I'll take a bolt for the country if I have to. If they have you in a tight spot and offer you a deal for me, take it. But if you can keep them running in circles until we can find Killian and run down the source of this rumor, we may be able to protect the Princess and keep our badges."

"You're asking a lot of the lad, Gelbard," said Hal.

"I know, Hal," Axhart sighed. "But we barely avoided a full-on revolution these past few days. We can't let the truth about Princess Rebeka get out, no matter what the cost."

CHAPTER EIGHT

Axhart dismissed Simon but asked Hal to stay and brief him on the Ironlands extradition case. It was now well after eighteenth hour and fatigue was again making Simon yawn. He returned to his own office where he found a neat pile of reports and messages that Lessa had placed on his desk before leaving for Weeksend.

He skimmed the reports but only two things caught his eye. The first was a note from Gervis Birchfield. He thought he had a lead on where Anika Sommerstag had been staying while in the capital. He'd assigned a duty team from the night watch to check it out and seal the location if the lead proved to be true.

The second was from the criminal records department. The Harsaka brothers had a long history of encounters with the law but nothing more recent than five years earlier. Both had done prison time, Lasko at the Bruno prison farm south of the city and Fortis at the Handleford maximum security prison in

Dundaria. What interested Simon was a hand-written notation that both files had recently been copied by a King's Prosecutor named Bendict Hammersmith, currently assigned to the antiterrorism arm of the Justice Ministry.

Simon sat back in his chair. Why would a couple of jimmy heisters draw the attention of an antiterrorism KP? He checked the date that the files had been copied ten weeks before the riots and a month before Rebeka's abdication. So, the KP's interest wasn't related to the Princess. Simon made a note to get in touch with Hammersmith after Weeksend. It was already after business hours and Simon doubted he'd be able to find a home number for him.

Another thought occurred to him. Why was there no trace in the criminal history of the Harsaka brothers for the past five years? Had they been out of the Commonwealth? Or just good enough to avoid detection? He made another note to have Birchfield look for any indication that they had been out of the country.

He considered the Mayor's manipulation of the investigation of Anika's death. Maybe it was as simple as a father wanting to find out what happened to his daughter. But Simon's gut told him otherwise. Aspenwald was a politician first; fatherhood was a distant second. There was some connection Simon was missing.

He blew out a long, tired breath as he looked at the timepiece on the wall. It was after nineteenth hour. *Enough for now,* he thought. *I'll take it up again in the morning.* He shuffled the reports into a semblance of order, made sure the large mirror on the corner of his desk was secured with his password and canceled the spell in the glowglobe overhead. The room was dark but for the light from the outer office. He picked up his letter case and tucked it under his arm. He made sure the outer office door locked when he closed it.

Axhart's office was dark when he passed it. The Ax and Hal must have finished and gone home. Simon descended the two flights of stairs to the booking level, thinking Hal might still be around but the desk Sergeant told him that Hal had left the building ten minutes ago. Simon nodded and headed for the stables to go home himself.

The next day was Weeksend. Simon knew there would be few people at Wycliffe House other than the duty crews and daywatch Civil Patrol. He slept late and stopped at a corner café just north of Tanner that he liked. Over fried eggs and spicey Azeri sausages, he reviewed his notes from the waterfront crime scene. He had already realized that the black pitch on Anika's shoes matched the same material on the Harsaka brothers' and his own boots. She had clearly been at the same pier before her death. He looked for some other connection, some reason for her to have been there but saw nothing new.

He'd received a message from Birchfield early that morning that there indeed had been a break-in and burglary at a warehouse a few doors down from the jetty where the Orc brothers had been found. Nearly a hundred weight of silver, a smaller amount of platinum, and some sort of specialty cold iron had been taken from a noble metals dealer who warehoused his materials near the docks on the Great Cut.

The warehouse had been well protected and warded. An armed guard made rounds every twenty minutes. Yet the thieves had gotten past the security system, canceled the Warding spells, and gotten away with the metals in the twenty minutes between guard checks. It was possible that the two Orcs had managed to get that much precious metal away by themselves, but Simon suspected they had at least one, maybe two assistants given the weight of the materials and the lack of traces found at the scene.

The lead on Anika Sommerstag's local address had not smelted out. A canvass of likely hotels and inns catering to foreign newsies had turned up no trace of Anika as a guest. It was still possible that she had stayed at one of a hundred other rooming houses and guest hostels in the capital, or even in the home of a friend or associate, but if that was the case, Simon had no leads.

A thought occurred to him and he jotted it down in a notebook he carried in his jacket pocket. Anika had been at two separate sites in the Hollows with no obvious connection and no obvious means of transportation. Could she have had a room in the Hollows, perhaps at some inn or rooming house? It shouldn't be too hard to check. An Elf in a Hollows flophouse would be remembered. He thought about having Birchfield check with Lily Ponsaka down at her inn on Canal Street but decided to do it himself. He and Lily shared history and Birchfield would be just another Bluebelly as far as Lily knew.

He checked his timepiece. It was just after ninth hour, plenty of time to go see Lily and still make it out to Glenharrow for Weeksend dinner with Hal and the family. He paid the bill for his breakfast and stepped out to the street and his sled.

He decided to go to Lily's place first before checking in at Wycliffe House. He was just unlocking his Oxley and cancelling the anti-theft spell when a dark green Hilten six-seater pulled up next to him, blocking the Oxley from leaving the curb.

Simon's hand went to the clip-on holster at the small of his back, but before he could draw the Czech and Hawley needler there, the tinted rear window of the big Hilten sled slid down revealing the face of Rondel Aspenwald.

"Lieutenant Buckley." Aspenwald's voice was

pleasant enough although the Lord Mayor was not smiling. "I had hoped for a progress report from you this morning."

"It's Weeksend, Mr. Mayor." Simon still avoided the more proper 'My Lord' when addressing Aspenwald. He knew it was petty, but the Elf's presumption of privilege bothered him. "My teams have the day off other than the duty crew. We have no new leads as to where Anika was staying while here in the city, nor how she got to the alley where she was killed. Do you have any idea where she may have been staying in Cymbeline? Any friends or acquaintances who might have put her up?"

Aspenwald shook his head, clearly annoyed at being questioned. "No. As I said, my daughter and I have had almost no contact in over ten years. When I ask for daily updates, I mean daily, even if you feel there is nothing to report. Is that clear, Lieutenant?"

"Aye, sir," said Simon. "And should I copy Lord Kershaw with my reports, or will you do that yourself?"

Aspenwald glared but said nothing. He waved a hand at his driver and the window rose. The big sled pulled away from the curb and glided down Tanner Street toward the government district.

Simon sighed and climbed into his Oxley. Baiting Aspenwald had not been smart. He knew that. But he was certain that there was more going on behind the scenes than he or Hal or even Axhart knew. Aspenwald's response to his barb about Kershaw was as good as a confession that there was some sort of collusion between the Mayor's Office and that of the Justice Minister. For now, though, all he could do was follow the leads he had on Anika and the Harsaka brothers and hope they led him to the connection between Aspenwald and Kershaw.

Simon followed the Hilten at a distance but turned south on Canal as the Hilten continued down Tanner toward City Hall.

Lily Ponsaka's tavern was deep in the Hollows but had been spared any damage during the riots. Simon didn't know if that was due to good fortune or to Lily's reputation as a peacemaker and neutral party in the gang rivalries that were a constant feature of life on the South Side.

Simon drove past the front of the tavern, turned right onto Knacker, and turned right again into the vacant lot behind the building that served as a parking area. This early in the morning, the lot was empty. Simon climbed out of the Oxley and set the warding spells before approaching the tavern's back door.

He knocked twice on the heavy green door and took a step back, holding his hands at his sides, palms out. Orc body language for peaceful intent. He felt rather than saw the eye regarding him through the small lens set halfway up the door. It swung open and Lily stood in the threshold, hands on her hips.

Simon gave her his best smile. "Good meeting, Mistress Ponsaka."

"What the hells do you want, Simon Buckley?" Lily's voice sounded more weary than angry. "I've got a hundred homeless Orcs camped out in my common room and no time for Keeper horse shit."

Lily Ponsaka was short, even for an Orc, with the olive skin and almond shaped eyes of the Azeri. She was broad shouldered and sturdy, her thick forearms heavily tattooed with Fish clan markings. She glared up at Simon but there was less anger and more sadness in her eyes

"Not looking to give you trouble, Lily," said Simon. "I just need a little information about a couple of Orcs, brothers, named Harsaka." He had decided as soon as he saw her face to save his questions about Anika. He'd bring it up later if he found a good time.

"Why?" Lily's voice was heavy with suspicion.

"I know there were a lot more deaths than just those two, but they were killed by illegal magic. That makes it my business." He paused. "And Kermal Brackenville came to see me with a message from the Old Men."

Lily stiffened at the mention of Kermal and the Cabal.

"They want me to make sure their deaths are 'properly investigated.'" Simon continued, making it clear by his tone that he was not taking their orders but would nevertheless do just that.

Lily sighed and looked away. "The Harsakas were jimmy heisters who had no problem stealing from their own people. They spent most of their time out in the East end. Had a legitimate plumbing business as a cover, but made a living breaking into other people's property. Word was, they were available for hire. If you needed something liberated from someone else, you could call the Harsakas."

"Did they do work for anyone in particular?" Simon asked. "The Old Men? Maybe one of the gangs?"

Lily shook her head. "Not that I heard of. They were Azeri, Serpent clan, but never really part of the Brigades. Too much money to be made on their own."

"Any connection to the Free States?" Simon asked carefully.

Lily's eyes narrowed suspiciously. "Is this about that Elf newsie?" She scoffed. "I might have known. How many Orcs died in the last four days? And all the Bluebellies care about is one Elf woman who didn't know her place."

Simon frowned. "Come on, Lily. You know me. I've never done less than my best in any investigation, Orc or not. I gave Brackenville and the Old Men my word, and you know what that means."

Lily folded her arms, her glare now angry. Simon returned it with his own. After a second, he sighed. "Look, you don't have to trust me, or even believe me, but I've got the Cabal looking for answers on the one hand and the Lord Mayor riding my ass on the other. I need help."

"What's the Mayor got to do with this?"

Simon lowered his voice, glancing behind Lily into the kitchen. "That Elf newsie was his estranged daughter. And the mage who killed her also killed the Harsaka brothers. I'll clear both cases if I can find that mage. It isn't that the Elf is more important to me, it's that so far, she's the best lead we have."

Lily glared at him for another second then sighed and looked away. "You'd best come in then. You'll be wanting to look through her things and take them to her family."

"She was staying here?"

"Aye, I thought that was why you came. She took one of the upstairs rooms a week ago. Said a friend from the city recommended she speak to me." She opened the door to the kitchen wide so that Simon could come in.

CHAPTER NINE

"Did she say who this friend in town was?" Simon asked as he glanced around the bustling kitchen. Ciara, Lily's cook, was ordering the scullery maids and assistants about as coffee pots bubbled on the big double stoves and cauldrons of porridge and soup hissed and steamed.

"No," Lily answered. "Like as not, it was a friend in Fredonia who had emigrated from here." She led him through the kitchen and into the crowded common room.

The big room occupied most of the ground floor of the building which itself spread over almost half a city block. Normally quiet on a Weeksend morning, it was packed with Orcs. They occupied every table and chair and many more were seated on blankets and pads spread on the floor. Whole families crowded together with bags and bundles of their possessions heaped around them.

Simon and Lily picked their way across the room

toward the staircase on the far wall. Most of the
Orcs exchanged small waves or nods with Lily while
studiously ignoring Simon. A few quickly averted their
eyes while others stared at him with open hostility.
For his part, Simon kept his expression neutral and
tried to avoid any eye contact. He didn't want to make
anyone feel they were the subject of official interest
and particularly didn't want to start any trouble. He
was out of uniform and had kept his needler concealed
under his shirt tail, but still everyone seemed to mark
him as a Bluebelly, a King's Peacekeeper.

They climbed the narrow stairs to the second floor.
A long landing ran back toward the front of the tavern
alongside the stairs. Two parallel hallways led away
from the landing at a right angle. A double handful of
tiny rooms lined each hall, five to a side.

Lily led him to the end room on the front side of
the building and opened the door with a master key
she drew from her apron pocket. Simon followed her
in and looked around.

The room was barely eight feet wide and ten long
but had a window in the wall opposite the door that
looked down on Canal Street. Cheery yellow curtains
framed the window and its panes gleamed spotlessly
in the morning light. A narrow bed was pushed against
the right-hand wall with a small storage chest at the
foot. On the opposite wall a small desk and a series of
pegs for hanging clothes completed the furnishings.

Simon was careful not to touch anything. "Has
anyone been in here since Anika was last here?"

Lily shook her head. "No. Chamber maid looked in,
but the bed hadn't been used so she locked up."

Simon looked carefully about the room. A traveling
case sat on the floor next to the small chest. It was
bigger than a knapsack but smaller than a full-on
trunk. The kind of case that could hold a week's
worth of clothing but still be easily carried. Clean silk

blouses hung from the wall pegs along with a short waisted Glenharrow wool jacket. Papers littered the desk, most of them covered with writing in a small neat hand. They were in Elfscript, which Simon could read, but made no sense. *More code or shorthand?*

Simon used his knuckle to slide the desk drawer open. It contained a battered leather notebook embossed with the initials AS.

Simon turned to Lily. "I'm going to call some of my lads down here to take custody of Anika's things. After we leave, lock the door. No one enters this room until Sergeant Birchfield and his team gets here."

"Not stupid, am I?" Lily retorted. "You lot will do your tests and dirty up my room with your powders and potions, then leave me and mine to clean it all up."

Simon gave her a wan smile as he took out his pocket mirror and entered Birchfield's private locus. A few seconds later, the Sergeant's face swam into view on Simon's mirror. He was obviously at home, dressed in shirtsleeves and a short kilt.

"Sorry to bother you at home, Gervis," said Simon. "We've had a break in the Anika Sommerstag case. I've found out where she was staying here in Cymbeline. Call the duty Crime Scene mage and get a team down to Lily Ponsaka's tavern, corner of Canal and Knacker."

Birchfield looked nonplussed, but to his credit, he recovered quickly and said, "Aye, LT. I'll see to it myself."

"I'll have Lily seal the room and get a uniform to sit on it until you or the team get here," Simon continued. "Call whomever you think you may need from your team. I know some of them are still on ninety-six hour stand-down but I'll see if I can square overtime pay for anyone you call."

Gervis nodded his appreciation. "I'll be there in thirty minutes. Birchfield out."

Simon summoned the duty desk for the Civil Patrol and requested a uniformed Peacekeeper be sent from any nearby patrol to secure the room.

He and Lily backed out and he had her relock the door. "The uniformed Patrol will be here in a little while. What can you tell me about Anika? Did she say what she was doing in Cymbeline?"

"Not my business, was it?" said Lily. "She paid for a week in advance, never caused trouble, took her breakfasts in the common room and was out all day, didn't come back until late. First day of the riots, she went to ground here along with half of South Canal street. Didn't see her again after that."

"How did she get about the city?" asked Simon. "Did she have a sled? Hire someone?"

"She had a flier," answered Lily. "Paid me half a crown a day to store it in the shed out back."

"Is it still there?"

"Not as I've seen. Last I checked was yesterday. Wasn't there then."

"May I look in the shed?" asked Simon.

Lily sighed and took the ring of keys out of her apron pocket. She handed one to Simon. "As you wish. Just make sure you lock up and give me back the key."

Simon had more questions but sensed Lily's impatience. Instead, he took the proffered key, nodded his thanks, and followed her to the stairs. They reached the ground floor just as a uniformed Civil Patrol agent stepped in from the street. He saw Simon and hurried over, throwing him a brisk salute.

"Patrol Agent Falstaff reporting, sir," the young man said. Simon thought he looked too young to be a Peacekeeper. *Or am I just getting old?*

Simon returned the salute and directed Falstaff to the upstairs room. "Keep the scene secure until Sergeant Birchfield arrives. After that you may return to your regular patrol or assist the forensics team in any way they may require.

"Aye, sir," said Falstaff, the excitement evident in his voice. Simon almost grinned. He'd once been a Patrol keeper as well and remembered the anticipation of being included in an important investigation.

"Go on upstairs, Agent Falstaff. And tell Sergeant Birchfield you're at his disposal. He may have duties for you."

The younger man snapped another salute and fairly ran up the stairs.

Lily looked up at Simon with a slight smile. "Gods, he makes me feel old." She rubbed a hand across her chin as if wiping the smile away. "Get on with yourself, then," she said. "I've real work to do."

Simon smiled back at her. "Yes, Mistress Ponsaka."

The shed leaned against the back wall of the tavern a few yards north of the kitchen door. The ten by ten-foot square interior smelled of cleaning fluid, dust, and damp cloth. Mops and brooms hung from pegs on the walls and tin buckets were stacked three high on racks at the back. The space in the center, maybe six by seven feet was relatively clear. Simon pulled out his torch and shone the bright light on the packed dirt floor. He could see the faint but distinctive indentations made by the tripod legs of a small flier. Shining the light around revealed nothing more of interest. He closed and locked the shed.

He thought about Anika riding a flier all the way down from the Free States and rejected the idea. It would be an arduous journey for even the most hearty flier enthusiast. She had more likely come in by commercial coach or passenger ship and rented the flier here in the city. It was another lead for Birchfield to follow.

He returned to the kitchen and found Lily overseeing the controlled chaos of several cooks and a dozen scullery maids working in the confined space. He handed her the key and thanked her for her help. She made a shooing gesture toward the door but didn't try to speak above the noise in the room.

Simon had just reached his sled when Gervis Birchfield checked in from Anika's room. The forensics team was still a few minutes out. Simon told him about the flier and Gervis said he'd check rental agents as soon as they opened the following day. Most were closed on Weeksend.

Simon glanced at his timepiece. It was just past midday. Without traffic, he could be in Glenharrow in forty-five minutes. For once he would be early for Weeksend dinner. He hoped Sylvie would be early as well.

CHAPTER TEN

Simon took the surface streets rather than following Canal south to the W205 highway. He went north to Tanner Street and followed it through All Gods Square with its six temples to the Commonwealth's dominant deities. In the side streets around the square were temples to many of the Orc sacred pantheon and the Temple of the Silver Lady favored by the city's Elves. He wound his way through the labyrinth of Westport where streets followed the banks and canals of the River Finnigan. He hit the approach to the King Harold Bridge at a few minutes past thirteenth hour.

The bridge emptied out onto Grand Avenue which cut straight through the warehouses and chandleries that made up most of the Westbank district of the city. Grand Avenue turned into Halfhelm Boulevard and wound its way up into the hills of Glenharrow.

Before Glenharrow had become a bedroom community for Cymbeline's management class, it had been the ancestral home of many of the

Commonwealth's most prominent Dwarven families. Huge multigenerational mansions, or halls, had been carved directly into the hillsides in the manner of the ancient underground cities like the Darrowdowns, only on a smaller scale.

Stonebender Hall was modest by ancient standards, but still large enough to accommodate the seven children Hal and Molly had raised there as well as the various grandchildren, nieces, nephews and other relatives who seemed to constantly stream in and out. Simon pulled his Oxley into the detached stables built next to the bulk of the hill. He noticed several other sleds in addition to the battered yellow sports model Hal favored. He smiled when he spied Sylvie's dark green Faleron four-seater parked off to one side. He parked next to it and crossed the circular drive to the big oak front door.

Just as Simon reached the door, it burst open and two little Dwarf girls dashed out, rushing past him, nearly knocking him over.

"Hi, Uncle Simon," they shouted in unison before dissolving into a hail of giggles. They ran across the drive toward the hillside opposite the stables where Simon knew there was a sand pit and several trees with rope swings rigged in the upper branches.

A moment later they were followed by a young Dwarf woman with a pretty freckled face and flaming red hair. "Jasmine and Glory," she shouted toward the girls. "Watch where you're going. You nearly knocked your uncle down."

"Yes. Mama," called Glory, the smaller girl.

"Sorry, Uncle Simon," called Jasmine, the big sister. Then they both dissolved into giggles again.

Simon grinned down at Meredith Hamnar Stonebender, his sister-in-law. "No harm done," he said. "It's good to see you, Mery. Is Wills here too?"

Simon bent over as Mery stood on her toes and

gave him a firm hug around his neck. "He's in the back with Hal and Molly. The girls were getting restless, so I brought them out here to play." She cocked her head and arched an eyebrow at him. "I met your fiancé, too. She's quite the Lady. Out of your class, that's for sure." She poked him in the chest so he would know she was teasing.

"But Sylvie and I aren't ..."

"Oh, stuff and nonsense," Mery scoffed. "Anyone can see she's over the moon for you. Marry her quick before she sees the ground. That's what your foster brother did with me and look where we ended up." She squeezed his arm as she passed and walked quickly after her daughters.

Simon walked into the large central hall of the house. Rooms opened on either side, large formal dining room to the right and comfortable, if oversized family rooms to the left. Wide staircases on either side of the hall led to the second story living quarters. Straight back, down a well-lighted stone passageway was the huge kitchen that was the center of family life in House Stonebender.

Simon was halfway down the passage when he heard the deep booming voice of his foster brother, Willston. He didn't hear the words clearly but heard laughter from several other voices.

He entered the kitchen as Wills turned and saw him. The Dwarf grinned and raised a pewter mug in Simon's direction.

"Speak of the crow, and here he is," said Wills. "Welcome, brother. I was just telling your good Lady a few stories from your misspent youth. Do you remember Master Helmsmith's farm?"

Simon held up his hands in mock horror. "Not the bull and the apple tree story again."

He saw Sylvie control her laughter. She caught his eye and gave him one of her dazzling smiles. She stood and came to him. He took her in his arms and they kissed. Wills roared his approval and banged his mug on the huge kitchen table.

"Enough of that, Willston Stonebender," scolded Molly from the other side of the room near the stove. "This is my kitchen, not some common tap room."

Wills lowered his head "Yes, Ma," he said, his voice the soul of contrition. He swiveled his head and winked at Simon and Sylvie, which made them all laugh again.

Molly looked back and forth between them with her hands on her hips trying but failing to look stern. "Well, Haldron," she said, smiling. "You wanted sons. Do something with these two."

Hall took a pull from his own mug and said, "Me? You're doing fine on your own, my love."

Molly made a face at him, but then smiled again and turned back to the stove.

Sylvie leaned close and spoke softly in Simon's ear. "We need to talk after dinner. Business."

Simon nodded. He walked with her to the big table and sat next to Wills. Sylvie kissed the top of his head and went to speak to Molly.

Simon accepted a mug of ale from Hal, then turned to Wills. "So, big brother, how's the defense advocate business?"

Wills cocked his head. "Don't start with me Simon. This is Weeksend dinner. You know how Ma feels about us arguing over a meal."

Simon held up a hand. "Rein in, Wills. I'm not looking to revisit old dross. Just wondering if you'd been in touch with your friend from Justice lately?"

"Bryan Andrews? No, not since the New Year's holiday. Why?"

Simon sipped his ale. "I'm trying to get a line on a KP with the antiterrorism office over there, an advocate named Bendict Hammersmith."

Wills laughed. "The Hammer? He's practically a

legend in the Ministry. I hear he's fearsome in the courtroom. I've not gone up against him. Don't ever want to. Why do you want to know about him?"

"His name came up in connection with a case one of my squads is working," said Simon. "What I'm wondering is why, and whether he's someone who'll give me a straight answer."

Wills shrugged. "Depends on the question. Hammersmith is as straight as they come. If anyone would talk to the Peacekeepers, he would. But he is an investigator with the antiterror squad. They're not famous for sharing information outside the Ministry." He paused, his eyes narrowing. "What sort of case?"

"The Harsaka brothers, a pair of jimmy heisters, got themselves drowned without ever getting wet. Some sort of water spell. The brothers had a criminal record but I think the last five years or so have been scrubbed. Hammersmith was the last person to check the records before me. I want to ask him if he knows anything about that."

"Harsaka," Wills repeated. "Azeri?"

Simon nodded. "Snake clan, but by all accounts not affiliated with the Brigades."

"If Hammersmith pulled the record," said Wills, "it's likely they have some connection to the Azeri Liberation Brigades. I don't see an advocate of his standing taking an interest in a couple of break-in sneak thieves."

"Aye," said Hal from the other end of the table. "And if it's a Ministry case, you'll get no ore out of Hammersmith, only dross and good wishes."

"You're saying I shouldn't contact him?" asked Simon.

Hal set down his mug and stroked his beard as he considered for a moment. "No, but go see him in person with the record in hand. It'll be a lot harder to show you a false tunnel if you have evidence he's involved. Who knows? If Wills is right, he may not be your usual Ministry lackey."

Before Simon could answer, Molly and Sylvie came over, their hands full of plates and cutlery.

"Enough Keeper chatter," said Molly, setting down a pile of plates. "Wills, go fetch Mery and the girls. Simon, make yourself useful and set the table. Sylvie, dear, would you go to the sideboard there and get out some napkins? And you," she pointed a finger at Hal. "Set down that mug and go to the cellar for a nice wine to go with this roast. Not that mead you insist on every week. There's those good bottles of Talien red that Sylvie brought two weeks gone. They'll do nicely."

"Yes, love," said Hal meekly.

Under Molly's direction the table was set, and the family seated. The joint of beef was carved and served with flatbread, mushrooms and rice, and some spicy mustard greens in cream sauce. Wine and fresh apple juice went with the meal.

Conversation was light—Molly allowed no "business" talk at her table. Much of it revolved around Simon and Sylvie with gentle and not so subtle hints that it was past time for them to declare a formal engagement. Sylvie smiled and gracefully deflected some of Molly and Mery's more direct questions. Simon lapsed into silence and refused to rise to Wills's teasing that he didn't deserve a woman of Sylvie's grace and beauty. He was about to declare a halt to all the speculation until he saw Sylvie gazing at Mery as she cut Glory's meat and poured her a glass of apple juice. Sylvie caught his eye at that moment and smiled.

Maybe it is time, he thought. *But how can I ask her to leave the Havens and give up her career? Axhart would take her as a Keeper in a heartbeat, but would she abandon Summerfield and the Rangers for me?*

When everyone appeared to have eaten enough, Hal rose and lifted his wine glass. Simon refilled his own glass and passed the bottle across to Sylvie who did the same. This was as much a tradition as Molly's no business rule. When everyone had a glass, Hal raised his own and said, "To House Stonebender, the Six Gods, and King Thorston." The adults echoed his words and everyone drank.

"Mery," said Molly. "Will you help me clear away and bring out that apple crumb cake you brought from home? We'll leave these four to talk business. Girls, you're excused. Go out and play and your Mama will call you when it's time for cake."

Sylvie nodded her thanks to Mery and Molly and moved her chair closer to Hal. "I have news from the Havens," she said without preamble, looking from Hal to Simon. "Galen Flandyrs has been spotted in Tintagel."

"He's back in the Havens?" asked Simon. "Has he been detained?"

"No," answered Sylvie. "And that's the other part of my news. It appears he's being sheltered in the Graystorm compound next to the High Tower. My father is protecting him."

CHAPTER ELEVEN

"Flandyrs?" asked Wills. "Is he important?"

"Remember the Alorton scandal last Midwinter?" said Simon. "Flandyrs was the Havens diplomat who suborned Alorton. His scheme was to manipulate the Brigades into inciting a war between the Commonwealth and the Azeri Empire. Flandyrs was an operative for the political arm of the SID, the Gray Rangers. He escaped the Commonwealth and has been in the wind until now."

"The SID disavowed him, of course, but the political department is controlled by the Traditionalist faction in the Havens High Council. Rulanis Summerfield is the last truly powerful Progressive in the Rangers, and his position is tenuous."

"The Graystorm compound, you say." Hal looked at Sylvie with concern in his voice. "Are you safe, lass?"

Simon wondered what Hal meant, until it hit him. If Sylvie's father, head of House Graystorm, a leader in the High Council, and cousin to the Steward, was openly harboring a fugitive, it meant he had the support, or at least consent of House Hightower, the Stewards of Tintagel. It meant that the Traditionalist faction in the Council had enough power to act with impunity. Well known Progressives, like Sylvie and Senior Ranger Summerfield could be in danger of reprisal. *Syr* Berland Graystorm had disinherited his youngest daughter many years earlier, but she still was a Graystorm, a name that commanded respect within the Havens. Simon didn't think her own father would be a threat to her, but many of his retainers might see her death as an opportunity to gain influence in the Traditionalist faction.

"I think I'm safe for now," Sylvie said. "I may need to prevail on you and Molly for sanctuary if things get really bad, but so far there's been little more than talk and no public declaration of Traditionalist rule. The Progressive faction still holds enough Council seats to keep the more strident Houses in check."

"You're family, lass. You have a home here if needs be." He glanced at Simon as if he expected him to say something.

"Aye," agreed Molly. "You needn't ask." The look she gave Simon was more of a glare.

Simon took a deep breath. *In for a penny, in for a crown,* he thought. He reached across the table and took Sylvie's hand. "You have a place with me," he said. "If you'll have me. We need to talk." He looked pointedly at Hal and Molly. "Privately." Wills had the good sense to say nothing.

Sylvie smiled and started to say something but caught to look in his eye and only nodded. "There's more," she continued. She reached under the table and brought up her well-worn leather travel bag. She took out a heavy object and set it on the table in front of Hal. He moved back slightly, as if she had set a venomous snake in front of him.

The object, made of polished wood and black cold iron, had a hexagonal tube about two fingers in width and the length of Simon's hand bound to a wooded stock and curving handle. Any Peacekeeper would recognize the grip and trigger arrangement as similar to his own sidearm, if heavier and less well made. At the end of the tube perched a flat triangle of metal, like a small pan next to what looked like a tiny claw hammer. Simon shivered slightly when he saw it. It was clearly related to the other-worldly weapon that he had hidden in his locker at Wycliffe House. He had seen first hand how deadly the strange weapon could be.

"What in the seven hells is that thing?" Wills asked.

"A weapon," said Simon. "It uses some unknown Fire propellant, non-magical, to shoot a lead projectile out of the tube. At least that's what the one I have does. This looks different, less well made, but I'd guess that it functions the same way." He looked at Sylvie for confirmation.

She drew a lead ball and a small bag of black granular powder out of the bag and set them next to the weapon. She pointed to the bag of powder. "That's the propellant. The little hammer on the weapon holds a shard of flint. It strikes a spark from the metal pan that ignites the powder" She looked at Simon. "And yes, it does as much damage as the smaller lead bits your weapon shoots."

"Where did you get this?" Hal asked.

"We took two hands of these things from a known jolt smuggler we picked up near the Free States, up around the northern border. He had them hidden in the frame of his sled along with a ten weight of this powder and three hands of lead balls." She tapped a finger on the thing's wooden handle. "The fact that he had ten of these things means this isn't a one-off. Someone is making these in quantity. And they're doing it all without modern magic methods. None of these had any signature aura."

"Why is that important?" asked Wills, his eyes fixed on the weapon.

"It won't trigger a security spell," said Simon. "With no aura, the spell won't recognize this as a weapon. If you could conceal it well enough, you could walk into King Thorston's throne room with this thing and nothing short of a full body search would detect it."

Hal picked the weapon up and examined it. "I see the similarity to the thing Simon found, but this is a single shot weapon. Simon's has the revolving wheel that holds six slugs. And the ammunition for Simon's weapon is more sophisticated, all self-contained." He stroked his beard with his free hand. "Whoever is producing these things found a simpler version that they could make by hand without magic. The question is why?"

"Not just why, but who," said Simon. "Who is having these things made? And how do they even know about weapons like this?"

"Did you learn anything from your drug smuggler?" Hal asked Sylvie.

"Nothing useful," Sylvie answered. "He's a courier for hire. He'll move goods for anyone who'll pay, no questions asked. He picks up and delivers at anonymous postal boxes or dead drops."

"What does your man in Fredonia know about this?" Hal smiled at Sylvie's surprised expression. "I have my own sources, don't you know? I've known for a while that you have an inside man in the Fredonia Militia."

Sylvie cocked her head. "Not sure how you know about him. Only Summerfield, Hamil Fairborn, and I are supposed to know who he is." Hal just smiled. Sylvie shrugged. "Nothing. Rumors of some new smuggling operation moving goods by sea from the

Azeris, either north around through Hybaria or the long way south via the Cape of Storms."

"So, nothing that isn't obvious," scoffed Hal.

"But, if these are being made in the Empire, why go through Fredonia and the Havens? Why not smuggle them across the Eastern border into Holdfast, or up from the South through Dundaria?" said Simon.

"Why assume they're meant for the Commonwealth?" Hal asked. "These are inert, but only good for one use. More of an assassin's weapon than a soldier's. Who in the Havens might need such a weapon?"

"My thoughts exactly," said Sylvie. "And I keep coming back to Flandyrs. I don't think he'd plot open warfare on the Great Houses," she picked up the weapon. "But he could cause a lot of devilment with these things."

"So why bring this thing here?" asked Simon. "Summerfield must think there's some connection to the Commonwealth or he wouldn't have asked you to bring us in."

Sylvie cocked her head at him but didn't deny it. "This thing may have been made by the Azeris, or even somewhere in the Free States, but the plans, the idea came from that other place. That other world where Simon's weapon came from. And that portal was opened here, in the Commonwealth, by Glendowyn Hightower."

"How do we know that someone else didn't open the same portal?" Hal asked.

"Not likely." Sylvie shook her head. "The skills to open such a portal are beyond most Earth mages, and the consequences of reaching through one would be fatal to Humans or Orcs, even with lead shields. Besides, who would even understand what to look for? Flandyrs probably did, but only after Simon got the weapon past Blackpool's security spell. No one else could know the potential of these things."

Hal frowned. "And Summerfield thinks Flandyrs still has a contact here? Someone who at least knows what Glendowyn and Blackpool managed to do."

"Gran Swampwater?" Simon speculated.

"Not likely," said Sylvie. "She only talked to us because of her son. I can't see her sharing anything with an outsider, especially with an Elf."

Molly and Mery returned at that point with plates and a tray of apple cake cut into squares. Mery carried a pot of coffee.

Molly cocked her head at Hal who nodded. She was a Keeper's wife and knew when to interrupt and when to leave well enough alone.

"Wills," she said as she set small clean plates on the table. "Go fetch the girls. Mery and I will set out their plates." She looked around. "Who else wants cake and coffee."

Talk of Flandyrs and strange weapons was replaced with Wills and Mery describing the trials and tribulations of building a new house on the other side of the Glenharrow Hills in nearby Steading. Simon could remember when Steading was considered rural and backward. Now it was becoming yet another suburb of the burgeoning capital.

Sylvie moved over to sit next to Simon as they ate apple cake, drank coffee, and finished with some sweet white wine. Conversation revolved around family news and Simon listened as Wills caught the family up on events with the rest of the Stonebender siblings. Sylvie slipped her hand into Simon's as she listened, enjoying the talk. Simon's other two foster brothers, Hervik and the eldest brother Thorston were also advocates, although they concentrated on corporate law. His three foster sisters were all in law enforcement in some way. Wren was a Lieutenant on the day watch in Northollow, one of the closer suburban townships. Ilsa was an agent with the Justice Ministry stationed on the Eastern Borderlands near Azeri Crossing, and Katya was a King's Prosecutor in the Northwest Territories.

By eighteenth hour everyone was sated, and the conversation lagged. Wills and Mery gathered up their daughters and bade the rest of the family goodbye. Molly suggested that Simon and Sylvie take advantage of the warm evening and go for a walk "to work off the apple cake."

"Hal and I can manage the dishes," she said. When Hal started to protest, she fixed him with one of her no-nonsense glares and he ducked his head and began clearing the table.

A few minutes later, Simon and Sylvie were walking hand in hand across the wide driveway in front of the Hall. Simon led the way to a copse of trees just behind the stables. There was a stone bench there with a view over the back gardens behind the main house. They sat down and Simon turned so he faced Sylvie.

He looked at her and for a moment his breath caught in his chest and his tongue felt thick. *How do I do this?* He thought. *What do I say?*

He took both of her hands in his and looked into her eyes. "Sylvie..."

She stopped him with a finger on his lips. "Yes," she said.

"Yes?"

"Yes, we should get married. Yes, I will leave the Havens and live here in the Commonwealth with you. Yes, my love. I want us to be a family."

"But," Simon stammered. "You'd be giving up everything back there. Your career, your family and friends, your Title, everything."

She kissed him. "None of that matters. My career is likely over anyway. If the Traditionalists have taken charge of the Council, Summerfield will be put out to pasture, if he's lucky. All of us in the Rangers who openly supported him will be quietly retired or shuffled off to remote or obscure postings, safely out of the way. I'd sooner wash dirty linen in a laundry than put up with the kind of 'duty' they'd assign me."

"Axhart will take you on as a Peacekeeper in a heartbeat," offered Simon. "If you want to keep working here, that is."

Sylvie smiled. "We'll see. As for family and title, my father disowned me years ago. I was never close to any of my siblings, being the youngest by over fifty years. You and Hal and Molly are more family to me than they ever were." She reached up and touched his cheek. "We share *ghiras* now. I don't feel whole when I'm parted from you. So, yes, Simon Buckley, I will marry you and live wherever you wish."

He took her in his arms and for a long moment there was nothing in the world but the sunset, the cool air, and their two bodies and minds intertwined in a long kiss.

CHAPTER TWELVE

Simon arrived at his office a quarter hour later than usual but still in time for the morning watch change. He had looked in on his teams and arranged a quick briefing with each of his Sergeants for later in the morning.

Lessa greeted him with a mug of coffee and a short stack of message flimsies. She smiled in a knowing way but said nothing other than her usual "Good meeting." Simon suspected Hal had already told her about his engagement.

He and Sylvie had gotten little sleep the night before. Their announcement of their decision had been greeted with a roar of approval from Hal and an "About time" from Molly. After that, the remainder of the evening had been spent mirroring the rest of the family and many of Hal and Molly's friends. Hal had then insisted on breaking out the 100-year-old Darrowdowns brandy he kept for special occasions and he and Simon had sat together far into the night drinking and talking.

Sylvie was on her way back to the Havens. She planned to resign from the Rangers as soon as she could arrange a personal meeting with Summerfield. She hoped to be able to move her personal effects and be back in the Commonwealth within a couple of weeks.

Simon sipped the coffee gratefully as he read through the morning's message traffic. Little of it related directly to his teams but it did give him a feel for the energy on the streets. One item did relate to his open cases; the extradition request for their fugitive in the Ironlands had been approved. He'd have to send Hal out there to take the Dwarf into custody which meant that the other cases Hal was working would be on hold or would be handled by his team reporting directly to Simon for the time being.

He was sipping the last of his coffee when Lessa stepped in and announced that Sergeant Birchfield was there to see him.

Simon glanced at his timepiece. It was almost eighth hour. "Thank you, Lessa," he said. "Send him in. And would you please draw up travel orders and a budget authorization for my signature? I'll need to send Sergeant Stonebender to the Ironlands for a fugitive pick-up. Also, see if you can get me an appointment to talk to a KP Advocate named Hammersmith. He's with the Justice Ministry Antiterrorism Office."

"Aye, LT," she answered with a grin. Simon smiled back. She was learning. Lessa stepped aside and Birchfield came in. Simon waved him to a chair.

"Good meeting, Gervis. What's the latest?" Simon asked.

"We found the flyer Sommerstag had rented," he answered. "It was on the roof of the furniture shop that backs up to the alley where she died. There's a ladder on the other side of the building. That's how she got down. Forensics is processing the flyer, but I don't expect much. There was black pitch on the landing struts but nothing else useful on it that I could see. At least we know how she got from the docks to the alley."

"What do we know about the furniture shop? Any connection to known gangs or the Azeri Liberation Brigades?"

"I've got one of my guys doing a records search on the address and the owner." Gervis checked his notebook. "An Orc named Starn Clearbrook, Fish Clan. He's been there for a good ten years, no complaints on record."

"What about Anika's room at Lily's place?" Simon asked.

"We haven't had any success with the notebook. It's some sort of private code or shorthand. There was a high-end imager and voice recorder in the trunk by her bed. Kyle Evarts is going over them. We found receipts for the flyer rental agency, several restaurants, a commercial coach company, and a number of other businesses scattered through the Hollows. My guys are checking each one out and we think we can put together a chronology of her movements for the time she was in town." He glanced at his notes again. "Nothing much new on the Harsaka brothers. No one wants to talk to us about them and I get the feeling they have some sort of high jingle connection."

"How so?" asked Simon. He hadn't mentioned his own suspicions that the criminal records had been altered.

"Nothing specific," Birchfield replied. "Just a feeling. One of my snitches out in the East End is a *kharo* for the Ox clan at the far end of Tanner Street. He shut me down when I asked about the brothers. Not unexpected. But he mentioned that I'd be better off asking around 10 West than far East Tanner."

10 West Tanner was a reference to the Justice Ministry, headquartered in the old Royal Mint building at that address. Simon only nodded, and Birchfield gave him a curious look.

"Do you know something I don't LT?"

Simon told him about the Harsakas blank criminal records for the last five years and his plan to speak to Bendict Hammersmith.

"You think Hammersmith turned them?" asked Birchfield. "Why would they interest the antiterrorism squad? As far as anyone knows they were jimmy heisters, not smugglers, and there's no hint of any connection to the Brigades."

Simon shrugged. "That's what I want to ask Hammersmith. I doubt he'll confirm or deny their connection, but it's worth a conversation."

Gervis grunted and checked his notes again. "The only other thing that's a bit curious is the list of stuff stolen from the warehouse down by the docks. It comes to 85 Standard weight of silver, 20 Standard weight of platinum, and 15 Standard of cold iron. The silver and platinum are easy to understand. Any jobber will take them at near thirty percent of market price and sell them on for seventy percent before the end of the day. But the iron is an odd thing to steal."

"Why would anyone steal cold iron?" asked Simon. "And why would the dealer have it locked in his warehouse?"

"This wasn't ordinary iron," Gervis answered. "It's what's called neutral iron. It's smelted and forged by hand using no magic, not even a Fire spell to start the forge fire. Research departments at universities and spell companies use it to dampen any residual spells in the lab so that new spells aren't influenced by ambient magic. There's no market for it outside of those places and they control the inventory very carefully. They aren't about to purchase from an undocumented source."

Simon felt a chill. He knew another use for such iron. He didn't say anything to Gervis. The magically inert weapons weren't part of the investigation, at least not yet, and Simon had a feeling the information should be kept as close as possible.

"Curious, yes," said Simon. "But easily checked. There can't be that many places in the city where a jobber could lay the iron off. See if anyone has approached them. But meanwhile, keep it close. I don't want details getting back to His Lordship the Mayor unless it's from me, understood?"

"Aye, LT," said Gervis as he closed his notebook and stood. "I'll do that inquiry myself."

He turned and left the office, passing Lessa on the way.

"Had you already contacted the Justice Ministry about seeing Advocate Hammersmith, LT?" she asked as she entered the office.

Simon shook his head. "No. I didn't even know the man's name until after the end of the day watch on Smitsday. Then it was Weeksend and I figured nobody would be in their office until this morning."

"Well, his secretary seemed to be expecting our call," said Lessa. "She didn't even check with her boss and gave you an appointment at half past thirteenth hour today."

Simon rubbed his chin and considered this. He hadn't spoken to anyone other than Hal and Willston about Hammersmith. He hadn't exactly told Wills not to speak to Hammersmith, but he hadn't asked him to either. *Professional courtesy, I suppose. Actually, this may not be a bad thing. If Wills has already vouched for me, he may be more willing to talk.*

"It's all good, Lessa. Somebody opened the tunnel for me."

Lessa nodded. "Sergeant Stonebender is here. I

have the travel orders ready for him." She glanced over her shoulder then leaned forward and whispered. "And congratulations, LT."

Simon smiled. Lessa passed a hung-over Hal as she left the office and closed the door. Hal groaned as he sat down and eyed Simon's coffee mug.

"Got any more of that?"

As if on cue, Lessa returned with a tray holding a full coffee pot and two mugs. She set it on the desk, grinned at Hal, and left. Simon poured for Hal and himself and they both drank gratefully. Hal set his mug down and rubbed his temples.

"The extradition paperwork came through," said Simon setting down his own mug. "Lessa has the travel orders and an expense voucher for you."

"I still think this is a bad idea," Hal grumbled. "Send someone else. You're looking at an IG beef that could cave in on your head, you've got the Mayor on your back about a high-profile case, and you've got nothing but a couple of junior sergeants to back you up. You need me here."

"I need you in the Ironlands," said Simon. "Their minister was pretty specific about only dealing with a Dwarf 'of standing.' You're all I've got. Besides, it was your case. You should see it through."

"Cleavestone can stick it up his arse," said Hal, referring to the Ironlands Justice Minister. "The Stonebenders were never good enough for his high and mighty grandfather back before the Wars. Now I've got 'standing'? Hypocritical old bastard."

Simon just sighed. Dwarven feuds were long. This one dated back at least three centuries and had endured long after House Stonebender had relocated to the Commonwealth.

"Bury it, Hal. You're going and you will be the very picture of diplomacy while you're there. Take someone from your team with you, your choice. I'd say Jack Ironhand since he's also a Dwarf, but he's your second. I'll need him as team leader while you're gone." Simon smiled as a thought occurred to him. "If you really want to stick it to Cleavestone, take Handel Brookstone. An Orc armorer in a Peacekeeper uniform will really set the old bastard off."

Hal grinned crookedly. "The look on his smug face when he sees Brookstone might just be worth the trip."

"And you'll both be under diplomatic cover. He'll just have to swallow it and be polite," said Simon.

"All good," sighed Hal. "I'll go. If we leave by midday, we'll be home in three. Watch your back until then."

"I will. Lessa has the paperwork. Now get out of here and tell Brookstone to pack a bag."

Hal stood and gave Simon a wry salute, which made him smile, then turned and left the inner office. Simon could hear him speaking to Lessa in a gruff tone, but she laughed, so he figured it was all good.

A few minutes later Lessa announced that Sergeant Hanks was waiting to see him. Jason Hanks was the newest Sergeant in the Magic Enforcement division, having been prompted to take Frank Killian's place after the Flandyrs affair. Simon hadn't known him well during his own time as a Sergeant. Events and cases had never really brought them together. Hanks had a reputation as a competent, if somewhat plodding investigator. His case clearance rate was acceptable but not stellar and his team tended to reflect his slow methodical approach. Simon liked him well enough but had never been able to make the same personal connection that he had with Hal or with Gervis Birchfield.

Hanks stopped in front of Simon's desk and saluted.

"Have a seat, Jason," said Simon. "How is your team doing?"

Hanks nodded and took a seat. "Well enough, LT," he answered in his slow Dundarian drawl. "And may

I say, congratulations on your engagement? I don't know Lady Graystorm well, but the squad room thinks she's pretty amazing."

"So, Hal and Lessa have been spreading the word." Simon shook his head. "So much for keeping things low profile for a while."

Hanks frowned. "Sorry, LT. I didn't know you minded."

Simon laughed and waved a hand. "All good Jason. Now, what's new with the team?"

"We're getting back on to the right path after the riots. We finally have a lead in the Weaver case. It looks like an Orc immigrant with some Earth talent was recruited by the Fish Clan to collapse the building. Should be moving on them with a warrant today." Hanks went on to detail several other cases his team was working, all moving forward. No flash, but solid procedural work.

"All good," said Simon as Hanks finished. "Anything else?"

Hanks squirmed slightly in his seat. "Well, we caught a new case this morning. I'm not even sure it's in our garden, but the arson squad asked us to assist. It involves a straightforward robbery of a specialty metals warehouse way out past the east end of Tanner, in the Clamath industrial area. The thief set fire to the warehouse, maybe to cover his tracks, although that doesn't make a lot of sense to me. Once the fire got good and hot, someone cast an air spell that sucked most of the oxygen out of the building. It damped the flames, but not the heat. As soon as the Fire Brigade opened the doors it set off a flashover that injured three firefighters and almost took out the Water mage on the scene. He's apparently one of their oldest and best and he managed to throw up a water wall that saved the whole team. He called us because he's convinced this was a trap to kill firefighters, not just ordinary arson."

Simon held a lid on his impatience. Of course this was in their garden and was probably just as the senior Water mage had suggested. Hanks should have led the briefing with this case. Instead he asked calmly, "What have you learned so far?"

"Nothing, really. All I've got is what I just told you. I'm sending Tunnelsmith out to meet with the Water mage and get a formal statement."

"No, do that yourself. And get a list of everything that was stolen. Get one of Kyle Evarts's men out to the scene for a forensic investigation and aural reading on the air spell." Simon paused as Hanks scribbled notes. *I shouldn't have to tell him this,* he thought. *He should be ahead of me at this point.*

"Aye, sir," said Hanks stiffly. "I'll get right on it."

"Who was the Water mage?" asked Simon.

Hanks glanced at his notes. "Fellow named Jaime Smithington. He's an assistant Chief, heads up all the Brigades in the Hollows and the East End."

"Why was he on the scene? Seems odd for a senior officer to respond to a routine fire."

Hanks nodded. "I thought so too, but my guys tell me that half the department is on stand down. They got hit hard with the riots, a lot of injuries and just plain exhaustion from working five days straight. Senior command has taken over a lot of the local Brigades so their men can get some rest."

Simon thought he recognized Smithington's name but couldn't place it. "All good, Jason. Get going and keep me posted when you have more information."

Hanks stood and saluted again then left the office in a hurry.

I'll need to have a talk with him soon, before his next quarterly review. Simon shook his head. This was the part of his job he hated. Rating his teams by statistics and judging people's abilities made him feel uncomfortable, like he was betraying a confidence.

Simon put those thoughts aside and spoke the incantation to start up the magic mirror on his desk. He flashed on the dictation function and began dictating a report to Mayor Aspenwald. He hoped the written report would satisfy the politician. He was in no mood for a face-to-face briefing.

CHAPTER THIRTEEN

Simon spent the rest of the morning doing paperwork, the bane of his existence. Much of it was simple reporting requiring little more than a brief reading and a signature. Some involved review of pending court cases his teams had cleared, and this required more attention. He'd never appreciated the role a Peacekeeper Lieutenant played in making sure the evidence sent to the King's Prosecutors was clear, concise, and well organized. Much of his time involved organizing his teams' reports into a form that could be easily followed in a courtroom, rather than the more realistic but often chaotic chronology of the actual investigation.

He put the work aside at half past midday and told Lessa he was going to get some lunch before his meeting with Bendict Hammersmith.

"I'll be available by mirror if you need me but try to hold any calls until I get back to the office."

Simon stopped at a tavern two blocks away for a

beer and a bowl of mutton stew. He took his time, considering how he would approach Hammersmith. He'd taken Hal's advice and brought the file on the Harsaka brothers with him. He figured it would be harder for Hammersmith to deny altering the record, if indeed he had, if Simon could show him the actual file. In the end, he decided to simply ask Hammersmith what interest he had in the Harsakas' background, since obviously he had checked out their records. He might deny altering them, but he had clearly signed for them and therefore had some interest.

10 West Tanner was within comfortable walking distance of Wycliffe House. Simon arrived at the main gate to the old fortress fifteen minutes early for his appointment. The building had been the Royal mint during the later days of the Magisterium but had been built 300 years before that as a Royal fortress, one of six that ringed the old city outside the Old Wall.

Simon showed his credentials at the guard post and was passed through the gate. He walked through the gatehouse into the bailey. The central keep had been broken during the final battles of the Wars a hundred and eighty years ago. Rather than preserve it, it had been razed and the bailey converted to a garden. The inner walls of the fortress had been opened and glassed with plate and lead panes in a style that had been daring 80 years ago but now looked quaint in comparison to the steel and glass commercial towers of Cymbeline's North Side.

The central garden was green, full of mature trees and lush bushes, and set with benches and low walls that created natural nooks and private sitting areas. Simon had no illusions about their actual purpose. All were carefully monitored with sound and image recorders. More than one confession had been recorded during 'private' conversations between KPs and suspects.

The guard had directed him to the west wall. There he found a lift and a directory. Hammersmith was listed as a Special Prosecutor in the Antiterrorism division with an office on the fourth floor.

Simon rode the lift up and found himself in an open lobby with a view through a curving wall of glass panels looking down on the central courtyard. A receptionist, a thin fussy looking man, sat behind a desk opposite the lift. As Simon approached the desk a broad-shouldered Dwarf stepped forward from his right. Simon turned to face him. He was a little taller than Hal with sandy hair and beard, a ruddy face and a ready smile. He extended his hand.

"Lieutenant Buckley?" he said. "I'm Bendict Hammersmith. Your brother told me you needed to speak to me. Shall we go to my office?"

Simon shook his hand. "So Willston did contact you."

Hammersmith nodded. "He did. He told me you were interested in a couple of Orcs and that you weren't the type to be put off by bureaucratic doublespeak." He grinned. "Not that I'd try that sort of thing."

Hammersmith gestured toward the right and set off walking at a brisk pace. Simon trailed behind him as they passed a series of office doors on the left and the rough stone of the old curtain wall on the right. About halfway along the length of the West wall Hammersmith stopped and opened the door that looked the same as half a dozen they'd already passed. Hammersmith's name was painted on the frosted glass of the door but otherwise there was nothing to mark it as any different.

Simon stopped in the doorway. The entire far wall of the office was glass, three wide panes bound together with thin lead strips forming a floor to ceiling window. Hammersmith pulled out a modern swivel chair and took a seat. He waved Simon to a leather bound chair opposite the black wood and steel desk. He noticed Simon's gaze and grinned again.

"One of the best kept secrets in the capital," he said. To Simon's puzzled glance he added, "The courtyard. Not many people know it's here. I guess those of us who work here forget how remarkable the place is."

Simon thought of the narrow window in his own office, really just a glazed over arrow slit, and had to agree. He sat in the chair, fingering the file folder in his lap.

"I assume those are the records of the Harsaka brothers." Hammersmith leaned back in his own chair and folded his arms. "Let me save us both a lot of time and verbal jousting. Yes, the Harsakas were working for Justice. Yes, I sequestered the last five years of their criminal records. It was part of the deal that got them in our tunnel, so to speak. And no, I can't tell you why we were interested in their assistance. It's part of an ongoing case with Crown Security implications. And no, I don't know who killed them."

"Well, Faith," said Simon, allowing his natural Westport docks drawl to surface. "I guess there's nothing for a poor Peacekeeper to do but go back to my little office and let my betters catch the real bad guys."

Hammersmith's grin vanished. "I've told you what I can, Lieutenant. No need to be rude. The Harsaka brothers provided some important information and I can't let what they told us get out." He held up a hand as Simon opened his mouth to speak. "No, I don't doubt your discretion, Lieutenant, but the fewer who know the scope of this investigation the better."

"What did the Harsaka brothers have to do with the Free States?" Simon asked in a neutral tone. "Specifically, Fredonia. Did they spend any time there?"

"That would be one of those things that I can't

discuss with you," said Hammersmith.

"Do you know what they stole from a nearby warehouse the night they were killed?" asked Simon.

Hammersmith uncrossed his arms and sat up straighter in his chair. "Why would that matter to me? We got information from the Harsakas. What they did on their own time was not my problem."

"What do you know about neutral iron, Mr. Hammersmith?"

Hammersmith smiled. "If you know what neutral iron is, you know that no jobber in the Commonwealth would touch it. So why steal it?"

"Let's not pretend you weren't interested in the iron." Simon's voice was hard. "The platinum and the silver were just sweeteners for the Harsakas, so they'd take the job. It was the neutral iron, and whomever was taking it off their hands, that you wanted." He paused. "What was in the files for the last five years? Did Lasko and Fortis spend a lot of time in Fredonia?"

Hammersmith's smile broadened. "Willston said you were good. Tell me what you know, or surmise about neutral iron and Fredonia and I'll tell you what the Harsakas were doing for us."

Simon looked at him for a long while. "I know that neutral iron carries no magical aura. That any device, or weapon, made with it would fail to register on a security screen or detection spell. I know that someone has made weapons like that. I know that the Free States are at least the conduit, if not the origin of those weapons." Simon paused and when Hammersmith didn't respond, he continued. "I know that the Harsaka brothers broke into a warehouse three days ago and removed a quantity of neutral iron and a substantial weight of other noble metals. Those metals, and particularly the iron, have not been found. Shortly after the theft, both brothers were murdered by a Water mage using a condensation spell. I suspect the Harsakas had connections to the Free States and those connections are what you leveraged to recruit Lasko and Fortis."

Simon didn't mention the death of Anika Sommerstag. He wasn't sure why, but he didn't want to reveal that and her connection to the Mayor unless Hammersmith seemed to already know about it.

Hammersmith turned half away from Simon and looked out through the glass wall at something in the courtyard below. He tugged at his lower lip for a few long seconds. He glanced back at Simon. "I don't suppose you'd just take my word for it that the Harsakas' deaths had nothing to do with the work they were doing for me?"

Simon shrugged. "Not unless you shared convincing information that ruled out a connection."

"Didn't think so," Hammersmith said with a wry smile. "What I'm about to tell you doesn't leave this office." He paused and Simon nodded. "About twelve weeks ago, Lasko Harsaka contacted one of our agents in Fredonia. He claimed to have information about Galen Flandyrs. There's still a substantial reward for information leading to his extradition. Lasko and Fortis wanted to deal Flandyrs for the money and a clean slate in the Commonwealth."

"They had charges pending here in the Commonwealth?" Simon's question was more of a statement. "How were they connected with Flandyrs?"

"Flandyrs hired them to do a job in Fredonia. He still has contacts in Snake clan. Even after you and Stonebender took down the Azeri Liberation Brigade here in Cymbeline, he maintained connections with the branches in the Empire and the Free States. So, Flandyrs reached out and found the Harsaka brothers. They were laying low after a high-profile heist in the Commonwealth but were open to contract work if the price was right. It was all arranged through a local *kharo* and the brothers didn't know who was paying until the time came for delivery."

"What did they steal for Flandyrs?" asked Simon. He was pretty sure he knew the answer but wanted Hammersmith to confirm it.

"Ten Standard of neutral iron," said Hammersmith. "But you knew that, didn't you?"

"No, not for sure. But it makes sense."

Hammersmith cocked his head. He reached into a drawer and drew out a short piece of metal. He set it on the desk in front of Simon. "Do you have any idea what this is?" he asked. "We found a crate of them mixed in with a shipment of Azeri rawhide at the Eastport customs station."

Simon picked the object up. It was a short iron tube, a little longer than his hand. "Neutral iron?" he asked. Hammersmith nodded and Simon continued. "It's part of a weapon. It fits into a wooden handle. The weapon uses a small explosive charge to shoot a lead ball down this tube with incredible force. The ball isn't much wider than a fingernail, but deadly."

"And you know this how?"

"I've seen such a weapon, fully assembled." Simon dropped the metal tube on Hammersmith's desk. "The Gray Rangers intercepted a dozen of them at the Free States Border, just southeast of Fredonia, a couple of weeks ago. They're mainly concerned about the trouble these things could cause in the Havens. But it looks like there's a problem here as well."

"You've seen these things?" Hammersmith's face paled. "They really work?"

Simon folded his arms. "Will you take my word for it that I have and they do? If we're trading information, fine. Otherwise, I'd rather not be too specific about how I know."

Hammersmith's smile was thin. "What do you want to know?'

"Why were the Harsaka brothers back in the Commonwealth? Were they still working for Flandyrs, or did they have another buyer for the neutral iron they stole here? And what's their connection with Anika Sommerstag?"

"Who?" Hammersmith looked nonplussed. "You mean that scandal sheet newsie from Fredonia who's been poking around the Hollows? What about her?"

"She's dead. Killed by the same Water mage who killed the Harsakas."

Hammersmith leaned back in his chair and said nothing for a moment. "I don't know what she was doing in Cymbeline," he said. "As far as we know, she had nothing to do with Flandyrs or with the neutral iron. The Harsaka brothers returned a couple of weeks before they died with no Commonwealth warrants outstanding. They reported in on schedule. They had the location of the warehouse and the means to contact Flandyrs's agent to take delivery. Anything they could steal in addition to the iron was supposed to be their fee. We planned to have a team on hand to scoop up anyone who took delivery of the iron. The rest of the metal would go back to the owners and the Harsakas would be free to go."

"If you knew where they were going and how they were supposed to make the delivery, then why are they dead and the iron and other metals missing?"

"Because the Harskas were cunning," Hammersmith said. "Not necessarily smart, but too clever by half. They saw the riots as an opportunity to make a tidy profit and still keep their contract with Flandyrs. They robbed the warehouse a day ahead of schedule."

Simon nodded. "You didn't have a team there. And then Flandyrs's man played them false and killed them."

Hammersmith sighed loudly. "We have no idea who the brothers' contact here in the Commonwealth was and now we have no conduit back to Flandyrs. He's in the wind again."

"So, you don't know of any connection between Sommerstag and the Harsakas?" Simon asked.

"Other than being in Fredonia before coming here, no." Hammersmith cocked his head. "Why the interest in Sommerstag?"

It was Simon's turn to pause. He wasn't sure if there was any real connection between Anika and the Harsakas other than the mage that had killed them. He decided to go with that.

"Anika Sommerstag was murdered by the same mage who killed the Harsaka brothers," he said. "They were both on the same dock down near the Great Cut, maybe at the same time, maybe not."

"Were they working together?" Hammersmith asked. "Did Sommerstag know anything about the weapons or the connection to Flandyrs?"

"I don't know," admitted Simon. "My teams are looking into her activities here in Cymbeline. We know she was already here working on some sort of story before the riots. We know she was interested in events down in the Hollows before that. But we don't know why she was here or what she knew about the Harsakas."

"As to Flandyrs," Simon continued. "He's been spotted in Tintagel. It appears he's under the protection of House Graystorm."

Hammersmith leaned forward. "You know this for certain? How old is your information? How reliable?"

"He was seen moving openly around the Graystorm family compound as little as two days ago. My source is completely reliable. He's being sheltered by the Traditionalist Party and I doubt the Steward has much motivation to enforce our extradition request."

"We'd heard the Traditionalists were moving more openly to take control of the Havens government," said Hammersmith tugging at his beard. "It seems events are moving faster than I'd anticipated. We don't know for sure if there's a plot to disrupt politics here. Only rumors of some sort of high level attack in the next few weeks. But if these things"—he pointed to the iron tube on the desk—"are here, then someone is planning to use them."

CHAPTER FOURTEEN

Simon left Hammersmith's office with an agreement to share whatever information either of them developed about threats to the Crown or the city. He didn't believe for a second that Hammersmith would share anything he considered important, but Simon's focus was on solving the murders, not on stopping terrorists. What seemed unimportant to the Antiterrorism squad might still be valuable to Simon and his teams.

He was thinking about Anika and wondering how she fit into this new picture. He didn't notice the dark blue Hilten sled until it pulled to the curb just ahead of him. A bulky Orc in an expensively tailored business suit got out and faced him.

"Lt. Buckley." The Orc said his name as a statement rather than a question.

"What can I do for you?" asked Simon as he took a step back and moved his hand toward the needler holstered at the small of his back.

The Orc held his hands out at his sides, palms

outward. "No harm, Lieutenant. Mr. Forsaka just wants a word with you."

Kalmish Forsaka was a *demilia,* a priest of the *demilvosk* animistic religious sect favored by many Azeris. He was also de facto head of the Cabal of Clans, the Old Men who ran most Orc affairs in Cymbeline.

"Then why didn't he send Kermal Brackenville?" asked Simon. "I'm not some lackey to be summoned. If Forsaka wants to talk, he can make an appointment with my secretary."

Simon started to walk away. The Orc moved his hand and faster than Simon could react, he found himself looking down the barrel of a Gowron bolt pistol.

"Brackenville is otherwise occupied," said the Orc. "I have my orders. My Boss didn't specify if he wanted you healthy, only that he wanted you." He sighed and lowered the weapon, but only slightly. "Look, Lieutenant. I can't say I blame you for not wanting to get into the sled. I wouldn't like it either. But I've had a tough morning, and I'd appreciate it if you'd let me do this the easy way." He raised the weapon again. "But easy or hard, we're going to see Mr. Forsaka."

Simon hesitated still. Forsaka wanted him alive, so he doubted his would-be escort would shoot to kill. More likely he'd aim for a leg. Simon's needler was loaded with sleeper darts, but he didn't think they'd take the Orc down before he put a slug in him. Worse, the dart might ruin his aim and the slug would hit something vital. In the end, Simon smiled and raised his hands chest level.

"Let's go see the *demilia,*" he said.

The Orc lowered the pistol and motioned toward the sled. Simon got into the passenger seat and the Orc climbed behind the steering yoke.

The Orc pointed to a compartment between the seats. "I'll need you to put your sidearm and mirror in here." He shrugged at Simon's hard look. "Boss's orders. You'll get 'em back after."

Simon swiped the front of his mirror and checked for messages before dropping it in the compartment. The needler followed. He didn't say anything about the dagger in his boot sheath. He doubted it would be much good against the Gowron, which may have been why his escort hadn't asked about it.

They drove south from Tanner on side streets, deep into the Hollows. Simon expected to be taken to Farska's *demilvosk* shop not far from Lilly's tavern, but to his surprise they went farther south and east, toward the Great Cut.

"Where are we going?" Simon asked.

"Where my Boss told me to take you," was all the reply he got.

They passed the warehouse and dock complex where the Harsaka brothers had been killed. A few blocks later they turned into a narrower street that ended in a small, closed square. Directly ahead lay a burned-out warehouse. At first Simon assumed it was yet another victim of the recent violence, but on second look, the blackened timbers and ash showed signs of weathering. This building had burned weeks, maybe months, ago.

The sled stopped and settled to the ground. The big Orc pointed at the building to the right, a narrow structure wedged between the derelict warehouse and a large chandlery. Simon climbed out of the sled. The door to the narrow building opened as Simon approached.

A petite well-proportioned Orc woman with jet black hair and brilliant green eyes regarded him with a wry smile. He recognized her but realized he'd never learned her name. She'd once led him through a maze of alleys to a meeting with the Cabal.

"Simon Buckley," she said with a soft Azeri accent

"Chief Forsaka is waiting for you." She turned and walked down a narrow corridor toward an open doorway.

Simon followed and they entered a well-lit room fitted out as an office. To his left, behind a battered desk, sat Kalmish Forsaka. The Orc Chieftain was dressed simply in an open necked shirt and camel hair vest. His arms were bare, and the Wind Clan tattoos stood out dark against his light-colored skin. On his right wrist he wore a thin gold bracer. A ring with a large aquamarine stone glinted from his left hand. The petite woman stepped back and closed the door leaving Simon alone in the room with the most dangerous Fire mage he had ever encountered.

Forsaka smiled at his discomfort. He gestured toward a chair. "Welcome Lieutenant," he said. "Please sit. Will you have tea?"

Simon exhaled sharply. He'd noted the porcelain tea service on the corner of the desk, but still couldn't believe Forsaka intended to observe the forms of hospitality after having him snatched off the street.

"You have your private muscle pull me off the street like some common thug, and then offer me tea?" Simon fumed, anger overcoming apprehension. "Where is Kermal Brackenville? You sent him to make contact about the Harsakas. Why not let him relay information to you?"

"Kermal is engaged in business outside the capital right now," Forsaka said pleasantly. "My apologies for the unusual circumstances, but I couldn't very well come to your office, and asking you to come to my shop could involve complications after the recent violence. Please, take tea and then we can discuss business."

Ritual, thought Simon. Food or drink offered and accepted before business could be conducted. He sat and Forsaka poured tea into small delicate cups. Simon sipped the fragrant brew and composed himself.

"Where is Kermal?" Simon asked. "Fredonia?"

Forsaka's expression didn't change, but Simon thought he saw the barest hesitation as the Orc lifted his own cup to his lips. Forsaka sipped and savored the tea.

"What have you discovered about the Harska brothers?" he asked, ignoring Simon's question.

"They were working for the Justice Ministry," said Simon, "but then you already knew that."

Forsaka set his cup down and tented his fingers. "There's a difference between knowing a thing and confirming it. What sort of work did they perform for the Ministry?"

"That's part of an ongoing investigation," said Simon. "I can't, won't, discuss that. I will tell you that it doesn't connect in any obvious way to the Cabal."

Forsaka laughed. "And what would you know of our operations or our interest in the Harsakas's activities?"

Simon felt another surge of anger. "I know that these riots caught you and the rest of your so-called Cabal off balance. Your *kharo's* didn't see it coming, couldn't control it, and have yet to offer any help to the Orcs harmed by it. I know Lily Ponsaka has done more for 'your' people than any Clan Chieftain has ever done. Investigating the Harsakas is my job because they were killed by illegal magic. I'm not your lackey or your ally. I'm willing to talk to Kermal Brackenville because he was my teammate and friend, but don't trade on that to try to manipulate me or so help me I'll make it my life's work to lock you in a cell for the rest of your days."

The old Orc's face reddened, and his eyes went cold. Then just as quickly his face returned to the neutral smile he'd worn when Simon first entered the room. "As you wish, Lieutenant. I accept your assessment of them for the time being." He sipped more tea. "And you're right about the riots. In fact, that's part of my reason for wanting to speak to you. To try to avoid further misunderstanding."

Simon drained his own tea and held the cup just above the tea service tray. If he set it down upside down, it would signal an end to the conversation and he would either leave the room or remain Forsaka's unwilling guest.

"I'm listening," he said.

"What do you know about the warehouse next to this building?" Forsaka's question took Simon by surprise. It didn't seem to relate to anything they had said so far.

"Nothing, other than it must have burned some weeks ago, not in the riots."

Forsaka nodded. "It fell victim to a series of arson fires in the winter and spring. Arson fires that destroyed a good deal of the jolt stockpiles of both the Canal Street Scalpers and the Knacker Loblollies."

Simone felt a chill. *Does he know about the Princess?*

As if reading his thoughts, Forsaka said, "We don't care about the identity of the arsonist. The important fact now is that the same Fire Brigade Chief who investigated those arson fires was the target yesterday of a trap deliberately set to kill the firefighters on the scene."

Simon's eyes widened. He groped for the name that Jason Hanks had given him just that morning. "Jaime Smithington?"

Forsaka nodded. "This trap wasn't set by us, or by any Orc in the Hollows."

"How can I be sure of that?" Simon asked.

Forsaka shrugged. "How can I be sure that the Harsakas haven't compromised me or my associates? You see? We'll just have to trust each other here."

"So who did set the trap?" asked Simon. "And why?"

"I don't know. But ask yourself, who would benefit

from Smithington's death? Not me or my associates. We didn't set those earlier fires, despite what Sergeant Killian wanted you to believe, nor did Killian himself, so he doesn't benefit either. Maybe Assistant Chief Smithington would have an idea."

"Why tell me this?"

Forsaka drained the last of his tea and set the cup on the tray, upside down. "Because I don't want any mistaken ideas about Orc involvement in an attack on the Fire Brigade. We have enough trouble down in the Hollows without adding Peacekeeper vengeance to the mix."

Simon set his own cup down. "My teams don't work that way."

Forsaka's smile was thin. "Perhaps not. But trust is in short supply down here. And as you say, they are your teams."

Simon heard the door open and turned his head. The young Orc woman stood in the doorway.

"Lisana will show you out," said Forsaka.

Simon nodded and started to follow her out. He stopped at the door and turned back to Forsaka. "The Harsakas were working for Galen Flandyrs as well. They stole a quantity of neutral iron for him." Simon paused, but Forsaka's face remained impassive. "The iron is here, and it's being used." Forsaka's cheek twitched but he held Simon's eye. "Help us find it."

"I can't help you with that, Lieutenant. You should talk to your old friend, Francis Killian." Forsaka turned away and Lisana led Simon out of the room. His thoughts spun, *Killian? Again? We should have put him in irons after the Flandyrs business. Is Frank working for him directly now?*

Lisana delivered him to the Hilten and the big Orc drove Simon away without comment. True to his word, he opened the compartment between the seats and returned Simon's needler and mirror. They stopped at almost the exact spot where Simon had been picked up, little more than an hour earlier.

As the big Hilten drove away, Simon took out his mirror and captured an image of the registry number. He doubted it would lead to anything, but one never knew, and he had a hunch.

He resumed his walk back toward Wycliffe house as he summoned Gervis Birchfield's mirror locus. Birchfield answered immediately.

"Gervis," said Simon without other greeting. "I need you to do two things for me. First, run this sled registry. Find out who owns it and if there's any connection to the agency that rented Anika Sommerstag her flyer." He read off the series of numbers. "Second, pull together anything you can find on Francis Killian. He was a Sergeant on a Magic Enforcement team up until last winter, then he got busted to Patrol. He resigned a few weeks ago and dropped out of sight. We need to find him. As of eight days ago he was separated from his family and living in a low rent hotel in Westport. I have a tip he may be the person who took delivery of the Harsakas' neutral iron."

"Aye, LT," said Birchfield. "Are you on your way back to the House?"

"Yes, but I'm on foot. Is there something important happening?"

Birchfield shook his head. "No. But we've worked up an idea of where Sommerstag went during the last few days before she died. I wanted to fill you in before end of watch."

Simon glanced at his timepiece. It was just after fifteenth hour. "Meet you in my office at half past sixteenth?"

"Will do. Birchfield out." He broke the connection.

CHAPTER FIFTEEN

Simon was back in his office by half past fifteenth hour. On his desk he found a series of reports from Jason Hanks. The first was a forensic analysis of the fire and the air spell that had been used to set the trap for the Water mages. Not surprising, the aural analysis was inconclusive. One of the problems with tracking air spells was the transient nature of their medium. When air and explosive fire were combined, there was almost no aura to analyze.

Next, were ten separate witness statements from the Fire Brigade mages, bystanders, and the Patrol Keepers who had been present for traffic control. None added much to what was already known.

More interesting, and also disappointing, was Hanks's interview with Jaime Smithington. It covered the incident and Smithington's insistence that it was an intentional trap for his men, but Hanks's questions seemed perfunctory and only covered the obvious. Simon could sense Smithington's frustration at not being asked for the deeper reason behind the trap. He resolved to speak to the Fire Chief himself. One exchange caught Simon's eye.

Smithington: This wasn't the first time we'd been out to that building. It nearly burned down a couple of months ago when someone set fire to a hundred weight of jolt the Scalpers had stored there. The warehouse was saved, but I wonder if the repairs were too expensive and someone decided to cut their losses.

Hanks: Who are the owners?

Smithington: Some consortium of High Street investors through a couple of shell companies. No one and everyone. They've a handful of slum tenements and run-down warehouses all through the Hollows. Arson's their preferred means of liquidation.

Simon sat back in his chair. He knew what Smithington was implying. *Does he know who actually set the fires? Or does he suspect arson for profit?*

He glanced through the rest of the interview. Appended to the end was a list of six properties that Smithington had given Hanks, all owned by the same shell company, and all involved in arson or fire incidents within the past year. The last address on the list sent a chill through him. It was the waterfront warehouse where Farsk Kronska and his men had burned. He needed to talk to Smithington, and soon.

"LT?" Lessa's voice caused him to look up. "Sergeant Birchfield is here."

"Send him in, Lessa. And has Sergeant Stonebender gone for the day?"

"Aye," she said with a nod as she opened the door wider for Birchfield. "He said he was going home at about midday and would start for the Ironlands from there." She grinned. "He took Agent Brookstone with him."

Simon grinned back. "I foresee consternation in the Ironlands." To Birchfield's puzzled look he said,

"Hal Stonebender is handling an extradition warrant from the Ironlands. The Magistrate there is an old adversary. Hal took Brookstone along as his second just to rub the Ironlanders's collective noses in it."

Lessa closed the door and Birchfield took a seat.

"What have you found so far, Gervis?" Simon asked.

"Well, I'm not sure if it's anything other than coincidence, but the registry number you gave me is for a Hilten six-seater owned by the same livery company that rented Sommerstag her flyer." He cocked his head at Simon. "How'd you know?"

"I didn't. Just checking a side tunnel. But I don't like coincidences." Simon paused and motioned for Birchfield to go on.

"The livery company is based in the East End and is owned by a shell company. The operation is run by a couple of Orcs." Birchfield glanced at his notes. "Ponsaka and Hensig, both Azeri, Fish clan. One is a second cousin to Lily Ponsaka but from what we could learn, they're not close. There've been rumors of smuggling and jobber deals through their stable, but nothing solid."

Simon rubbed his chin. "But Lily might have sent Anika to them if she wanted to rent a flyer, right?"

Birchfield shrugged. "Sure, it's possible. Want us to check it out?"

Simon shook his head. "Not likely to be important, even if she did. What did you learn about Anika's movements over in her last couple of days?"

Birchfield again looked at the notebook. "So, based on receipts and conversations with people near the places she went, it looks like she roamed all over the Hollows, from the Great Cut to the Old Wall, but mostly along Canal and Knacker. Almost all of the places we can verify were in Scalper territory."

Simon slid the list of arson locations across his desk. "Cross reference her known locations with the places on this list."

Birchfield glanced at the list and started to pick it up. He paused and looked closer. "Simon, one of these places is just down the street from the alley where she died. It's within a half block of the furniture store where her flyer was found."

"Did you interview the store owner?"

"Yes. "Birchfield nodded. "One of my guys talked to him this morning. He had never seen Sommerstag and had no idea her flyer was on his roof."

"We'll need to check out that location," Simon checked the list. "That warehouse, first thing tomorrow."

"You want to ride along?" asked Birchfield.

"Yes, come collect me after morning muster." Simon said. "In the meantime, what have you learned about Frank Killian?"

"Not much more than you gave me. We checked out the hotel, the Hybarian, on Kestril Street in Westport. Not high class, but clean and well run. Mostly a place where ship's officers stay when they're in port for more than a couple of days. Killian stayed ten days. He paid for the first week up front, in cash. Then, eight days ago, he dropped out of sight. He cleared out all his things and stuck them with three days unpaid room charges."

"Frank skipped on his bill?" asked Simon.

"Well, that's the strange part," answered Birchfield. "Two days after he pulled out, someone came in and paid his bill, again in cash."

"Who?"

"The manager didn't know. A clerk took the cash and canceled the bill. All he could tell us was that he was tall, human or half-Elven, well dressed and paid in gold."

"And that's it?"

Birchfield smiled. "Not quite. The hotel has a pretty

good set of Warding spells on the front desk including weapons detection, counterfeit currency telltales, and cashbox imaging."

"We have a picture of the guy?"

"A partial. The imaging spell is focused on the cashbox to prevent theft, not on the customer. But we have a partial profile and a clear image of his hands. And he's got a distinctive scar on the right. A puckered half-moon shape in the web space between the thumb and first finger."

"Fingerprints?" asked Simon.

Birchfield grimaced. "Boss, it's been a week. Hundreds of people in and out of that place. There's no way we could isolate his. But if we find him, we can confirm based on the scar."

"There's no crime in paying a bill for someone," said Simon. "But I'd like to know who'd be helping Killian, and where he's gone to ground for the past week and a half."

"What's so important about Killian, Simon?" asked Birchfield. "I didn't know the man well, but the rumors and gossip were all over the squad room."

Simon didn't answer immediately. He held Birchfield's eye, measuring him. Birchfield didn't look away. Finally, Simon spoke. "What I tell you doesn't leave this room, understood?"

"Aye, LT."

"Killian was bent. He was on the cuff to a gang chieftain in a deal to corner the drug trade in the Hollows. He was allowed to resign rather than stand trial for reasons that are above our rank—lots of high brass jingle." Birchfield nodded but said nothing. "Still, the Force kept an eye on him. He had connections to some very bad people down in the Hollows. Two weeks ago, he dropped out of sight. Then, just today, a source I don't trust but consider reliable, told me to ask Killian about the neutral iron the Harsakas stole."

"About that, LT," said Birchfield. "We canvassed all of the labs and research departments who use the stuff. No one knows anything about an illicit market for it. It has no use outside of spell research."

"Not quite, Gervis." Simon's tone brought his Sergeant up short. "This is the part that stays under rock until I say different. Neutral iron can be worked into weapons. Weapons that aren't detectable by any Warding or Security spell. I've seen them. A shipment was intercepted in the Gray Havens a little while ago, and we have good evidence that they are being made here as well."

"Gods above and below, Simon. What if someone snuck some of those things into Parliament, or into the Throne Room?"

"Exactly," said Simon. "We need to find out who got that iron and where it is now. If Killian knows, we need to talk to him."

"Understood, LT," said Birchfield. "We'll keep looking." He shifted in his seat. "Did you find out anything from the Ministry?"

Simon smiled. "Aye, I did. This is also close hold, understand?" Birchfield nodded. "The Harsaka brothers were informants for the Ministry. They had been offered amnesty in exchange for information about Galen Flandyrs."

"Flandyrs! He's been located?"

Simon held up a hand to quell Birchfield's enthusiasm. "He has, but he's got heavy protection. What's important for our case is that Flandyrs hired the brothers for a job in the Free States, one involving the theft of neutral iron. I think they were doing the same thing on their job here."

"So, we're now investigating a plot to overthrow the Commonwealth," said Birchfield with a lopsided smile. "No pressure at all."

Simon smiled as well. Birchfield was proving to be

a solid Keeper. "Look, Gervis. You've done good work on this so far, but you're new to leading a team. I'm impressed with your handle on things, but if you ever feel you need back-up, help or support, with your team or with the brass, don't hesitate to call on me. There's too much at stake here to let pride or indecision get in the way."

Gervis nodded. "Understood, LT. I'll keep the guys on Killian. And I'm going to take another look at that warehouse break-in."

"Good. But first, go and get some rest. Hal Stonebender always harped on me about pushing too hard. 'Sleep is a weapon' he'd say. Now I'm telling you: Go home and get some rest."

"Aye, LT. See you in the morning." Birchfield got up and left the office. As if on cue, Lessa stuck her head in.

"Is there anything else, LT?" she asked.

"No, thank you Lessa," Simon answered. "Go on home."

CHAPTER SIXTEEN

Simon was back at his desk by half past sixth hour the following morning, thirty minutes before muster. He'd slept well, if only for about five hours. Hal had checked in just after midnight from the Ironlands. He and Brookstone had arrived and had an early morning meeting with the Ironlands Justice Minister.

"Now that we're here, I'm actually looking forward to seeing what happens when they meet Brookstone," Hal had said.

"Behave yourselves," Simon answered.

"Always, lad, always," said Hal. "Any news on Killian?"

"Nothing firm," said Simon. "We got some surveillance from the hotel where he stayed. Someone paid his bill two days after he left. No clue where he went, though."

"How about the IG?" asked Hal.

"No word," Simon answered. "You sure they're still interested?"

"Who knows? The weasel squad does things on their own time. Just watch your ass until I get home."

"Will do. Don't start an international incident while you're there."

Hal had signed off with a laugh and Simon had tried to get some sleep.

Lessa arrived a few minutes before seventh hour with a steaming mug of coffee and the reports from the night watch. He thanked her and sipped the coffee as he leafed through the papers. Nothing caught his eye until he glanced at a report of a break-in by spell nullification in Westport. Someone had used a Keeper spell to cancel the door Warding on a side entrance to the Hybarian Hotel. A search by the staff didn't find anyone in the building who didn't belong and there was nothing missing from the office, safe, or store rooms. The spell was a common one, and although restricted to the King's Peacekeepers, it was also used by a number of commercial security firms. Since nothing was stolen, no aural analysis was done.

Simon thought about Birchfield's report on the man with the scarred hand. He was certain that the break-in had been prompted by the team's inquiry; and that all images of the scarred hand had been purged.

Lessa opened his door and announced Sergeant Birchfield.

Gervis swept in just after her. "Ready to go, LT?"

"Aye," said Simon, rising from behind his desk. "I hope you have a copy of the image from the Hybarian. The hotel had a break-in and I'm betting their images from the Warding spell have been stolen or purged."

Birchfield rocked back. "I have a copy, but what the hells, LT? Who would care about someone covering Killian's bill?"

Í don't know, Gervis. But I think they just made a mistake. They've just confirmed that whoever paid the bill is important to them. We might have let it go, but now we know it matters to someone. Let's find out who."

Gervis smiled. "Will do, LT."

They rode in a black Keeper sled, heading south on Canal. The rest of Birchfield's team followed in a tactical sledge along with a forensics team of two CSA mages. Simon and Gervis had already agreed that whatever they found at the warehouse, they wanted a forensics team on site.

The warehouse was half a block north of the furniture shop where Anika's flyer had been found. Simon looked south as he climbed out of the sled. He could see the roof of the shop and its clear sight line to the front of the warehouse.

He turned to look the building over. The fire damage was still evident in the older brickwork, but the front had been rebuilt and the big roll-up doors facing the street were new. The investors had clearly invested some money in refurbishment.

Birchfield joined him and walked up to the right-hand door. He rubbed his badge to cancel any Wards then reached down and tugged at the lifting handle. The door didn't move. He tried the other door with the same result.

"Seem to be locked from the inside, LT," he said.

"Right," said Simon. "Have the team wait here. You and I will go around and find a side door."

Birchfield shouted some orders to the rest of the Keepers before falling in beside Simon as they made their way along the narrow alley on the north side of the building.

Old broken glass and congealed ash underfoot and heavy scorch marks on the wall above them showed that the money spent on the front had not found its way to the rest of the building. There was still a faint smell of ash and smoke in the still air and, Simon noted, a faint whiff of something else.

There was a side door about halfway along the length of the building. The heat from the old fire had warped the frame and the door didn't close completely. Birchfield rattled the knob and the door popped open. What had been a faint whiff of odor swept over them as a miasma; the unmistakable sickly sweet smell of decay.

Simon glanced at Birchfield and they both drew their sidearms. Birchfield entered first, sweeping to the right while Simon stepped through behind him, sweeping to the left.

The dim interior was a single open space with a central row of iron pillars supporting the roof. Just inside the left-hand roll-up door sat a grounded sledge. Simon peered over the sight of his needler but nothing moved.

"Clear," he called.

"Clear!" Birchfield answered.

Simon slid the needler into the holster at the small of his back and approached the sledge. The smell was stronger there. Even before he reached the sledge, he saw the rust brown stain that spread like a fan across the concrete floor.

The body lay in a heap on the far side of the sledge. The pale flesh had become swollen and bloated in the week since the man had fallen. Simon couldn't see his face, but he recognized the jacket the man wore. He had one just like it from his Civil patrol days—a serge jacket, short waisted, dark blue with gold lettering across the back, a service number and a capital WH. They had found Francis Killian.

"Call the Forensics team, Gervis," Simon said. "This is a crime scene now."

"Aye, LT. Who's the dead man?"

"We've found Frank Killian," answered Simon. "Looks like he died about the same time as Anika Sommerstag."

Birchfield grimaced. "Smells about right. What is that stain?"

Simon glanced at him. "I thought you studied the crime scene images from the Sommerstag murder."

Birchfield blanched. "But Anika's blood pattern was shaped like her body."

"She was standing next to the wall. Frank had his back to an open room when the spell took him." Simon turned to look in the bed of the cargo sledge. A heavy canvas covered the bed and he lifted the edge with the back of his hand. Bars of black iron lined the area he revealed.

Gervis returned with one of the crime scene mages. Simon instructed him to start with the doors and work toward the back of the warehouse.

"Get those doors processed and then open them, clear out some of this stench," Simon said.

Gervis stood looking down next to Killian's body. "What do you think, LT? Did he stumble onto whoever hired the Harsakas to steal this stuff?"

"Maybe," answered Simon. "But why leave the stuff here? Kill a man, and then leave the loot where we can find it? A sensible person would want it as far from here as possible."

"The warehouse is locked up, and no one knew Killian was here," Gervis pointed out.

Simon shook his head. "Too risky. This place reeks of death. Anyone walking down the alley would notice. Unless they were sure no one would be checking on this place, they wouldn't risk leaving the sledge here. Driving it out wouldn't even have aroused suspicion."

"So, was Killian in the wrong place at the wrong time, or was he in on the robbery somehow?"

"I don't know, Gervis," said Simon as the crime scene mage signaled that he was done with the door and started to crank it up with the winch attached to the wall next to it. As the cool fresh air from outside wash over his face, Simon realized he did know. Killian had been involved. He had no proof or even evidence of that, but the feeling in his gut told him it was true.

"Help me with this," Simon said to Gervis, pointing to the canvas. Together they rolled it back taking care to wear gloves and handle it only by the edge. Next to the bars of iron were oblong shapes wrapped in heavy paper. Through small rents at the corners, Simon could see the glint of gold. He pointed it out to Gervis.

"Not much doubt this is the stuff from the robbery," Gervis said with a nod.

"So we have a direct line from the docks where the robbery took place and the Harsakas were killed, to the alley near the furniture shop where Anika died, to this warehouse where the loot ended up and Killian was also killed. All four people were murdered by illegal magic," said Simon. "I'm betting by the same mage. But the why of it is what doesn't track for me. If we assume this mage killed the Harsakas in some sort of double cross, then why kill Anika?" Simon paused and rubbed his chin. "We know she was on the docks at one point because of the pitch on her shoes. Did she witness the killing of the Harsaka brothers? But if she was killed because she could identify the mage, then how does Killian fit in? Was he there as well? Then how did he end up here with a sledge full of stolen metals?"

Gervis knelt and checked Killian's feet. "There's some sand and black pitch stuck in the treads of his boots. LT." He swiveled to look at the skids of the sledge. "There's more here on the left skid. Looks like both Killian and the sledge were on the docks somewhere. Maybe not where the Orcs were killed, but what are the odds?"

"Not likely to be anywhere else," Simon agreed. "Forensics will prove it, but for now, we accept it. But what does that mean? That both Killian and Anika witnessed the Orcs being killed and the mage went after them as well? But if Killian wasn't involved with the heist, then why is he here? And if he was, why was he killed?"

Gervis shook his head. "I don't know, LT. And you're making my head spin."

"Think, Gervis," insisted Simon. "I can see eliminating the Harsakas. They could talk and whoever wants that neutral iron doesn't want word to get around. If Anika saw the murders, I can see going after her. But if Killian is here, it implies he was in on the heist or the delivery. Why kill him and leave the metals here? Something doesn't track."

"I still don't get why Sommerstag was on the docks that night," said Birchfield. "We've tracked her movements pretty well. They seem to follow a general path eastward from the River to this area along Canal Street or Tanner, but before the night she died there's nothing to indicate she went south as far as that dock on the Cut."

"After we finish here, get one of your guys to show her image around Westport, especially around the Hybarian Hotel. Maybe someone saw her there." Simon looked down at Killian again as more of the CSA team came into the warehouse. "What do we know about Sommerstag before she came to the capital?"

"Not much, LT," said Birchfield. "She mostly did fluff and scandal stories; who's sleeping with who, who just got caught with their knickers down or in a flat that wasn't theirs, who's getting married or divorced. Stuff like that. She didn't do serious news."

"Not much society scandal down on the docks," Simon observed.

There was little more Simon and Gervis could do in the warehouse. Simon left Birchfield with the CSA team and took the sled back to the House. Anika's presence in Cymbeline bothered him. Why was a scandal sheet newsie poking around the Hollows? The alley where she had died was uncomfortably close to a warehouse that the Princess had set afire during her ill-conceived campaign to burn out the jolt trade. Simon wanted to go over what information Birchfield's team had about Anika's movements and cross reference that with the arson sites. He had a bad feeling that they would match up.

CHAPTER SEVENTEEN

Simon arrived back at Wycliffe House just before midday. He climbed the stairs to his office, pausing briefly in the squad room to let Rob Steelhelm, the new day watch commander know about Killian and the sledge at the warehouse.

He opened the door to his office and Lessa looked up sharply from her desk. Her eyes widened and she made a shooing gesture with her hands. Simon stepped into the office, puzzled. Then a loud voice called from the inner office.

"Is that Lieutenant Buckley, Miss Greenwater?" the voice asked.

"Aye, sir," she answered. To Simon she whispered, "It's the Weasel Squad. Some Inspector named Lowell and two Sergeants."

Simon nodded thanks to Lessa and went through to the inner office. Two men in Sergeants uniforms sat in the chairs facing Simon's desk. They swiveled their heads to look at him as he entered. Simon recognized the one on his left as Giles Machemer, formerly from the Civil Patrol and a toady of Frank Killian's. The other was a Dwarf he didn't recognize.

A third man, tall and lean, sat on the battered couch to the left of the desk. The couch had previously been in his cubicle when he'd been a Sergeant and he'd brought it with him after his promotion. The man rose to his feet as Simon entered and pulled a badge wallet from the inner pocket of his jacket. He wore a well-tailored business suit of dark blue breeches, matching short waisted jacket, light blue shirt and hose, and a blood red cravat.

"Good meeting, Lieutenant Buckley. I'm Spencer Lowell, King's Inspector General." He showed Simon his badge and identification card. "These are Sergeants Machemer and Forge from my staff."

Forge nodded politely in Simon's direction but said nothing. Machemer's glare was an unmistakable challenge.

"What can I do for you, Inspector?" asked Simon as he walked around his desk to sit down. *Stay calm, stay focused,* he told himself. *This guy is smooth and looks smart, but he brought Machemer here for a reason, and that has something to do with Killian. The two of them were tight.*

"I'd like to talk to you about the warehouse fire that killed Farsk Kronska some weeks ago." Lowell made a show of replacing the badge wallet in his jacket and resuming his seat on the couch, crossing his long legs. "And about the immolation death of Biran Stillwater. I understand you were involved in both of those events?"

Simon looked at Machemer rather than Lowell. "Involved in the sense that both events occurred in the course of an investigation into the use of illegal Blood magic, yes. But Stillwater's death was part of a gang war over control of the jolt trade down in the

Hollows. And although the fire that killed Kronska was arson, there's no evidence that it was connected to my case nor has the Fire mage who was responsible been caught. That investigation is still active."

"Horse shit," growled Machemer. "You and your pet Fire mage killed both Orcs and set a good Keeper up to take the fall."

"Frank did that all by himself. He didn't need my help." Simon turned to Lowell. "What do you want to know?"

Machemer started to rise from the chair but sat at a wave of Lowell's hand. The dwarf said nothing and sat impassively. Lowell smiled slightly.

"And yet, Agent Aster resigned and ran off to the Free States immediately after the fires, thus avoiding any official inquiry into his actions," observed Lowell.

"Liam made a choice to accompany Princess Rebeka to the Free States. He was hardly avoiding anything, quite the contrary," replied Simon, careful to keep his anger in check. "The last I heard from Liam, he and Rebeka were happily married and starting a new life in Fredonia."

"We have no extradition treaty with the Free States," observed Lowell.

"And so Aster is free and clear. He may be untouchable, but you aren't," said Machemer. "You and Axhart planned the whole thing. Take down the gangs. Kill the witnesses and then pin the whole thing on a good man. Where is Frank Killian, Buckley? What did you do to make him drop out of sight?"

Simon looked from Lowell to Machemer to Forge who continued to sit silent. *That's his role here,* thought Simon. *Say nothing, then offer to talk to me on the side after I get into a fight with Machemer. Get me to point the finger at Axhart or throw the rest of my team under the rockpile.* He looked at Lowell and saw a small look of satisfaction flicker across his face.

"And how am I supposed to have done that, Macscreamer?" asked Simon, using the snide nickname Machemer had earned when he had been on a Magic Squad team before being recruited by the Weasel Squad.

Now the other man did come out of his chair, leaning in with both hands on the desk to get close to Simon's face. Simon could smell the residual of last night's beer and this morning's coffee on Machemer's breath.

"First, you and that Elf bitch from the Havens concocted the story that Azeri terrorists were going to blow up the city with fire grenades. Sure, Stonebender brought in Barsaka, but where were these famous grenades? Nobody's ever seen them. But that dog and fish story was enough to get Frank demoted." Simon glanced at Lowell who sat on the couch, elegant legs crossed and showing no signs of intervening.

"Then," continued Machemer, having taken a breath. "You set up the ambush on Stillwater, convinced Killian to vet the meeting, and left him hanging on to the dirty end of the shovel when your pet half-breed and your Fire mage took out Stillwater and his security guys."

"And how do you know what went down in that tavern, *Sergeant*?" Simon laid the emphasis on his rank to remind everyone who the ranking Keeper was in the room. "Were you there? I don't remember seeing you with Killian's squad. Did I miss something?" Machemer paused, his face going purple, but Simon pressed on, not letting him regroup. "You haven't done your homework, Giles. You didn't prepare for this interview. But you go ahead with that idea, Machemer. I'll be able to pull a dozen different witnesses, who actually were there, who will know exactly how that night went down and what Frank did, or more importantly, didn't do there."

"Where is Frank Killian? What did you do to make him disappear?" snarled Machemer through gritted teeth.

"You're a day behind events, Macscreamer," said Simon. "Killian's dead. One of my teams found his body along with a sledge full of stolen goods in a warehouse down in the Hollows this morning."

The color drained from Machemer's face and he settled unsteadily back into the chair. Simon gave him no quarter. "You didn't talk to any of the Keepers who were there, did you? Because you know that everyone in that squad room thinks people like you are the bottom feeders of this Force. They've got more respect for the people they lock up than for the Weasel Squad, and you know that, don't you Macscreamer." Simon turned to Lowell, who, to his credit, showed no reaction. "What's this all about, Inspector? I thought we were talking about a couple of Orc gangsters who were burned by Fire magic."

To Simon's surprise, it was Forge, the Dwarf, who spoke next. "And the same arsonist is linked to both events, as well as a series of fires in the Hollows before the meeting with Stillwater. Fires that you were aware of before you approached Killian about the meeting. How do you explain that?"

Simon looked more closely at Forge. He had the ageless face of a mature Dwarf, although his beard was trimmed shorter than the usual fashion. His uniform was crisp but the belt and scabbard at his waist were well worn brown leather and his badge hung from a lanyard of tarnished brass. Simon would have bet that his badge number was not much higher than Hal's.

"I don't need to explain anything," said Simon. "You guys have nothing. Why don't you come down to the holding cells and I'll show you how to conduct a real investigative interrogation? Killian is dead and the evidence links him to a warehouse heist down at the docks by the Great Cut. How do you explain that, Sergeant Forge?"

Forge held his gaze, his face impassive. "As you just said, Lieutenant, I don't have to explain anything. I'm not the subject of this investigation."

"What investigation?" asked Simon. "All I've heard so far is a bunch of jailhouse rumors. If you have evidence that I or anyone on my teams have done something improper, bring it out. Otherwise get out of my office and let me get back to real Keeper work."

Forge remained impassive. "What did Gelbard Axhart tell you to say about the fires?" he asked. "Did he order your Fire mage to burn that warehouse and kill Kronska? Did he promise you a promotion in return for your cooperation in this scheme?"

Simon looked from Forge to Lowell, ignoring Machemer. *So he's not going to play the good guy. He's supposed to move in for the kill once Machemer put me off guard.* He caught Lowell's eye and there was a moment of recognition. Lowell knew that Simon had seen through the ploy, but clearly didn't care. *He's too smug. He knows what really happened but can't prove it without me or Axhart. But how could he know? And who else does?*

"I'm deferring to your age and seniority by not physically throwing you out of this office," said Simon forcing calm into his tone. Forge gave him a wry smile. He turned to Lowell. "Am I under caution here? Should I call an advocate and my Association representative?"

Lowell smiled, but it was cold and didn't reach his eyes, which bored into Simon's. Simon forced himself to be calm and return the stare.

Lowell shook his head. "No need for that, Lieutenant. It's early days yet. We'll continue our inquiry through other channels for now." He stood. Forge did as well. Machemer stayed seated, glaring at Simon until Forge laid a hand on his shoulder and pulled him out of the chair.

They don't know how important an interview with a suspect can be. Simon thought. *They didn't prepare. You need to know the answers to your questions before you ask them and be ready with follow up if there's new information.* The Weasel Squad had for so long relied on the sheer intimidation of their presence that their investigators had forgotten that lesson. He looked at Lowell. *Well, most of them. What did he learn from this?*

"Until we meet again, Lieutenant Buckley," said Lowell, extending his hand.

When Simon took it, he looked down. There, in the space between the thumb and first finger, he saw the curved puckered scar. A cold chill ran down his spine. He looked up but Lowell's eyes betrayed nothing.

"As you say, Inspector," said Simon, hoping his voice didn't break.

Lowell turned and left the office. Forge and Machemer followed, the Dwarf pushing the taller man ahead. Machemer turned at the door to glare at Simon but said nothing more.

Once they were gone, Simon flopped into his chair and took a deep breath. Lessa stepped into the office.

"Are you all good, LT?" she asked tentatively.

Simon passed a hand over his face, calming himself. "Yes, all good, Lessa. Would you see if Captain Axhart is in the House and if he'll see me?"

Lessa's eyes widened, but she just nodded her head and ducked back to the outer office.

Ten minutes later, Simon was in front of Elvira Cairns's desk as she entered Captain Axhart's inner office to announce him. She emerged a few seconds later and waved him in, closing the door behind him.

Axhart sat behind his desk, some papers in his hand but his eyes focused on Simon. "Come in Buckley," he said. "I understand the Weasel Squad paid you a visit today."

"Aye, sir. But that's not why I wanted to see you; well, not entirely," Simon answered. "What do you know about an IG Inspector named Lowell?"

"Why do you ask?"

"Because he has a half-moon shaped scar between the thumb and forefinger of his right hand." To Axhart's puzzled look, Simon went on, "A man with that same scar came into the Hybarian Hotel out in Westport and paid Frank Killian's outstanding bill two days after Hal lost track of him. One of my teams found Killian in a Hollows warehouse this morning. He's dead, killed by an exsanguination spell. There's a sledge full of stolen neutral iron and other noble metals in the warehouse with him."

Axhart pursed his lips and narrowed his eyes. "You think Lowell has something to do with Killian's death?"

"I don't know, sir," Simon replied. "He clearly knew where Killian was staying and didn't want his disappearance to attract notice, even from an unpaid bill. Maybe he had Killian on a string to give evidence against me and my team in the IG case. Maybe Killian had offered some other evidence that Lowell wanted quiet for the time being."

Axhart frowned. "What kind of evidence?"

Simon spoke cautiously. "I have a gut feeling that Lowell knows about the Princess, or at least has a strong suspicion that she's a mage. Remember when I said Killian may have been able to add two and three and get five? Whatever his sins, he was a sharp investigator. He knew about the warehouse fires before the meeting with Stillwater; he knew Liam and the Princess were at Lily's when Stillwater was killed. He would have been able to find out that the same Fire mage set the earlier fires as well as the one that killed Kronska. Maybe he told Lowell about his suspicions."

"If that's so, it would be concerning." Axhart set down the papers and gestured for Simon to take a seat. "Lowell was in charge of the Mayor's security detail during the last administration. He and the former Lord Mayor had some kind of falling out and Lowell resigned. He went to work for Rondel Aspenwald during his campaign and, after the election, Justice Minister Kershaw appointed him to the IG's staff."

"You said yourself, sir, that Aspenwald was a favorite of Lord Kershaw," said Simon. "Lowell would be an obvious choice to head an investigation aimed at you, especially if he had Killian willing to make an accusation."

"And yet you think this has something to do with the Princess?" asked Axhart. "What did Lowell say or do that indicated that?"

"I don't know," said Simon, frustrated. "He just seemed too smug, like he knew something the others in the room didn't. He let one of his lackeys, Machemer, lose control and attack me over Killian's demotion and didn't interrupt when I took Machemer down. The other Sergeant there, a dwarf named Forge, made all of the actual accusations—that I'd taken a promotion in return for conspiring with you and Agent Aster to kill Farsk Kronska and cover it up. Lowell should have backed his man, but he didn't. Like the accusation was unimportant to him. Like he just wanted to see how I'd react to a visit from the IG."

"I'm inclined to trust your instincts, lad." Axhart leaned back in his chair stroking his chin. "I'm not surprised to hear Hanson Forge is on this one. He and I have been on bad terms since I was his Sergeant on the Borderlands Patrol many years ago. I knew he'd made Sergeant but didn't know he'd joined the IG's staff. Be careful around him. He's been a Keeper for almost as long as Hal Stonebender and is sharp as they come."

"What should I do, Boss?" asked Simon.

"Nothing for now. Hal is off in the Ironlands, right?"

"Aye, sir," said Simon.

"Good," said Axhart. "He'd want to jump in and might do something we'd regret. Can you get in touch with Aster?"

"I can," said Simon.

"See if he and the Princess have had any unexpected visitors, contact from the Commonwealth, anyone snooping around that they don't know, that sort of thing."

Simon nodded. "I have a private mirror locus for Liam. I'll summon it tonight."

"When do you usually file your reports with the Mayor's Office?"

Simon blinked. "Late afternoon. Do you want me to report Killian's body and the stolen metals? I've been downplaying Anika's connection to the Harsaka brothers and the docks in my reports."

"No, actually I was thinking more about reporting the IG investigation," said Axhart. "Use it as an excuse to limit your daily reports. Too much time consumed in trying to comply with the IG's office and so on. See if Aspenwald takes the bait. If he's really interested in Anika Sommerstag and has any influence with the IG, he may pull some of the heat off you. If the IG doubles down, then maybe his interest in Anika is something other than fatherly."

"Maybe," said Simon skeptically. "I always thought there was something wrong about his interest in the investigation. As Hal would say, the stone seemed rotten somehow."

Axhart laughed at that. "By the gods, I swear you're half Dwarf. Just don't let that sense of stone blind you to the unexpected."

"Never have, Captain."

Simon took his leave. He spent the rest of the day

in his office, reviewing the reports from his teams and writing up a missive to the Mayor along the lines of what Axhart had suggested.

The final half-hour of the watch was spent in a frustrating discussion with Sergeant Hanks about his upcoming performance review. Jason couldn't seem to understand Simon's recommendations for action and kept insisting that he was following protocol and didn't see what more Simon expected of him.

In the end Hanks left the office confused and Simon left it frustrated.

CHAPTER EIGHTEEN

It was just after eighteenth hour when Simon parked his Oxley in the stables across from his flat. He had placed his saber in the rear compartment before leaving Wycliffe House and decided to leave it there. He still had his sidearm in the rear belt clip holster under his uniform jacket.

He crossed the short yard and unlocked the door to his flat. Immediately his badge vibrated. He took a half step back and drew the needler. He'd upgraded the Warding spells on the door and the vibration meant that someone had overridden them since he'd set them that morning.

Simon pushed the door open with his foot, still standing back from the threshold. He saw no one in the entry vestibule. He stepped inside, needler held before him in a two-handed grip.

"I'm in the front room, Simon. Don't shoot me." Kermal's familiar voice came from around the corner.

Simon stepped into the doorway and swept the

room. Kermal stood with his hands at his sides, palms forward and visible.

Simon sighed and holstered the needler. "Gods, Kermal. Can't you just summon my mirror like a normal person?"

"What's the fun in that?" asked Kermal as he sat down in Simon's favorite chair, his jacket draped over the chair back. "I see you've upgraded your security spells."

"Your advice," said Simon, suddenly very tired. "Why are you here? Last I heard, you were in the Free States."

"Just got in an hour ago," Kermal replied. "I came directly here. There are some things we need to talk about."

Simon paused for a second in the process of hanging his jacket on the peg near the door. He turned from the front room and entered the small kitchen. "I'm getting myself a drink," he called over his shoulder. "Can I get you anything?"

"I wouldn't say no to a beer," Kermal said.

Simon pulled two bottles from the chiller under the sink, uncapped them and returned to the front room. Kermal had shifted to the smaller side chair. Simon handed him a beer and sat in the armchair. He took a long gulp from the beer and sighed.

"So, what couldn't wait until tomorrow?" Simon asked.

Kermal grimaced, rolling the bottle back and forth between his hands. "You know Galen Flandyrs has reappeared I take it?" Simon nodded and Kermal went on. "He's in the Havens, but not many weeks ago he was in the Free States. The Cabal dispatched me there to find him; kill him if possible."

Simon frowned at that but Kermal went on, "I won't argue with you on that right now, Simon. Suffice it to say, he was long gone by the time I got there. But in looking for him, I ran down people who had known the Harsaka brothers. Flandyrs had hired them to steal some neutral iron from a dealer in Fredonia." Kermal paused. "I assume you know what neutral iron is?" Simon nodded and he continued, "The brothers completed the job and Flandyrs arranged a meeting with someone from the Commonwealth who wanted a similar job done."

"They finished that job just before they were killed," said Simon. "We found a sledge today with the goods still in it. Some gold, platinum, and a quantity of neutral iron. We also found Frank Killian. Dead. Killed by the same mage who murdered the Harsakas and Anika Sommerstag."

"I can't say I'm sad about Frank Killian. What was he doing with a sledge full of stolen goods?"

"Nothing certain," said Simon. "Ask me, I think he was taking delivery for someone else, but I don't know who."

"That's why I needed to talk to you." Kermal took another long pull from his beer. "Sommerstag and Flandyrs and the Harsaka brothers met regularly in the back room of an inn in Fredonia. We don't know all that they were planning, but our source in the inn did confirm that Flandyrs was planning to somehow eliminate opposition to the Traditionalist faction in the Havens Council. There was also a plan to coordinate the move in the Havens with some sort of attack on the Royal family."

"Your source?" asked Simon.

Kermal smiled. "One of our people is a serving girl at the inn. No one pays attention to the Orc who brings the drinks and clears away the empties. She made it a point to be in the room whenever the four of them met."

"So, what is the threat to the Royal family?"

"We don't have the specifics. Apparently Flandyrs

has a high placed ally here in Cymbeline, but we don't know who it is. Flandyrs plans an assault on the Haven council with some sort of secret weapons, but the logistics of getting such things into the Commonwealth seem to have been more complicated than he expected. He and the Harsakas had a loud argument about it just before they left Fredonia. Our girl couldn't overhear the specifics, but she did hear that they would have to settle for Sommerstag's approach over what Flandyrs called 'direct action.'"

"We've got a good lead on what the Harsakas were after but as I said, we don't know who was supposed to receive the goods," said Simon. "What was Sommerstag up to?"

"Something to do with the Princess," Kermal replied. His eyes narrowed when he saw the look of concern that briefly crossed Simon's face. "You know something."

"Aye, but not something I can share right now." Simon drained the rest of his beer. "Did you speak to Liam and Rebeka?"

"No. I didn't feel it was my place; not given how I left the Force. I figured you would get a better reception."

Simon leaned forward. "Liam would understand, Kermal. He might not approve of your choice, hells, I don't approve of it, but he would understand. You are still a teammate, still a Keeper in our eyes."

"As may be," sighed Kermal. "But I never said proper farewells, never explained my reasons for leaving the team."

"Hells, Kermal. No one said any farewells. Liam and Rebeka were out of the country so fast, nobody on the team got to say good parting. The team pretty much fell apart until Hal put it back together."

Kermal's eyes narrowed, and Simon realized he'd revealed more than he'd intended.

"Why so fast?" Kermal asked. Simon met his eye

and gave a small shake of his head.

"That's another thing I can't discuss right now. But you already know there's more to Rebeka's departure than the public tale."

"There have been rumors," Kermal confirmed. "Sommerstag was forcibly ejected from the estate King Thorston bought for his daughter on the outskirts of Fredonia."

Simon knew that despite her loss of title and lands, the Princess was not without wealth. The King had used shell companies to provide support as well and, more importantly, security. "I'm having to reevaluate my assessment of Anika," he said. "Up until now, I'd been thinking of her as a victim. It seems she was more of a participant in whatever has been going on."

"No victim that one," said Kermal. "She has a reputation in the Free States as a scandal monger who wasn't above manufacturing controversy where there was none."

"Which makes me wonder how much of the Mayor's interest is fatherly concern," Simon mused.

Kermal shrugged. "I don't have any information about the Lord Mayor, other than his public stance on Orcs. The Old Men haven't made any moves in that direction."

"Speaking of the Old Men," said Simon, steering away from any more talk about the Princess. "Why do they want Flandyrs dead? What's he to the Cabal?"

Kermal squirmed in his chair but met Simon's eye. "Chief Forsaka doesn't often share his thoughts with me, Simon."

"You were just following orders? Horse shit! You're better than that, Kermal. You wouldn't take the job if he hadn't given you a good reason."

"That's something I can't share right now." Kermal quoted Simon's words back to him. "I'll just say that the Cabal doesn't want to see the Royal House disrupted right now. They've no love for the King but have even less for the Havens and the likes of Rondel Aspenwald."

Simon exhaled sharply in frustration. "Gods, Kermal, why so cryptic? If there's a real threat to the Royal Family, I need to know."

"Nothing that definite," said Kermal, holding up a hand. "There's the usual chatter from the remnants of the Brigades and the Azeri Empire's hangers on. But we know Flandyrs is part of something bigger, we just don't have any specifics."

"Is Flandyrs the prime mover?" asked Simon. "Is that why the Cabal wants him dead?"

"I don't know, Simon. Forsaka is my clan Chieftain. If I'm only half Orc, that half is still tied to the clan. He gave me enough information to convince me that killing Flandyrs was the right thing to do. Unfortunately, he's in the Havens now; under the protection of House Graystorm no less." He shrugged. "As to Aspenwald, he's a snake, but more than that, the Chief seems to have a special interest in him. He may be connected to Flandyrs through his daughter, but all indications were that they weren't close."

Simon regarded the empty beer bottle in his hand. He wanted another but decided against it. He had several mirrors to summon before he could sleep and he wanted his head clear. "Anything else you can tell me, Kermal?"

Kermal drained his beer, taking the hint. "No, just watch your back. These are deep waters." He stood. "I'd better report to the Chief. I'll keep our talk to myself."

"Don't worry about it. Tell Chief Forsaka that I will be talking to Jaime Smithington tomorrow."

Kermal gave him a curious glance but didn't ask. They shook hands at the door and Simon closed it as the half-Orc enforcer walked away.

Simon pulled out his mirror as he went back into the front room. He summoned Sylvie's mirror first. It had been two days since they'd parted and he already missed her. It was as if now they'd decided to spend their lives together, (*well at least the rest of my life,* he thought) he couldn't bear an even brief parting.

Sylvie answered right away. "Hello, love," she said, smiling broadly. "Miss me already?"

"I missed you as I watched your sled disappear down Hal's street." Simon smiled back at her then grew serious. "Are you safe? Did you speak to Summerfield?"

"No, he's been recalled to Tintagel," said Sylvie. "Borderlands Station is being isolated. The *Syr* for Justice on the Council has pulled all the Rangers he considered loyal to the Traditional camp back to the capital as well. He's put Genna Silverthorn in temporary command, and Hamil Fairborn and I have been relieved of field duty and assigned desks watching over the holding cells." She frowned. "I'm worried about Summerfield. He's in Tintagel without any backup."

"Rulanis Summerfield can take care of himself," said Simon. "I'm worried about you. If the Traditional camp has gotten that bold, you need to get out of there. Summerfield will understand."

"I know, love," said Sylvie, glancing over her shoulder. She lowered her voice. "There are rumors that they are going to close the borders. Hamil and I are going to try to get across tomorrow, after shift. I know you can't speak for Fairborn but you've met him. You know he's solid."

"No worries, Sylvie. I'd go to the ring any time for Fairborn." Simon answered. "I'll vouch for him with Axhart. Just get out of there as soon as you can."

"We will, Simon. I'll message you from the Borderlands. Stay safe. I love you."

With that she signed off. Simon looked at the

mirror for a few moments. Then he entered another summons.

"Hammersmith here," Bendict Hammersmith said as he activated his mirror. His eyes narrowed as he recognized Simon. "Buckley, what can I do for you?"

"I have some information for you, Bendict. The weapons we spoke about are only part of the problem. Flandyrs was working with a newsie named Anika Sommerstag. She had developed evidence about some kind of scandal involving the Royal Family. I have an idea about it, but it's not definite and I won't share it now." Simon paused but Hammersmith seemed to be listening. "The Harsakas delivered the stolen neutral iron to an ex-Agent named Frank Killian. He and the Harsakas were killed by the same mage during the last night of the riots. Killian and the stolen goods were found in a warehouse on Canal, near where Anika Sommerstag was killed. The killings are all connected and several sources tell me that something big is going down soon."

Hammersmith rubbed his chin. "Not very specific," he said. "What is going to happen? When? Soon isn't enough. How am I supposed to mount an operation based on that?"

"I know it's thin." Simon agreed. "But it isn't likely to be a direct attack on the Throne or on Parliament. My information is that Killian's death and the logistics of getting the secret weapons into the Commonwealth made a direct attack impractical. Whatever they are planning, the target will be outside of the Palace or Parliament."

"All good as far as it goes," said Hammersmith. "But again, short on specifics."

"Not much more I can tell you," said Simon. "Other than it will likely be timed to match an open move on the Havens Council. I know that's not your garden, but you should expect blowback from it here."

"Right," Hammersmith nodded. "We have information of our own about that. Looks like Flandyrs is providing the weapons and muscle for the Steward and his party. The Council has been the only check on the Traditionalists for the last two or three years. Enough of the *Syrs*, especially those from border areas like Talien and Portalis, profited from cross border trade and technology to keep the worst of the Steward's cronies in check. But their margin has always been slim and depended on Graystorm as a neutral go between. If Graystorm is harboring Flandyrs, then that balance of power has shifted."

"I may have other information for you by tomorrow. I have a few more summons to send tonight. Can I meet you at the Ministry tomorrow around ninth hour?"

Hammersmith glanced down for a second, likely checking a schedule. "Make it closer to tenth. I have a briefing with my operational staff at ninth. Shouldn't take long."

"Until tomorrow then," said Simon, closing the connection.

Simon checked his timepiece. It was half past nineteenth hour, so half past twenty-first in Fredonia. A little late to call but not too late. He entered the locus to summon Liam's private mirror.

Liam's face swam into view in Simon's mirror. The young mage's face lit up with a smile that was half pleasure and half relief.

"Simon! Good to see you safe and whole." He half turned away from the mirror and called, "Becky, it's Simon!" Turning back, he lowered his voice. "Is everyone all good? No one hurt in the riots?"

"All good here, Liam. I'm well, and so are Hal and Jack. Kermal sends his best, although he was just up in your patch. I don't suppose he stopped in?"

"No, I'm sorry he didn't. Business for the Old Men?"

Simon cocked his head. "You know about that?"

"Stenson Harold briefed us a week after we arrived here. He came up with the security detail the King assigned to us." Liam looked to his right. "Here's Rebeka, Simon."

The image shifted to reveal Rebeka Fangbern, only daughter of King Thorston Fangbern. "Sergeant Buckley, no, excuse me, Lieutenant Buckley." Her smile was brilliant. "So good to see you again."

"And you, Your Highness," said Simon with a small bow of his head. "You're looking well."

"Oh, drop the Highness," Rebeka said with a laugh. "I'm just Rebeka Aster now."

"It seems to suit you," Simon noted.

"It does. I thought I'd miss the power, the attention. For the past year I had been so frightened of what I had become, not to mention the pressure to keep my secret, that I didn't realize how lost and miserable I was." She laid her hand on Liam's shoulder. "Liam changed all that. I'm happy here."

"Then I apologize in advance if this call is upsetting." He glanced between Rebeka and Liam. "What can you tell me about Anika Sommerstag? I heard she had a set to with your security detail."

Rebeka's eyes flashed and Liam frowned. "What has she told you about it?" Rebeka asked.

"Nothing," said Simon. "She's dead. We found her exsanguinated in an alley off of Canal a few days ago. The same mage who killed her, also took down a couple of Orcs the same night; a pair of brothers named Harsaka."

Both Liam and Rebeka looked pale. "The Harsakas and Sommerstag are all dead?" Liam asked.

"That's what I just said, Liam. What do you know about these people?"

Liam looked at his wife. "Becky?"

"Tell him, Liam. We don't know who else she may have talked to."

Liam looked back at Simon. "About three weeks ago Becky and I were out in the back of the compound. She was working on some directional spells. We keep the security team away when we're practicing. The fewer people who know about her talent the better, and I'm a known mage, so the fireworks aren't unexplained." Liam shrugged. "We don't lie to them and we don't keep them from doing their job, but we try to avoid putting them in the position of having to lie for us."

"All good, Liam," said Simon. "Tell me about the Harsakas."

Liam nodded. "As I said, we were practicing some directional spells. I had a containment field up with a bank of flame and Becky was sending bolts at various targets. She had targeted a dead tree near the compound fence. The thing was hollow and exploded in a shower of sparks and splinters. It also knocked both of the Harsaka brothers senseless. We called the security men who came and ejected them. But we're pretty sure they saw who cast the fire bolt, and they knew it wasn't me."

"So, they guessed that Rebeka was a mage," said Simon.

"Aye," said Liam. "And they told Sommerstag. She had no proof, but she had an eye for a good scandal. She took to snooping around the edges of the compound and badgering us for an interview."

"We've been asked by media for such from day one," Rebeka put in. "Most of the legitimate local and international news groups have respected our request for a few weeks of adjustment before we start answering the public interest circus. But a number of the scandal sheets have already started putting out salacious speculations about us. Usually, the unwanted pregnancy rumors or the 'poor Princess seduced by an adventurer' stories. We'll need to answer them soon."

Liam nodded. "Not to mention the diplomatic queries. King Thorston made a public statement that Rebeka had abdicated her title and any official standing with the diplomatic service, but they still want to stop by for a brief chat about this or that trade initiative or border situation."

"What was different about Anika?" asked Simon.

"She implied she knew the 'real' reason we'd left the Commonwealth," answered Liam. "And she wouldn't take no for an answer. She showed up at the gate almost daily insisting to the security men on duty that we'd agree to see her. She even scaled the back fence and came knocking on the back door. Becky almost burned her with a fire bolt, she was so angry. In the end, the security force bodily ejected her, and we went to the local magistrate to get an exclusion order filed against her. After that, she stopped coming around. We'd heard she'd left Fredonia but didn't know where she'd gone."

Simon was silent for a moment, considering what to tell Liam and Rebeka.

"I think you should start talking to the media and be prepared to get ahead of the story," he said. "I'm almost sure that Sommerstag told Galen Flandyrs about Rebeka. I also suspect that Frank Killian worked it out and may have told an IG Inspector named Lowell. The more people who know about this, the less likely it is that we can keep it under the basket."

Rebeka simply nodded, although Liam looked grim. She spoke first. "We've discussed this with Father. If there are more than just rumors and it looks like the real story will break out, we'll call a meeting with the major news groups and tell the truth. I don't care if the public knows. I've already abdicated. But I still won't let what I've done bring down my father's government. I'll confess to killing those men if it will stop further violence." She smiled wryly. "Besides, there's no extradition treaty between the Commonwealth and the Free States. All manner of shady characters end up here."

Once again Simon was struck by Rebeka's poise and courage, far beyond what he would expect from someone her age. *But then, she was raised in a political family,* he thought. *The wonder is that she is so sensible.*

"Hopefully, it won't come to that," said Simon. "The Harsakas, Anika Sommerstag, and Frank Killian are all..." Simon broke off as the fact registered. "Liam, what was the exact date that the Harsakas were caught inside your perimeter?" Liam thought for a second, then named a date two days short of three weeks earlier. Simon jotted it down and said, "Liam, I want you and Rebeka to be very careful over the next few days. Something big is happening in the Havens and we're expecting blowback here in the Commonwealth as well." He held up a hand to Liam's questioning look. "I don't know anything specific, but it may involve what we've just been talking about. Be ready to make a statement, but don't do anything until you hear from me or the King. All good?"

Both Liam and Rebeka nodded. After a few goodbye pleasantries, Simon signed off. He felt a chill. If what he suspected was correct, then he, Axhart, and anyone else who knew the truth about Rebeka could be in real danger.

His summons to Axhart went unanswered, so he left a message. He considered trying to reach Hal in the Ironlands but decided to wait. Hal should be checking in before long anyway, if he and Brookstone were on schedule.

CHAPTER NINETEEN

Simon slept fitfully. He awoke at half past fourth hour and gave up on further efforts at slumber. He showered and shaved and dressed in his blue serge uniform. It was spring but the weather was still cool and the blues lent an air of authority that he wanted when he went to meet with Hammersmith.

Axhart had not answered his summons. Nor had Hal checked in. Simon paced for a while in frustration before taking his jacket from the peg by the door. He checked his needler, opened the door and plunged out into the early dawn light.

There was virtually no traffic on the streets until he reached Wycliffe House. He parked in the stables and walked up the stairs, past the subdued activity of the night shift squad room, and up to his own office.

He sat at his desk and considered what he now knew with certainty. Someone was killing anyone who knew or might know the truth of Rebeka's abdication. He pulled out a blank sheet of paper and began making a list and a timeline.

He started with the names of everyone who knew or could be suspected of knowing that Rebeka was a mage. Himself, Liam, Hal, Axhart, Sylvie, the King and Queen, Stenson Harold, and George Latham had all been part of the initial group that confronted the Princess and got her out of the Commonwealth. He added the names of Lasko and Fortis Harsaka, Anika Sommerstag, and Galen Flandyrs. After his conversations with Liam and Kermal, he was certain that they had been aware of the secret and were preparing to use it to embarrass the Royal House, or perhaps try to force some concessions from King Thorston. At the bottom of the list went the names of Frank Killian and Spencer Lowell, both with question marks after them. After a moment's thought, he scratched out the question mark after Killian's name.

Next to the list he drew a timeline starting with the fire that had killed Farsk Kronska and had been his first confirmation of Rebeka's responsibility for the arson fires in the Hollows. He linked the dates to when each person on the list had learned about the Princess. There were two distinct clusters, one around the night of her abdication and a second starting three weeks later. He placed Killian's name off to the side. He didn't know when Killian had worked things out, but was certain he had, probably within a day or two of the announcement of Rebeka's abdication.

He drew lines to Anika, Killian and the Harsakas from the date five days earlier. This he broke down into hours. Forensics put the Harsakas' deaths at around half past eighteenth hour and Anika's at just before twentieth. He hadn't seen the report on Killian, but given the degree of decomposition and the dried nature of the fluids, Simon reckoned the man had died at about the same time. The exact hour was less important than the fact that all three deaths had occurred the same night and within a fairly tight time frame.

He looked at the other names on his list. Hal was out of the country and likely out of reach of his mystery Water mage. He'd need to warn George Latham and Axhart to be on their guard. Stenson Harold was head of Palace security and the Palace itself was well protected. The King and Queen were under constant guard and he doubted there would be any opportunity for someone to get close to them. He'd discuss his findings and suspicions with Hammersmith later today and then get in touch with Harold.

That left Lowell. Simon stared at the name for a long time. He couldn't be sure that Lowell knew the truth about Rebeka, but there was an undeniable link between him and Killian. Why would Lowell pay off Killian's bills unless he was cultivating him as a witness? Maybe Killian had approached the IG's office in the first place, looking for some kind of compensation or reinstatement. Simon doubted Forge and Machemer were aware of the true basis for the investigation. Their actions in his office were too genuine. Lowell, on the other hand, had acted as if their questions and Simon's answers didn't matter. The last thing Simon wanted to do was confirm Killian's story by warning Lowell.

He rubbed his eyes. *Gods, I wish Hal would check in. I really need his advice on this.*

The door opened and he looked up. Lessa stood there, a stack of messages in her hand.

"Oh, LT," she said in surprise. "You're here."

Simon glanced at the timepiece on the wall. It was half past sixth hour. He smiled. He knew Lessa came in early but hadn't paid much attention until now.

"Good meeting, Lessa," said Simon. "Is there any coffee?"

She set the messages in front of him. "Two minutes.

I'll be right back."

He leafed through the stack of papers and message flimsies. The top paper was the forensics report on Frank Killian. Aural analysis showed that his time of death was within 30 minutes of Anika Sommerstag's. It confirmed his impression of events that night. The chain had started at the docks, traveled to the warehouse and likely had ended in the alley. One mage, four deaths, all in a tight time frame and all revolving around the sledge full of precious metals.

But why was the sledge left in the warehouse, untouched? The gold and platinum were worth enough to tempt any thief. But Forsaka had implied that the neutral iron had been the target and Killian had been involved. As the link between the Harsakas and whoever wanted the iron? Simon nodded to himself, now even more certain that Killian was the delivery man. He drove the sledge from the docks to the warehouse but hadn't had the chance to complete the delivery. The Harsakas had been killed before they could pick up their share—the bulk gold and platinum. And Killian had died before he could pass the iron on.

Lessa returned with a mug of coffee. Simon sipped gratefully and thanked her. She stood in the doorway, wringing her hands.

"Is there something else, Lessa?" Simon asked.

"That Inspector from the Weas—from the IG's office just summoned. I told him you weren't in yet. He wants to see you, here, at fifteenth today." She looked back at her desk. "Should I tell him you're in court or something, put him off?"

Simon smiled. "No, Lessa. Tell him I'll be here at fifteenth, with an advocate and my association rep. Let me know what he says when you tell him that."

Lessa grinned. "Will do, LT."

After she returned to the anteroom, Simon summoned George Latham's private mirror. He had kept it after Latham had coordinated Rebeka and Liam's exit from the Commonwealth.

Latham answered on the second tone. "George Latham," he said briskly. His face grew serious when he saw Simon. "Lieutenant Buckley. To what do I owe this pleasure." His tone said he was anything but pleased. He was still in shirtsleeves but clearly had been dressing for court. He had his trademark red cravat around his neck, but not yet tied.

Simon smiled in what he hoped was an apologetic expression. "I'm sorry to bother you, sir, but there's been a serious development. Rebeka's secret has been compromised." He went on to relate the information he had about the Harsakas and Anika Sommerstag. Latham listened without comment. "So, sir, I'm concerned that you may be in danger."

Latham pursed his lips but didn't answer immediately. When he spoke his voice had the sonorous tone that had made him a formidable advocate and litigator. "Have you considered your own safety, Lieutenant?"

"Aye, sir, but I have a job to do," answered Simon. "I'm being as careful as I can and still be effective."

Latham smiled at that. "Have you also considered that none of the people who are, shall we say, authorized to know about Rebeka have been harmed or threatened? The dead are all criminal conspirators who were acting against the Princess."

Simon sat stunned for a second. He'd not thought of that fact. He spoke carefully. "Are you saying these killings are part of some protective action?"

Latham held up a hand. "No!, No, I have no information about any such thing." He must have seen the look on Simon's face, for he went on in a lower tone. "Seriously, Lieutenant, I don't know of any Security Service actions over the past few days. I'm not being evasive. I'm just pointing out an obvious connection between the people you mentioned. Perhaps coincident, or perhaps not. In the meantime, I will take your warning to heart and be careful. Have you informed the Palace of your concerns?"

"Not yet. I'm meeting with an advocate from the Justice Ministry at tenth hour today and will be talking to Lieutenant Harold after that."

"All good, Lieutenant," said Latham, nodding. "Give Stenson my regards."

"I will, sir," said Simon. He added quickly before Latham could close the connection. "If I may, sir, I'd like to ask a favor."

"Ask away."

"I may be in need of an advocate, or at least the appearance of having one," said Simon.

"My fees are fairly steep, Lieutenant." Latham smiled. "Perhaps you should tell me why you need my services."

Simon outlined the IG investigation and his upcoming meeting with Lowell later in the day. "The thing is, sir, I suspect that Killian was on the cuff to Lowell and told him about the Princess. Lowell covered his outstanding hotel bill. He didn't stick up for his men when they botched my interrogation. Now he's coming at me again. It's pure intimidation, and I need to show him I'm not going to roll over easily."

"And a well-known advocate in your corner could put him on the defensive," Latham agreed. "All good, Lieutenant. What time are you meeting this Inspector Lowell?"

"At fifteenth hour, sir," Simon replied.

"I'm in court today until midday but have nothing scheduled after thirteenth. Shall I meet you in your office at quarter before fifteenth?"

"Yes. Sir," said Simon. "Thank you."

"Don't thank me yet, Lieutenant," chuckled Latham. "You haven't seen my bill." He closed the connection.

Simon tried Hal's mirror locus again but got no reply. He checked his timepiece again and considered the time zone change. If Hal and Brookstone had made the pickup, they might already be on the road back. Simon put his mirror away, struggling for patience, and tried to finish reviewing the papers Lessa had left on the desk. Most of them were routine communications and memos from other departments. There were a couple of updates from Gervis Birchfield and Jack Ironhand and a long, tedious report from Jason Hanks that added little to his investigation of the backflash fire. Simon made a note once again to interview Jamie Smithington himself.

At the bottom of the stack was a short note from the Lord Mayor's Office to the effect that despite any unrelated IG inquiry, Aspenwald still expected Simon to pursue the investigation into Anika Sommerstag's death and report daily on his progress.

Simon held the note in his hand and rubbed his chin. On the one hand, he'd expected this response. It might indicate fatherly concern, or it might simply be arrogance born of power. There was no offer to intervene with the IG but again, that wasn't surprising. The Mayor's Office had no direct command over the IG, who answered directly to the Justice Minister. But Simon knew how politics worked, and he was fairly certain that Kershaw and the Mayor were close acquaintances, if not friends. He also knew that Lowell had worked for Aspenwald in the past.

Aspenwald could have intervened without causing much comment if he'd thought it would help the investigation, Simon thought. *Does that mean he doesn't really care about solving the murder, only about whether it could blow back on him? Or is he being overly scrupulous about calling in a favor because he doesn't want to compromise the investigation?*

He tossed the paper aside and rubbed his eyes. He

drained the last of his coffee and checked his timepiece yet again. *Gods above and below, where in the seven hells is Hal?*

As if in answer the summoning tone on his mirror chimed. He snatched it up and swiped his hand across its surface. The face that appeared belonged to a Dwarf, but it wasn't Hal's. The Dwarf wore a Peacekeeper's uniform and the shoulder lanyard of a Sergeant. He was fairer than Hal with reddish brown hair and a close trimmed beard.

"Simon Buckley here," Simon said. "Who are you?"

"Good meeting, Lieutenant," the Dwarf said. "I'm Sergeant Georg Stonehelm, day watch out of Eastmark. Jack Ironhand gave me your name and mirror locus. I have a DB here on my patch that I thought you lot should know about. He's a Keeper, Magic Enforcement out of Wycliffe House. Fellow named Giles Machemer."

Simon felt a chill in the pit of his stomach. "How did you know to reach out to me, Sergeant?"

"Didn't," said Stonehelm. "I reached out to Jack as an old friend because the dead man is Magic Squad. Jack's the one who set me onto you." He paused and scratched his beard. "Look, LT, all I know is that this guy was fished out of the Finnigan a mile downstream from the Great Cut. He has a couple of iron bolts stuck in his chest and a Keeper's badge in his pocket. My team is handling the investigation and I need to know what he was working on that might have brought him east of the Cut."

"Machemer wasn't in my chain of command. He was detached to the IG staff under an Inspector named Lowell." Simon paused to look Stonehelm in the eye. "And just so all the dice are on the table, he liked me for killing another Keeper, his former Sergeant; a man named Frank Killian."

Stonehelm scoffed. "If he was tight with Killian, it might explain the two bolts in his chest."

"How so?" asked Simon.

"I've got a couple of snitches in the Orc neighborhoods around East Tanner who tell me Killian's been recruiting ironworkers and blacksmiths for some sort of secret project, promising big payoffs when it's done. He took along a couple of Snake Clan hardboys to back him up, but he pissed off a bunch of Guild masters from the Wind clan and they threatened to introduce his head to their tap hammers."

"The Harsaka brothers?"

Stonehelm's eyes narrowed. "Yes. How did you know? Was he working undercover for the Squad? I'd heard he was kicked off the force for being on the cuff to a bunch of jolt dealers."

"He was definitely not working for us. In fact, I think he was working for Lowell in a bid to try to take down Gelbard Axhart."

Stonehelm held up a hand. "Whoa, that's way above my rank. I don't want to get dragged into some feud between the IG and the Ax. I just want to finish a quick murder investigation and keep my head down."

"Any word on what this secret project was?" asked Simon.

"Nothing that makes any sense. Some sort of hand work making tubes from iron bars, but the smiths couldn't use any spell work or machinery. Why work that hard when a spell powered borer could do the job in a tenth of the time?"

Simon knew the answer to that. "I'm not sure I can be of much help, Sergeant. Machemer wasn't working any official case in your patch that I know of. He may have been poking around for the IG's office. Maybe he asked the wrong people over there about Killian and the Harsakas."

"Might could be," Stonehelm said slowly in a now evident Dundarian accent. "The Guild masters talk tough, but I never thought they had a killing beef with Killian or the Harsakas. Just the usual clan turf rivalries. Those never amount to much more than cracked heads and property destruction." He cocked his head as he looked into his mirror at Simon. "You say he had a personal gripe with you?"

"Aye," said Simon. "He blames me for Killian's getting the boot. But if I'd done for him, I wouldn't have left traceable bolts in his chest and I'd have weighted the body better. Any idea when he died?"

"Not yet," replied Stonehelm. "Aural analysis is still out, but he hadn't been in the water long, and the body hadn't been weighted at all. Why? You looking to establish an alibi?" Stonehelm smiled as he said it, but Simon could see he was still considering the possibility that Simon was a killer.

"Well, it must have been after fourteenth hour yesterday, because up until then, Machemer was in my office accusing me of conspiracy to kill Farsk Kronska and take over the drug trade down in the Hollows." Simon smiled back at Stonehelm. "His boss is coming back to have another run at me at fifteenth today, so if you've got suspicions about me, you'd better get in line."

The Dwarf laughed, for real this time. "Actually, my forensics mage guesses he went in the water about seventeenth yesterday. He needs more time to nail it down to an exact time of death. I'm pretty sure your watch staff can vouch for you at that time?"

Simon just nodded. He wondered if Lowell knew about Machemer and whether that was why he wanted to interrogate him again.

"I'll be in touch, LT," said Stonehelm. "Thanks for the info on Machemer."

CHAPTER TWENTY

Stonehelm broke the connection and Simon set the mirror on his desk. *Why Machemer? He didn't know anything. He was a donkey's ass but he had no real power. Unless somebody thought Killian had confided something dangerous to him. But what?*

It was now into the day watch and his team leaders started to check in. Gervis Birchfield had little new to add to the information he had shared the day before. He planned to look first at the warehouse from which the neutral iron had been stolen, but didn't expect it to yield much. He had also put in a request with the business fraud teams to see if they could trace ownership of the warehouses that Smithington had listed as belonging to the same consortium. Maybe there was a connection to one of the players in their case. Finally, the forensics mages had determined that the small ebony stick that had been in Sommerstag's bag was from an imager, not a handheld mirror. They were working on retrieving any pictures that might be on it and could tell the team what Anika had been looking for in her travels around the Hollows.

Jack Ironhand came in next and asked if Stonehelm had been in touch.

"Sorry to set him on you without warning, LT," he said. "I should have given you a heads up but I've been trying to get through to Hal and Brookstone since fourth hour and they aren't answering. Have you heard anything?"

"No," Simon answered trying to hide his own concern. "But I'm sure they're all good. It was just a routine extradition pickup. Hells. The perp wasn't considered dangerous, just stupid."

"If you say so," Jack said. "But you never know with Ironlanders. Touchy bastards, they are. Always on about some sort of tradition or breach of etiquette."

Simon grinned. "And we did tweak their beards by sending Brookstone along. Gods. I hope we don't have to try to get the two of them out of some dungeon."

Jack grinned back. "They'd have a job of it, trying to hold Hal. Oh, hells, I suppose your right, there could be a dozen reasons why they haven't checked in."

He went on to catch Simon up on the rest of the active cases his team was following, then stood and took his leave.

Jason Hanks's Second reported in next. Hanks was in court that morning to give testimony on an earlier case. Simon only half listened to the reports, something about tracking all the registered Air mages who had been in the city on the day of the backflash fire, before dismissing the man. He wondered idly if Hanks's case had anything to do with Latham's court appearance. If so, he actually felt sorry for the young Peacekeeper Sergeant.

It was nearly ninth hour by that time, and he had finished his third mug of coffee on an empty stomach. He could feel the lack of rest and the anxiety churning into acid. He knew he'd better eat something soon or the fire would become unquenchable and make him miserable all day.

He told Lessa that he'd be out for the rest of the morning and went to find some breakfast before walking over to the Justice Ministry for his meeting with Bendict Hammersmith.

By quarter to tenth, bolstered by a plate of fried eggs and soda bread with butter from a small restaurant midway between his office and Hammersmith's, he approached the gated entry to the Justice Ministry courtyard. He waited while the guards carefully checked a hand cart heavily loaded with three large barrels. One scrawny Orc in coveralls stood between the front shafts used to pull the cart and a larger one stood behind the cart leaning on the pusher plate as a guard stood in the bed and looked into the center barrel.

"What's this stuff, then?" Simon heard the guard ask.

"Fertilizer, guvner, for the flower beds," the large Orc answered. "Them roses has got the wilt. This stuff'll perk 'em right up."

The guard jumped down and waved them through. "All right, clear the gate. Just don't block the walkways with your cart."

"Right, guvner," said the Orc. "Heave, Taska!" The smaller Orc leaned into his harness, pulling on the shafts with thin, wiry arms as the larger one threw his shoulder into the pusher plate. They were obviously a team that had worked together for a while, as the cart moved smoothly and swiftly through the gate and along the center walkway.

Simon stepped up to the gate and showed his badge. "Simon Buckley," he said. "I have a meeting at tenth hour with Mr. Hammersmith."

The guard ran his eyes over Simon, noting the glow

of the security spell as it picked up Simon's needler in the hip holster and the dagger in his boot. He checked Simon's badge and glanced down at a note board before nodding. "Aye, sir. You're cleared to go on up to his office. Do you know the way?"

"I do," answered Simon. He pointed to the two Orcs who were pushing their cart off the walkway and up against the wall just below Hammersmith's office. "What was that all about."

"Gardeners," said the guard. "We see them a few times a week, but they have their tools in a shed at the back of the courtyard. They don't usually bring stuff in."

"What's in the barrels?"

"Fertilizer, they said," answered the guard. "Some kind of processed manure, I imagine. It was black like manure but was dry like powder and didn't stink."

Something about black powder made Simon stop. He looked down at his feet where a dusting of the powder had fallen from the cart. He stooped and picked some of it up between his thumb and forefinger. It was coarse. More like sand than flour. He lifted his fingers to his nose and sniffed. He smelled carbon and sulfur and an acrid scent that triggered something in the back of his mind.

He turned to the guard, speaking quietly but urgently. "Call your Guard Captain. Clear the building, now." The man didn't move. Simon slapped him on the shoulder. "Now!"

The guard spoke into his Farspeaker bracer as Simon drew his needler. He walked through the gate and crossed the green lawn toward the two Orcs.

They stood next to the cart which was now pushed up against the west wall of the courtyard. To their left was the lobby door to the offices on the upper floors. To their right was the west gate from the courtyard, really just a small door leading to the alley between

Tanner and King's Road.

"King's Agent!" he shouted, lifting the needler in a two-handed grip. "Stand away from the barrels and show me your hands."

The smaller Orc scuttled toward the west gate. The big one pulled a lighter from his pocket and struck it into flame.

"Don't!" Simon shouted. The Orc smiled and tossed the flame into the open barrel.

Simon pulled the trigger of his needler too late. The world dissolved into a flash of yellow flame and a hammer blow of sound and shock that threw Simon across the courtyard, slamming him against the east wall. Blinding white light filled his vision only to be replaced an instant later by blackness.

He returned to an awareness of noise; shouts, screaming, and the distant warble of a siren filled his ears while his eyes refused to focus. His vision cleared from the center outward, as if he were looking down a slowly widening tunnel. His head ached. There was a sharp pain in his back at the base of his ribcage and he was breathing in short gasps.

The west wall was gone, replaced by a smoking hole surrounded by shattered brickwork. The remains of the glass that had been the wonder of the courtyard space hung in ragged shards from twisted and broken ironwork.

Simon struggled to his feet, bracing himself against the east wall. He looked toward the Tanner Road gate. The guards were down but moving, stunned but not dead. He shook his head to clear it. He realized he'd only been down for a minute or two. As he watched, other guards began to converge on the courtyard and an Emergency Services sled pulled up outside the gate.

He looked around for his needler, found it a few feet away, and returned it to his hip holster. He took out his mirror, flipped through the directory scroll, and summoned a locus.

"Harold," a voice answered. The mirror was set to privacy mode.

"Lieutenant Harold, it's Simon Buckley. This is an emergency. Where is the Royal Family?"

Harold's scarred, lopsided face appeared in Simon's mirror. "Buckley, what's going on?"

"Bomb at the Justice Ministry," said Simon. "I think it's part of something bigger. Where are the King and Queen?"

"The King is on his way to address Parliament," said Harold, nonplussed. "The Queen is in her conservatory preparing to receive a delegation from the Hybarian Relief. The Crown Prince is in his chambers answering correspondence."

"Get them all under protection, now," said Simon.

"What the hells, Buckley? What do you know?"

"Nothing definite and there's no time to explain. If I'm wrong, the King can have my badge with a personal apology." Simon began running toward the hole in the west wall, remembering that Hammersmith's office had been directly above the blast.

Harold growled softly in frustration. "All good. I'm triggering the alert protocols now. You'd better be right about this."

"Thanks, Stenson," said Simon and broke the connection. He reached the site of the explosion and stopped. There was nothing left of the cart, the barrels, or the two Orcs. He was surprised to see that other than blackened grass and stone, there was no crater. The force of the blast had all been directed upward into the face of the building. Despite the noise from the street and the gate area, here next to the wall it was strangely quiet.

Simon looked around, not sure what he should do. Fire Brigade and Emergency Services personnel were arriving and spreading through the courtyard. One young medic rushed up to him, touching him gently on the shoulder.

"Sir, are you hurt? Is everything all good?" he asked.

Simon turned to him, showing his badge. "Yes. I'm Lieutenant Buckley, Magic Enforcement. I was supposed to meet . . . to meet Bendict, um, Bendict Hammersmith." He suddenly found himself on the ground gazing up at the sky.

The medic was kneeling beside him, checking his pulse and looking at his eyes. Simon tried to lift his head, but the world spun and his stomach lurched.

"Easy, LT," said the medic. "You've had a shock. I think you have a concussion. Just lie still and we'll get you to the hospital in two shakes."

"Hammersmith," said Simon. He pointed to the west wall. "He was in there."

"Lie easy," said the medic placing his hands on Simon's shoulders. "Teams are starting to clear the building. If he's in there, they'll find him."

Simon struggled weakly and very briefly. His head spun and his stomach lurched again, so he lay back as instructed. He closed his eyes, and while he remained conscious, his awareness was fragmented and confused. He was aware of a great deal of activity around him. At some point he was moved out of the courtyard to a large tent, presumably set up in the street. He may have slept, or at least lost track of time for a while.

He opened his eyes to a bright but diffuse light filtering through the white fabric of the tent. He gingerly turned his head, and while he still had a headache, he no longer felt dizzy or nauseated. He lay on a cot, in a row of similar cots under a white fabric roof. Two of the tent sides were rolled up and he could see the flashing orange and green lights of Keeper and Emergency Services sleds all around. He looked to the cot next to his and was relieved to see the face of Bendict Hammersmith.

The Dwarf's eyes were closed and there was a bandage wrapped around his forehead. Splints held both of his arms at his sides and his fine business suit had been cut away to reveal scraped and burned legs, but his chest rose and fell regularly as he breathed. He was alive.

Simon sat up slowly, swinging his legs over the side of the cot. His head spun briefly but then stopped and his vision cleared. He took a deep breath and felt sharp but bearable pain in his left chest area. He actually felt surprisingly well. His head was clear and he had more or less bearable pains in his back and legs, but he was alive and reasonably functional.

A medic noticed him and rushed to his side. "Lie down, LT," the man said. Simon recognized him as the man who had first reached him in the courtyard.

"I'm fine," protested Simon. He glanced at the man's nametag. "Medic Huntress, right? You were in the courtyard just after the blast."

"Aye, sir. And you have a concussion and a couple of broken ribs. You need to lie down until the ambulances can take you to hospital."

"No, no time for that," said Simon as he carefully got to his feet. He only swayed a little before steadying himself. "What's the situation?"

"Stable." Huntress eyed him warily, as if he expected Simon to fall down any second. "The rescue teams have cleared the building. The most seriously injured have been evacuated already. You are in the second group of stable patients who can wait for transport. Please, LT. Lie down."

Simon ignored his order and pointed to Hammersmith. "Will he be all good?"

"Aye," said Huntress. "A couple of broken arms and a concussion, but he's stable. We gave him a pain tincture and the healer put a sleep spell on him. He'll be fine."

"What's the butcher's bill?" Simon asked, regretting his coarseness when Huntress flinched.

"Twenty dead, forty-five injured," Huntress answered, deadpan. "You should be going to the hospital yourself."

"Do I need some specific treatment?" asked Simon.

"Well, no, likely not. But the protocols say we should observe you overnight."

Simon ignored him and reached into his pocket. "Where's my mirror?" he asked.

"It's in the property bag, under your cot, along with your badge and weapon."

"Get them out for me, will you?" Simon asked with a small smile. "My head's telling me I shouldn't bend over just now."

Huntress reached down and lifted a paper bag onto the cot. Simon quickly extracted his badge, needler and mirror. He checked the magazine and spell charge on the needler before sliding it into his hip holster. He activated the mirror and swiped on the recall function.

Harold answered the summons immediately. "Buckley! Thank the gods you're all good. We heard you were at the Ministry when it was bombed."

"I'm alive," said Simon. "A bit shaken, that's all. What's the situation with the Royal Family?"

"All safe and together in the Refuge under guard," Harold replied, his face growing grave. "How did you know? More importantly, if you knew there was a threat why didn't you inform me? I thought we were past all that interdepartmental horse shit."

"I didn't know anything until the explosion at the Ministry," said Simon. "What happened?"

"A bunch of Orcs, part of the official delegation to Parliament from the Clans down in the Hollows, were armed with strange weapons. They killed the

Parliamentary Master at Arms and two of his men before they were taken down. Whatever those things were, they evaded our security scans. Fortunately, they only could shoot once. But the Orcs clearly wanted to use them on the King when he addressed the joint session about the recent riots."

"And the Queen?" asked Simon.

"My people searched the delegation from Hybarian Relief and found two more of those accursed weapons. On Humans! Orcs I get, but Humans turning on the Royal Family? Anyway, the entire delegation is in lockup until we can sort this out." Harold paused and took a shuddering breath. "Gods above and below, Simon. What the hells is going on?"

"I'm still not sure," admitted Simon. "Since the riots, I've been chasing four interconnected murders that are tied somehow to Galen Flandyrs, some stolen neutral iron, and a state secret involving a certain young woman."

"Why wasn't I informed about this?" Harold's tone was carefully neutral, but his eyes and the set of his jaw revealed his anger.

"I wasn't sure myself until late yesterday," said Simon. "I had an agreement with Bendict Hammersmith to share information. I was at the Ministry to brief him first, then I had planned to call on you at the Palace. I never expected any action this soon. Hammersmith and I had suspicions, but thought that any operation was still in its early stages."

"Maybe it was." Harold's face looked more thoughtful than angry. "These threats were serious, but they seem a bit improvised, like they were put together on the fly. Maybe your investigation made them move too soon. Flandyrs, you say? He's resurfaced?"

"Aye," said Simon. "And he's got powerful protection in the Havens. But he must have people working this side of the border. He can't show his face in the

Commonwealth."

"Do you have any leads?"

"Nothing firm." Simon lowered his voice. "I have some bad feelings about some important people that I'd rather not discuss over the mirror. We need to meet in person, preferably with Axhart as well. I'd want Hammersmith to be there, but he's been hurt in the bombing and is likely out of action for a while."

"I'll be tied down here for most of the day," said Harold. "Can you set something up for this evening."

Simon nodded. "I'll summon Axhart as soon as we sign off. I'm sure he's in the Command Center by now. I have a meeting at fifteenth today anyway. Can you come to Wycliffe House after watch change, say eighteenth hour?"

Harold turned away from the mirror and said something Simon couldn't hear to someone nearby. He turned back to Simon a second later. "I'll try. I'll get a message to you if I can't make it. I have to go now. The King wants to be briefed on the situation, and Prince Henrik is insisting on touring the bombing site personally." Harold's face betrayed what he thought of that idea. "Be careful, Buckley."

"You too, Stenson." Simon swiped his hand across the mirror to sign off. He fished in the bag until he found his keys, his timepiece, and his purse. Then he walked out into bright sunlight and chaos.

CHAPTER TWENTY-ONE

Simon found Axhart at the Command Center in the lower levels of Wycliffe House, below the stables and behind heavy cold iron security doors. Simon had flashed his badge and asked for Axhart. To his surprise, he'd been hustled inside and directly to the situation room where Axhart sat at a desk flipping through reports and message flimsies.

"Simon," said the old Dwarf as soon as he saw him. "I heard you were injured, on the way to hospital. What the hells are you doing here?"

Simon looked around. The Command Center was filled with agents and mages. A bank of mirrors faced Axhart's desk. More workstations and mirrors lined the walls. Agents spoke in low voices into Farspeaker connections and jotted notes on papers that were passed to the desk in the center of the room, the desk where Axhart sat.

"I have a firsthand report on the bombing, and I think it connects with the attack on Parliament," said

Simon as he looked around the room. He stepped closer to the desk and said, "I need to speak to you confidentially, sir. I don't know if you've heard but that IG inspector Lowell is going to take another run at me today at fifteenth hour. And Giles Machemer was fished out of the river with two bolts in his chest early this morning. I think Lowell's going to try to set me up for it."

Axhart nodded. "I knew Lowell was coming back, but hadn't heard about Machemer. Does Lowell have a case?"

"Doubtful, but he'll bluster and threaten. I can handle him. The thing is, I think he's connected to these attacks. If I'm right, it may implicate some important people. Can you be at a meeting with Stenson Harold and me at eighteenth today? We need to coordinate our efforts with the Palace and the Justice Ministry."

Axhart crooked a finger at one of the nearby Agents. The man hurried over. "Falcon, sit down with Lt. Buckley and take his report. He was at the Justice Ministry. I'll see you at eighteenth in my office, Lieutenant. Let Elvira know so she can put it on the schedule." He grinned. "I'll be there."

Falcon was a Civil Patrol Sergeant, who took Simon off to a corner and recorded his report on the bombing. Simon stuck to the bare facts, avoiding any speculation about motives or who might be behind the attack. That was for later when he met with Axhart and Harold. Falcon looked over his notes, shut off the recorder, and told Simon that it would do for now.

Simon sat for a few minutes, watching the controlled chaos of the Command Center. From what he could overhear, the only major attack had been on the Justice Ministry. The assassination plots against the King and Queen had been thwarted, but none of the Orcs and only one of the Humans involved had allowed themselves to be captured alive. The Parliament was locked down and the news outlets had been kept in the dark about the danger to the Royal Family. The borders had been closed, Westport Docks were under lockdown, and all transportation in and out of the capital was being searched and cataloged.

Simon's head pounded and his stomach continued to turn somersaults as he finally stood and made to leave. He checked his timepiece and was surprised to see that it was half past fourteenth hour. He stopped by the dispensary for a pain tincture before climbing the stairs to his office.

He had barely settled behind his desk when Lessa looked in and announced that George Latham had arrived.

"Show him in, please Lessa." Simon rubbed his eyes and rolled his neck before sitting a little straighter in his chair.

"Thank you, Miss." Latham nodded courteously as he passed Lessa. He was dressed immaculately, as usual, in a dark blue business suit with a wide red cravat. He carried an eelskin letter case and a willow wood cane with a dark garnet embedded in the grip.

Simon rose in greeting but had to grip the edge of his desk to steady himself. He extended his other hand and Latham shook it.

"Thank you for coming, Mr. Latham." He waved the advocate to the armchair that faced the desk.

"No thanks needed, Lieutenant," answered Latham. "We both know that this is really about protecting the Princess. If helping you with the Inspector General furthers that end, all good." His face and tone hardened. "But make no mistake, if the price of her safety and the Royal Family's reputation is your head, I will serve it up myself."

Simon swallowed hard. "Understood, sir."

"Are you all good for this meeting?" asked Latham. "I hear you were injured in the Justice Ministry attack. I can intercede as your advocate and put this interrogation on hold until the Healers can evaluate you."

Simon shook his head, which he immediately regretted. "No, sir. It's important that this happens today."

Latham looked doubtful as he settled into the armchair. "Now," he said smiling again. "Tell me what this Inspector Lowell has said and done so far. Not what you suspect he may know, but what has actually been said by him or in his presence."

Simon related the last interview with Lowell, Forge, and Machemer; Lowell's odd failure to direct the questioning, even after it was clear that Machemer was following a blind tunnel.

"Giles Machemer was fished out of the Finnigan a few miles downstream from the Cut early this morning. There were two bolts in his chest, so this wasn't just a drowning, nor a suicide," said Simon. "I have a feeling that Lowell is going to try to put his murder on me somehow. It was pretty clear from Forge's comment yesterday that Captain Axhart is the real target here, but if they can put me in a squeeze, they may think that I'll roll over on him, or on whatever secret they think we're holding."

"That being the truth behind Rebeka's abdication," said Latham. "Does Lowell have any evidence that could implicate you?"

"Not that I know of. I was at home at the time Machemer was killed. Depending on when they fix the time of death, I may have people who can vouch for me, but I'd rather not involve them."

"You may need to." Latham narrowed his eyes. "Why would you be reluctant to have them come forward?"

"Because two of those people are the Princess and Liam Aster. We were speaking over the mirror, and I'd rather not open the subject of our talk to discovery," answered Simon. After a pause, he added. "I also had a guest in my flat earlier in the evening but again, there are reasons why it would be awkward to say who it was."

"Care to share what those reasons are?" Latham's tone suggested he suspected a woman that Simon wanted to protect.

Simon smiled wryly. "I have contacts within the Orc community, specifically with the Cabal of Clans. Given today's events, I'd rather not have to discuss that with the IG."

"I see," Latham said with a frown. "Did this contact know anything about today's attack?"

"Not directly, but his information is part of the bigger picture I'm starting to put together." When Latham's frown deepened, Simon went on, "Galen Flandyrs is behind the conspiracy to expose Rebeka as a mage and discredit the Royal House. He also has been acquiring neutral iron in order to make weapons."

Latham held up a hand to interrupt. "I'm afraid you just lost me. Neutral Iron?"

"Iron that has not been touched or influenced by magic. If hand forged into weapons, again without spellwork, the weapons are not recognized by modern security spells." Simon paused as Latham considered that. The older man paled as the implication dawned on him. "Weapons like that have been intercepted at the Northern Frontier of the Gray Havens. The components for them have been found by the Justice Ministry here in the Commonwealth. Bendict Hammersmith, an advocate from the Anti-terrorism section, was the lead investigator. I believe he was the target of the bombing at the Ministry."

"And the weapons?" Latham's voice was quiet, just above a whisper.

"They were used today in separate attacks on the King and Queen. Fortunately, Palace Security thwarted both attempts. Unfortunately, only one of the would-be assassins survived." Simon said. "I'm worried that this is only part of a bigger conspiracy. I suspect Lowell is involved and possibly even the Lord Mayor."

Simon had to give Latham credit. He took the revelation with little more than a twitch of the corner of his mouth and a shift in his seat.

Lessa opened the door and interrupted them before Latham could respond. "Inspector Lowell is here, LT. He has two uniforms from the Civil Patrol with him."

Simon looked at Latham who nodded. "Thank you, Lessa. Show him in."

Latham shifted in his seat so that he could see the door. Lowell swept in followed by a pair of uniformed Patrol Agents. He started across the office toward Simon but stopped when he noticed Latham. The two uniforms stumbled awkwardly as they tried not to run into him. Simon didn't rise this time.

Lowell seemed to recover quickly. He stepped forward and sat in the chair opposite Latham, uninvited. Latham leaned back in his chair, his cane held with one hand off to the side, looking comfortable and unconcerned. Simon sat silent, determined to match Latham's air of unconcerned waiting.

The uniformed agents took up station behind Lowell, trying to look grim, but clearly uncomfortable in the presence of the advocate. Simon suspected they had been commandeered by Lowell at the last minute and expected to be effecting a simple detention.

After a long minute of silence, Lowell cleared his throat and asked, "Lieutenant Buckley, can you account for your movements between first and fourth hours this morning?"

"Why?" asked Simon. "Do I need to?"

"You've heard about Giles Machemer." It was a statement, not a question.

"I've heard that he's a toad who sold his soul to the Weasel Squad for power and money. But you know that." Simon answered, holding Lowell's gaze, deliberately trying to unbalance him.

"Giles is dead." Lowell's voice was harsh with anger. He frowned briefly before continuing in a calm, even tone. "He was shot twice in the chest with a D'Stang bolt thrower. The bolts trace back to a weapon he checked out of the armory at Wycliffe House two days ago."

"He managed to shoot himself twice with his own weapon?" Simon said. "He had more talent, or at least more dexterity, than I gave him credit for."

Lowell shot to his feet. "You think this is a game, Buckley?" he shouted. "By the gods, I'll have you in irons before the day is out."

"On what charge, Inspector?" Latham's deep baritone wasn't loud but it cut across Lowell's shout like a sharp blade.

Lowell turned to face Latham. "Murder. I intend to detain Simon Buckley for the murder of Giles Machemer."

"I see," said Latham, still the picture of calm. "That's a serious charge. As Lieutenant Buckley's advocate I must ask, do you have a warrant for his detention?"

"I don't need one," replied Lowell. "I have evidence. The murder weapon was found in Buckley's own flat. That's enough to detain him pending a formal charge."

Simon was out of his chair in an instant. "You were in my flat? You son of a gnome, what the hells are you playing at?"

Latham sat up in his chair and held a hand up to Simon. "Be quiet, Simon." His voice was not loud but had the snap of command. Simon closed his mouth.

Latham gripped his cane in both hands as he leaned forward. "I assume you had a warrant to search Lieutenant Buckley's flat. May I see it? Which

Magistrate issued it?"

"It'll be forthcoming," blustered Lowell.

"What do you mean 'forthcoming'?" Latham's voice was cold.

"Exigent circumstances," said Lowell. "I went to inform Lieutenant Buckley of Giles Machemer's death and to question him about his whereabouts. He wasn't in his flat and the door had obviously been forced. I entered the flat on the presumption that a crime was in progress and that Buckley might be injured."

Simon laughed out loud, but Latham held up a hand again. "And you found the bolt thrower in plain sight?"

Lowell actually squirmed. "It was under the bed. I immediately left the flat and called a uniformed agent to secure the scene until a warrant could be obtained and a forensics team called."

"What Magistrate would issue a warrant after the fact based on that flimsy tale?" scoffed Simon. "Even Justice Saverna at his most rabid would laugh you out of his chambers."

"The warrant came from Minister Kershaw himself," sneered Lowell. "My squad reports to the Ministry, not to the Courts. He issued permission for the search over the mirror and intended to file it afterward. The attack on the Ministry HQ has had him a bit preoccupied since then." He turned to Latham. "So, yes, it will be forthcoming."

Lowell nodded. "But until it does, the search is not sanctioned and any evidence developed from it is invalid." He swept a hand toward Simon. "You may go ahead and detain my client, but once the search is invalidated he'll be released and I will file a motion to suppress any evidence brought forward as a result of your illegal search. Or you can produce the warrant and we can go to the courts to challenge it. Either way, detention of Lieutenant Buckley is temporary and problematic for your case. Your choice, Inspector."

Simon only half listened to Latham. He was struck by the mention of Kershaw. *Why would the Minister involve himself in a murder investigation? Why would he even respond to a request from Lowell? High brass jingle. Lowell is Aspenwald's man and Aspenwald has some serious influence over Kershaw. He got the Minister to order Axhart and me to feed information to the Mayor's Office.*

"Why don't you two go see Lessa in the outer office," Simon said to the uniformed Agents. "I'm sure she can find you some coffee or something."

The two Agents looked at each other before hastily retreating to the outer room. Their relief was evident. They had expected an easy detention, not a high-level political fight.

"Both of you sit down and we'll find a way to speak like adults," said Latham.

Lowell glared at Simon but resumed his seat. Simon settled into his chair as well.

"Now," said Latham looking at Lowell. "I am here as Lieutenant Buckley's advocate. You don't have to talk to me. We can end this now and you can walk out of this office and pursue whatever case you think you have."

Lowell nodded. "And I will pursue it. Count on that."

"At exactly what time did you enter Lieutenant Buckley's flat?" asked Latham.

"Just after eighth hour," said Lowell. "I learned about Machemer about half an hour earlier. We already had this meeting set and I wanted Buckley to know why Giles wouldn't be here."

"I heard Machemer was dead an hour before that. I'd been here for some time already," said Simon. "Dice on the table, Spencer. Who told you about Machemer? And was my door really open when you came to my flat to try to shake me up?"

"All good, dice on the table," said Lowell. "You're a liar and are concealing the identity of an arsonist. You and Axhart and others"—he looked pointedly at Latham—"know who killed Farsk Kronska and set numerous other fires throughout the Hollows. That Fire mage is connected to the Royal Family and I intend to charge you and the rest of your cronies with obstruction of justice, accessory to murder, and criminal conspiracy."

Simon held his hands out, wrists together. "Be my guest, Spencer. If you had a case, you'd have detained me by now. What did Killian tell you? Did he give you an actual name?"

Lowell blinked at the mention of Killian's name but otherwise showed no reaction. "I don't know what you're on about," he said. "I never met Frank Killian. He was Machemer's obsession, not mine. Giles was convinced you were the one who set him up and somehow got him killed."

And now I've got you, thought Simon. *The images of your hand paying Killian's hotel tab are the hook I'll use to hang you.* He started to speak but stopped himself. *No, not yet. I can connect Lowell to Killian and Killian to the stolen iron, but we still don't have the whole picture. Was Lowell the one who was going to pick up the metal, or was it destined for someone else?*

Latham spoke up at that point, covering Simon's awkward pause. "Aside from the dubious allegation of a bolt thrower illegally obtained from Lieutenant Buckley's home, do you have any other evidence of a crime? Who can corroborate this conspiracy you claim to know about?"

"Captain Gelbard Axhart, Liam Aster, and I have reason to suspect Princess Rebeka Fangbern has direct knowledge as well." Lowell's face held a smug smile, almost as if challenging Latham to respond to the mention of Rebeka.

He knows, thought Simon.

Latham returned the smile with one of his own. "Since both the Princess and former Agent Aster are currently out of your reach, I suggest we move this conversation up to Captain Axhart's office. I'm sure he'll take time out from the current crisis to respond to your accusation."

"No," answered Lowell. "This isn't the time." He turned to Simon. "Watch yourself, Buckley. This isn't over."

"You're right," said Simon. "It isn't."

CHAPTER TWENTY-TWO

Lowell stood and left the office. Simon remained stone-faced and motionless until he was gone. Latham looked relaxed and even gave Lowell a small wave as he reached the door. As soon as it closed, he frowned and looked at Simon.

"What about it, Simon," he asked. "Does he know about Rebeka?"

"I think he does, but he can't confirm it," said Simon. "I believe Killian figured it out and used the information to involve himself in this plot to discredit the King. He thought his story would be confirmed by Anika Sommerstag and the Harsaka brothers. I think Killian was supposed to be the go between for Lowell to take delivery of the neutral iron so that Anika and the brothers wouldn't know who was actually running the plot from the Commonwealth side. Anika only met Flandyrs in the Free States and wasn't told who was in charge here. I think a lot of her time here was spent looking into it. She was an investigator, after all."

"You mentioned Rondel Aspenwald," observed Latham. "Why do you think he's part of this plot?"

"Gut feeling," admitted Simon with a shrug. "But Lowell's Aspenwald's man. He ran security for the Mayor's campaign and, just after the election, Minister Kershaw approved his appointment to the IG staff as a full Inspector. Aspenwald also got Kershaw to break policy and instruct Axhart to update the Mayor on an active investigation. That's so unusual that the IG should be looking at that and not at me."

"Do you think Aspenwald knows about the Princess as well?" Latham asked.

Simon pulled at his lower lip as he thought about that. "I doubt it. I think he was telling the truth when he said he and his daughter weren't close. That doesn't mean they were estranged, though. I think Anika was supposed to deliver some key information or message from Flandyrs to either Aspenwald, or someone in his circle. That's why he's so keen on keeping up with our investigation."

"A lot of speculation without much evidence," Latham said quietly.

"I know," said Simon with a rueful smile. "But it's all I've got so far. I have a team looking for any connection between Sommerstag and either Lowell or Aspenwald, but they haven't found it yet. There's also a stick from her imager, which may hold some information. The forensics mages have it but, again, no reports."

Latham nodded and seemed to consider something for a long few seconds. Then he used his cane to lever himself out of the chair and picked up his letter case.

"Thank you for an interesting afternoon, Lieutenant Buckley," he said. "I should let you get on with the investigation. Meanwhile, I think I will call on Minister Kershaw and deliver a stern lecture on the rights of the accused and the proper issuance of search warrants."

"Thank you for coming, Mr. Latham." Simon stood and extended his hand. Latham shook it with a smile before turning and walking briskly out of the office.

Simon exhaled slowly and looked at the timepiece on the wall. It was nearing sixteenth hour and his team Sergeants would be reporting in soon. Simon knew many Lieutenants didn't take afternoon reports and perhaps he too would dispense with them when he'd been in the job a bit longer and had a better feel for his team dynamics. For the time being, though, he preferred to keep up with events as closely as possible.

Gervis Birchfield checked in first. He'd spent the morning looking again at the crime scenes down by the docks and at the Canal Street warehouse where they'd found Killian. His frustration at the lack of any new information was evident.

"Any better luck in tracing the partners in the consortium that owns the warehouse?" Simon asked by way of distracting Gervis from his annoyance over the wasted morning.

Gervis brightened. "Well, yes," he said. "The corporate papers list several holding companies and investment funds as the sole stockholders. Two are legitimate fronts for wealthy Gray Havens families who have hedged their wealth in case they lose favor back home. One is a property company with legitimate holdings all over the Commonwealth. I spoke with the advocate who manages this particular investment and he was quite open about their position. They were approached by a smaller investment fund they've done business with before and agreed to put up a minority share of capital in return for a guaranteed option on a piece of open suburban land. That smaller investment fund holds the majority of the consortium shares and lists our good Lord Mayor as a shareholder under trustee proxy."

"Trustee proxy?" asked Simon.

"It's a common maneuver for politicians who want to avoid a conflict of interest inquiry," answered Gervis. "They put assets under the control of a neutral party—an advocate or a fund—who manages their wealth as a trustee but keeps them at arm's length when it comes to strategy or decision making."

"So Aspenwald puts his investment in trust," mused Simon. "But what if the trustee doesn't keep him at a distance?"

"Nothing to stop secret orders, as long as there's no record," agreed Gervis.

"So we could make a case for connecting Aspenwald to the warehouse where the stolen goods were stored," said Simon.

"We could, but without evidence of collusion we'd never get it past the King's Prosecutors," said Gervis, just as frustrated as he'd been before.

"We may not need to. A conspiracy is only as strong as its weakest member. A few words and a strong threat to the right person may bring the rest down."

"Do you have someone in mind?" asked Gervis.

Simon shook his head. "Better not to ask yet. High brass jingle. But the connections are falling into place and the person I'm thinking of is already rattled."

Gervis still looked frustrated, but he nodded in agreement. Simon went on.

"Tomorrow I'd like you to get someone out East to talk to a Patrol Sergeant named Stonehelm. Giles Machemer, a former Magic Squad Agent who went over to the Weasel Squad, was pulled out of the Finnigan downstream from the Cut with a couple of iron bolts through his chest. He was a mate of Frank Killian's. The murder could have been some unconnected private beef, but maybe he'd been asking the wrong questions about Killian's last few days. Stonehelm said Killian had been shopping around for smiths willing to do hand work without spells. Promising big payoffs if they'd do a job strictly without magic. Ring any bells?"

"The neutral iron," said Gervis, now fully alert. "You think Killian was shopping for someone to forge it into weapons?"

"That's what I want you to find out," said Simon. "Fair warning, though. The Wind Clan Guild Masters weren't happy about Killian shopping on their turf. They won't shed any tears about his death. Be careful out there."

Simon had expected Jason Hanks to be in shortly after Gervis, but he didn't come. Simon thought about contacting him but rejected the idea as overly intrusive. He'd always hated direct calls from his LT when he was a Sergeant. He considered asking Lessa to remind him of the usual afternoon briefing but rejected that as well. A call from Lessa would make it seem even more like a command performance. In the end he chalked it up as just one more thing to discuss at Hanks's performance review.

At half past seventeenth, Lessa looked in. "Will there be anything else, LT?"

"Yes, Lessa. On your way out, ask the desk Agent to send Lieutenant Harold up to Captain Axhart's office. He'll be looking for me. Then go home. I'll see you in the morning." Simon waved her away. He spent the next half hour trying to organize some notes. He gave up after a few minutes and sat at his desk, fists clenched, struggling to control his rage. Despite his show of indifference in front of Lowell, he was shaken. Talking to Gervis had distracted him, but now, alone in the office, the anger kept resurfacing.

They were inside my home. They knew I was out. There must have been a watch on the flat. Gods, what if they saw Kermal go in? The bastards were inside my home.

They could try to hang Machemer's murder on him.

Lowell likely had the steel to try it. Even if Latham got the search invalidated, the accusation would still be there, like a low tunnel with rotten shoring. Any time he needed the high brass to back him, it could cave in like shale and bury him. He felt like he was now on borrowed time. *The bastards were in my home.*

He watched the seconds tick down on the timepiece hung on the wall to the right of his desk. At eighteenth hour he rose, shut down his desk mirror and left the office for the command suite at the end of the corridor.

He found the outer door open and Elvira Cairns's desk empty. He could hear voices from the inner office and stepped uncertainly that way.

"Is that you, Buckley?" Axhart called from the inner office. "Come in. The others are already here."

Others? Simon walked into Axhart's inner office to find Stenson Harold already there. The tall man was a decade older than Simon with an old burn scar twisting one side of his face and a stub of a left ear. He sat easily in his green and gold working uniform on one of the couches that flanked the dark green rug in front of Axhart's desk. Axhart himself sat in an armchair he had moved from its usual place against the wall and set in front of the desk facing the door. He smiled and waved Simon in.

"Sit," the dwarf commanded, pointing to the other couch. Simon paused in surprise when he noticed the person already sitting at one end of that couch.

Bendict Hammersmith looked much the worse for wear, but he smiled up at Simon. His head was still bandaged and both eyes were beginning to show dark bruises around them. Both arms were encased in plaster casts that reached above the elbows.

"I'm surprised to see you out of the hospital," said Simon as he took the other end of the couch. "Are you well enough to be out and about?"

"Not really. But I'm a Dwarf. We have standards to

live up to." Hammersmith eyed him. "I could ask the same about you. You look like hells."

"It has been a long day," replied Simon with a wry smile.

"If you two are finished," said Axhart with a smile, "I think we should get on with this. Simon, you wanted this meeting. You start."

Simon took a deep breath. He'd organized his thoughts on the way from his own office, but his head pounded and he now groped for clarity.

"This morning at about tenth hour there was a coordinated attack by Orc and Human terrorists on the Justice Ministry and the Royal Family. These attacks were carried out using magically inert materials that evaded our security scans but were nevertheless deadly. Without going into detail, these things are made without magic at any stage. The knowledge to create these nightmares comes from a different world, like ours but not. Portal magic can access this place but only at great cost. I don't know how to make the black powder that destroyed part of the Justice Ministry. I do know that it's the same stuff that powers these single shot slug throwing weapons used in the attack on the King."

"How do you know about them?" asked Harold.

"I have a much more sophisticated version in my personal locker. But to answer directly, a dozen of these were confiscated by the Gray Rangers near the border between the Havens and the Free States. Sylvie Graystorm showed me one this past Weeksend."

"And you didn't tell me?" Harold interrupted. "Or Hammersmith? Or someone outside the Magic Squad? Gods, Simon! The King and Queen might have been killed."

Hammersmith waved one of his plaster encased arms. "Simon did tell me, early the next day. I had seen the metal components for the weapons but had no idea what they were. At the time, we didn't expect that any attack was imminent."

"Well, it's just damned luck that the King is still breathing," Harold fumed.

"Aye, luck," said Axhart. "And a timely warning from Buckley." He looked pointedly at Harold, who glared back for a second before nodding and controlling himself. "What's the status of the Royal Family now?"

"They are back at the Palace with double guards and a complete lockdown of the grounds," said Harold. "Neither the King nor the Crown Prince are happy about it, but her Majesty has talked some sense into them. We've contained the story of the attack so far, but it won't be long before the news services figure out that the assassins had weapons that could get by our security spells. We need to have something to give them when the questions start."

Axhart nodded. "That's for the Prime Minister. For our part, put it out that we're investigating the weapons and the people involved, all the usual statements."

Harold went on. "For what it's worth, we have no good identification on the Orcs involved in the attack on Parliament. They weren't the same people who had been approved for the delegation. We're trying to identify who they actually were, and Civil Patrol is tracking down the Orcs who were supposed to be in the delegation. Same with the Humans involved in the attempt on the Queen. We have one of them in custody but he's not conscious right now."

"My team may be able to help with that," said Hammersmith. "We have dossiers on a number of known troublemakers, both Orc and Human. Send me fingerprints and aural recordings and I'll see if any match." Harold nodded his thanks. "After my initial meeting with Simon we went back and interviewed sources in the Hollows and along the Eastern Borderlands. Unfortunately, the information was long on rumor and short on solid information. The pattern that emerged suggested something imminent to build on the spontaneous explosion of the Hollows riots but coordinated with action in the Azeri Empire and the Gray Havens."

"Any names?" asked Simon.

"Galen Flandyrs," said Hammersmith. "And Bijan Alorton."

"But Alorton resigned after the Flandyrs affair last winter," said Axhart. "He's not Foreign Minster any longer."

"No," said Simon. "But he still has a lot of influence. Especially, with the Justice Ministry." He looked at Hammersmith who nodded agreement.

"Kershaw is Alorton's brother-in-law, and my team has had concerns about his objectivity for some time," Hammersmith agreed. "There's talk that Kershaw does nothing without Alorton's approval. We don't have enough hard evidence to impeach the Minister, and I'm not sure the Prime Minister would listen if we did. Alorton, Kershaw, and Rondel Aspenwald control a lot of Human law-and-order votes in Parliament. The King may not like them, but he needs them if any of his programs are going to go forward."

"So, Aspenwald is part of Alorton's circle?" asked Simon.

"I think so, although there's no direct evidence of collusion." Hammersmith shrugged. "Different crows, same rookery."

"And that's worrisome," Axhart put in. "Just before we started, I was briefed by the Foreign Minister, Lord Helmich; he's Alorton's successor, King's man to the core. There's been a lot of international reaction to today's attacks. The Ironlands have closed the border to all passage into or out of their territory." He held up a hand as Simon started out of his seat. "Hal and Brookstone are all good. They're interred at the border station, but are safe, just unable to communicate except through the consulate. The Ironlanders assure us they'll be released when the situation 'stabilizes'"

"That explains why Hal hasn't responded to my summons," said Simon.

Axhart nodded. His tone became more concerned. "The real problem is in the Havens. The Steward has disbanded the Council and has had most of the Progressive *Syrs* detained under house isolation. Galen Flandyrs has been named to head a newly created post as Minister of Internal Security. It looks like he's going to round up any at-large Progressives and their families. The Foreign Ministry has received almost a hundred applications for asylum since this morning." He seemed to note Simon's growing concern. "Have you heard from Lady Graystorm?"

"Not since yesterday," replied Simon, voice tight but controlled. "She and Hamil Fairborn planned to stay at the Borderland Station for the night, then make a move to the border, hoping to cross near Portalis. She was going to contact me once they reached West Faring on this side of the border."

"No word?" asked Axhart.

Simon shook his head. "She does have the family name, but her father is a rabid Traditionalist and tight with the Steward. He disowned her years ago, and I doubt he'd stand up for her now."

"Right, Sylvie Graystorm is tough and smart. She'll get through," said Axhart. "The final fly in the pudding is the Azeri Empire. They've moved a couple battalions of Imperial Guards to the border near Holdfast. They claim it's a scheduled training exercise, but Holdfast is also the gateway to the Lordiss Valley, the natural pathway into the Commonwealth through the Karkassis Mountains. The King is ordering the Homeguard to Wrothway, just west of Holdfast. Close enough to be mobilized but far enough to avoid looking provocative."

"Gods, Captain," said Simon. "Are we going to war?"

"Not our call, thank the Mother," Axhart replied. "We're Peacekeepers; Foreign Policy is outside our remit. But these bastards struck at us in my city. That won't stand. This was clearly a coordinated attack. It may have failed because we all got lucky, or because we were helped by a guardian spirit. It looks to me like whoever killed Anika Sommerstag and Frank Killian, not to mention the Harsakas, interrupted their timetable. From what Lieutenant Harold tells us, the attacks on the King and Queen appear hastily arranged and poorly executed. If the intent was to destabilize the Monarchy, they have failed and may have had the opposite effect."

Axhart looked first at Simon, and then at Harold. "I think Mr. Hammersmith needs to know the entire story."

Simon nodded. Harold frowned.

"What story?" asked Hammersmith.

Simon spoke first to Harold. "Stenson, I've spoken to both Rebeka and Liam within the last few hours. They are willing to go public if the Monarchy is at serious risk. Rebeka will testify that the King had no knowledge of her status or actions prior to her abdication."

"Will it come to that?" Harold's face was pale, his voice hoarse with emotion.

"I hope not. We've been granted some breathing room, I think. But we need Justice in this dig, especially if Alorton is pulling Kershaw's strings."

"What story?" demanded Hammersmith.

"Princess Rebeka is a Fire mage," said Simon. "That secret is known only to the Royal Family, George Latham their personal Advocate, and the people in this room." Simon didn't mention Kermal Brackenville. He trusted Kermal, but telling the rest that an enforcer for the Cabal of Clans knew Rebeka's true nature didn't seem a good idea.

Hammersmith looked puzzled. "Why the secrecy? She's already abdicated as the law requires. Why not let the public know and at least salvage some of her reputation? She's being ridiculed by the newsies as a silly, spoiled girl and an example of everything that's wrong with the Nobility."

"Because before she abdicated, before she'd learned even basic control of her magic, she set several warehouse fires down in the Hollows. At first it was jolt stockpiles that the Scalpers were sitting on. But the last fire was the warehouse where Farsk Kronska and his top hard boys had gone to ground. Just the suggestion that a Human mage had started that fire touched off the riots of a few days ago."

Hammersmith sat back frowning. "I get why the King wants this kept secret, but arson involving death is a serious crime. She escaped trial and punishment because she's a Royal? That's not how our system is supposed to work."

Simon shook his head and gestured around the room. "Believe me, we've all had those same thoughts. Stenson was ready to go into exile with her. Captain Axhart wanted to 'wring her Royal neck,' I believe his words were. Even the King required a good deal of persuading. In the end, the good of the country outweighed everything else. Rebeka's motives were pure, if her methods and the results were not. I'm not sure she completely controlled the fire until that last one. I saw the result once when she got emotional and nearly lost control."

Hammersmith still looked doubtful. "You say she's willing to make a public confession?"

"Yes," responded Simon. "But I don't think this is the time, and I'm not sure it would ever be in the Commonwealth's best interests. Think Bendict. The

Hollows were a tinderbox before the warehouse fires. If it had been revealed six weeks ago that Rebeka had killed Orcs by burning them alive, the whole country would have gone up in flames. Last week's riots would have been a rowdy Name Day party by comparison. That could still happen. Flandyrs planned to expose Rebeka publicly at the same time that the Traditionalists took power in the Havens. I think he tried to get the Azeris to try something more blatant at the Eastern border as well. If the Monarchy were crippled by the revelation of the Princess as a murderous Fire mage, and the country was up in arms, what could the Traditionalists do if they coordinated with the Empire? War? At the least it would be months or years before there'd be any repercussions to affect the Steward or the Azeris."

"Simon's right," said Axhart. "But again, diplomacy isn't in our garden. Right now, we need to find the rest of Flandyrs's crew here in the Commonwealth and stop them from causing more trouble. Can we count on you, at least until this is over?" Hammersmith nodded reluctantly. "Good. Get your dossiers to Harold. Meanwhile, get with Simon on Kershaw. If you and he can find evidence to link Alorton through Kershaw to Aspenwald or Lowell, we can squeeze Kershaw to give up the whole lot of them."

"My source in the Cabal confirms that Sommerstag, Flandyrs, and the Harsakas were all together in Fredonia just before the riots," said Simon. "My teams are looking into Sommerstag's movements leading up to her death. Our working theory is that she was bringing some sort of proof about the Princess to the conspirators here in Cymbeline, so that its release could be timed to the takeover in the Havens. She was killed before that could happen."

"You have..." Hammersmith stopped at a sharp look from Simon. "You think Aspenwald is her contact?" asked Hammersmith, recovering quickly.

"I do now. He denies any recent contact with her, but his demand that he be updated doesn't square with simple fatherly concern."

"How does Lowell fit into this?" asked Axhart, also ignoring Simon's remark about the Cabal. "If he's Aspenwald's man, why would he go after you for covering up Rebeka's arson?"

"He wants you, sir," answered Simon. "If he gets me to implicate you, then you'd be tainted. The King couldn't take full responsibility and appeal to Parliament for immunity under the Accords. You'd be forced out and Kershaw could install someone more sympathetic to Alorton's program. The King would be forced to go along with it."

Axhart grunted. "Bloody hells. That's not going to happen."

"It may still happen if we don't get to Lowell," said Hammersmith. He turned to Simon. "You say Lowell knows about Rebeka?"

"I'm convinced he does but have no proof."

"Then I suggest we start with him and try to work up to Kershaw," said Hammersmith.

"Agreed," said Simon. "I may have a way to get at him. He just made a big show of trying to pin a murder on me, but George Latham was there and shut down his illegal search. I think he's getting desperate. He was supposed to have Captain Axhart and me off the board by now and his superiors can't be happy with him."

"How does that give us a hook in him?" Hammersmith asked.

"If my team can trace Giles Machemer's movements before he was killed, we can show I wasn't involved. We can get him for attempting to plant evidence. Hells, for all we know, he killed Machemer himself."

Hammersmith still looked dubious but nodded. "I'll put a surveillance team on him. If he meets with

Aspenwald we'll get pictures. Maybe we can use that as well."

Simon looked at Axhart. "All good, Captain?"

"It's all as thin as moonbeams, but it's all we've got right now," Axhart grumbled. "Get to it and keep me informed."

"Aye, sir." Simon rose and lent an arm to Hammersmith helping him lever himself off the couch.

"Send me those prints first thing," Hammersmith said to Harold. He turned and made his way gingerly out of the office.

Simon extended his hand to Harold who shook it gravely. "The Princess would probably appreciate a call from you, Stenson," said Simon. "Let her know her family is safe and tell her that you'll support whatever she decides to do."

Harold rose and nodded. "You have a way of finding yourself in deep waters, Simon. Be careful."

CHAPTER TWENTY-THREE

The next morning, Simon awoke in pain just before dawn. His head hurt. His back hurt. His ribs hurt. He even hurt behind his eyes. About the only part of him that didn't hurt was his feet, and they were numb.

He checked his timepiece. Just after fifth hour. He could sleep for another hour or so, right? He tried to roll over and groaned as a sharp pain stabbed through his back. *No, maybe not.*

After several minutes of slow agony, he managed to stand. Five minutes of slow walking got him to the shower. The hot water released much of the tension in his tortured muscles and, after he gulped a mouthful of the pain potion the medics had given him the day before, he managed to get into his uniform.

By the time he walked out the front door he was moving fairly comfortably. One look at his Oxley convinced him that he would never be able to climb out of it, if he even managed to get into it.

He took out his mirror and called the duty desk at

Wycliffe house. He asked the desk sergeant to have a patrol sled pick him up on the way back to the house at end of shift. Thankfully, the Sergeant didn't ask questions.

He managed the stairs to his office without falling or having to stop, but the climb was slow. Lessa was already at her desk in the outer office when he lurched through the door. She looked at him with concern.

"Gods, LT," she said. "You look rough. Are you all good?"

"Been better, Lessa," answered Simon. "Is there any coffee?"

"Of course." Her tone was slightly scornful, as if offended that he could doubt her.

He smiled his gratitude and started for the door to his inner office. He paused with his hand on the door. "Could you see if you can find where a Fire Chief named Jaime Smithington would be today? I need to interview him."

"Can do, LT."

Simon eased into his desk chair a few seconds later, resting his elbows on the desk and his head in his hands. He was already tired and it wasn't even seventh hour yet. He didn't notice that Lessa had come in until she slid the tray in front of him. The smell of hot coffee filled his nostrils. In addition to the steaming mug in the center of the tray, there was a full coffee pot next to a plate of oatcakes smothered in honey glaze.

"Thanks, Lessa." Simon smiled as he picked up the mug. "Who's first on the schedule today?"

"Sergeant Hanks," she answered. "But I told him to wait for half an hour. Finish your coffee and eat some oatcakes, or I'll call Mistress Stonebender and have her talk some sense to you."

Simon didn't know when Lessa had learned the trick of invoking Molly Stonebender. He suspected

Elvira Cairns had clued her in. Nevertheless, the coffee smelled wonderful and the oatcakes looked as good as Molly's own.

Half an hour later, he'd finished two of the oatcakes and two mugs of coffee. His ribs still hurt and his back was stiff, but he felt better, almost human. Lessa looked in and noted the empty mug and missing oatcakes. She smiled.

"Sergeant Hanks is here, LT," she said. "Shall I send him in?"

"Please, Lessa," said Simon. She cocked her head at him. "I'm all good, Lessa. At least when I'm sitting down. Please, send Hanks in."

She nodded and stepped back. A second later, Jason Hanks entered. He nodded to Lessa before crossing to stand in front of Simon's desk, not quite at attention.

"Oh, sit down, Jason," said Simon. "What have you got this morning?"

"We got a conviction in the Hale Street arson case. That's where I was yesterday." The pride in his voice was evident. Simon realized this was the first case on which Hanks had been the lead investigator. He remembered the feeling he'd had the first time an investigation of his had led to a conviction. He smiled.

"You didn't by chance go up against an advocate by the name of Latham, did you?" asked Simon.

"Who?" asked Hanks.

"Never mind," said Simon. "Congratulations."

"Thanks, LT." Hanks returned Simon's smile.

After a slightly awkward pause, Simon asked. "What else have you got?"

"We managed to find the Air mage who cast the spell at the warehouse where Smithington was almost killed. The team found him out east in Hagadorn; they're bringing him in now."

"When do you expect them here?" asked Simon.

"Should be here by tenth hour." Hanks eyed Simon. "Do you want to sit in on the interview?"

"Yes, I do," Simon replied. "When do you plan to question him?"

"Probably around thirteenth," said Hanks. "We'll need some time to get him processed and to let him stew for a while."

"I'll be there," said Simon.

Hanks nodded and went on to outline several open cases. Simon noted once again the methodical but rather dull progress. Nothing new but no major problems. Hanks finished and promised to keep Simon informed when the Air mage was picked up.

Hanks and Gervis Birchfield passed each other at the door, exchanging friendly greetings. Gervis asked after Jason's mother, whom Simon gathered was ill. He felt a pang of guilt for not knowing anything about Hanks's family.

Gervis sat where Hanks had been and looked closely at Simon. "Are you all good, LT?" he asked.

"I'm fine," snapped Simon more sharply than he'd intended. *Gods, get a grip, Buckley.*

"I'm fine," he repeated in a quieter voice. "I got knocked about a bit yesterday and have pains in places I didn't know were places." He sipped some coffee to clear his throat, which suddenly felt thick. "Any new developments?"

"Some. The forensics mages have been working on that image stick that was in Sommerstag's backpack. We thought it would open with the imager that was in her room, but no joy. The spells aren't compatible. Most storage sticks are standardized, but this one is either proprietary or encrypted. Kyle Evarts is working on it. Hopes to have something by end of watch today." Gervis paused when Simon closed his eyes and rubbed his forehead but went on when Simon looked up again. "I've sent a couple of my guys out to the East End, like you asked. I'll check with Evarts and then head out that way myself."

"Be careful," Simon cautioned. "Keepers aren't welcome out there in the best of times. Don't hesitate to call for backup if things get tense."

Gervis nodded and took his leave.

Lessa stepped in as Gervis left. "Agent Ironhand sent a message that he was in Court this morning, LT. Do you want him to check in later?"

"No need," said Simon. "I've taken his team out of the rotation until Sergeant Stonebender returns. They're too understrength to be very effective."

"All good," said Lessa. "I found Chief Smithington. He'll be in his office at the All Gods Square station all morning. Do you want me to call and set up a meeting?"

"No, thanks. That would make it official. I don't want to undermine Sergeant Hanks. I just want to ask Smithington a couple of questions." Simon checked the timepiece on the wall. "As a matter of fact, I think I'll go see him now."

The coffee and oatcakes seemed to have helped. Simon was still sore but didn't feel like a walking corpse by the time he reached the stables and spoke to the Patrol Agent on duty. He checked out an unmarked four seat sled. He stopped by the armorer and drew his personal D'Stang, stowing the bolt thrower in the rack between the front seats.

It was nearly tenth hour when he parked on a side street near the square about a block and a half from the firefighter's station. He showed his badge to the duty officer in the kiosk next to the huge roll-up doors that fronted the street. He was directed to a side entrance and up a flight of stairs to the administrative suite.

Smithington's office was small but well furnished. A large window in the outer wall looked over All Gods

Square with its gleaming temple complex and central aspen grove. On the inner wall, another window looked down on the main floor of the station where two large pumping sledges and a full ladder unit sat ready for call out.

Simon recognized Smithington at once as the scene commander at the fire that had killed Farsk Kronska and set off the whole chain of events leading up to the riots.

The grizzled Water mage stood and stepped around his desk to extend a hand to Simon. "Lieutenant Buckley, good meeting," he said. "The last time I saw you, you were a Sergeant. I've been expecting you."

"Good meeting, Chief Smithington. Sergeant Hanks told me your name, but I didn't make the connection until just now," said Simon. "I meant to come by earlier, but we had a busy day yesterday."

"We all did." Smithington's face grew grave. He waved Simon to a chair and sat down again behind his desk. "Most of my Search and Rescue teams were at it all night. I think we finally declared the scene secure at about fourth hour this morning. You were there?"

"I was," Simon replied. "I saw the wagon with the explosives go in but didn't make the connection to the black powder until it was too late."

"Bad business," agreed Smithington. "But you didn't drop by to talk about that. What can I do for you?"

"First, I wanted to give you an update on the turkey trap that almost took out your team. We found the Air mage who cast the oxygen evacuation spell. He's an Orc named Morningstar Pantosch. Ever heard of him?"

Smithington pursed his lips. "No, can't say I have. Is he connected to any of the Hollows gangs or to the Brigades?"

"A couple of prior arrests is all; no known gang connections. By his name, I'd say he's Hybarian, not Azeri." Simon paused. "Know anyone else who'd want you dead?"

Smithington laughed. "Not in the circles you're talking about. I've had a few set-tos with politicians who think firefighting is nothing more than water and spell power but don't see those as killing arguments."

"No, I suppose not," agreed Simon. "We're working on tracing the ownership of the warehouse, as well as the others on the list you gave to my Sergeant. That's led to some interesting connections, but none that I can discuss right now."

Smithington narrowed his eyes. "Anyone in particular I should worry about?"

"No, I doubt you'd have encountered any of them. No reason to think you're at risk from them."

"But as you said," Smithington replied. "Someone wanted me and my team dead. What about the Brigades? Or one of the gangs?"

"Not that we can see," said Simon. "I have a reliable source that went out of his way to assure me that none of the gangs or organized groups in the Hollows had anything to do with the attack. I can't go into more detail than that."

"And yet you say the mage was an Orc," insisted Smithington.

"Aye, and that's one of the things I'll be asking him about later today." Simon held out a hand, palm up in a gesture of placation. "I don't have all the answers, Chief. But I trust my sources. I'm asking you to trust me for a day or so."

Smithington nodded but still looked concerned. "As you say. Is there anything else?"

"Well, yes there is," said Simon. "I have an intersecting case that involves four murders, all committed by the same Water mage; two by dry drowning and two by transcutaneous exsanguination. The aural pattern isn't in any of our registries, or any of the international registries we can access. The mage is either a rogue, or from somewhere outside the Accord nations. Can you give me any idea how that can be?"

Smithington laughed. "There are more unregistered mages out there than you know, Lieutenant. Latents who never developed their talent, immigrants from places outside the Accords, mages who started training but never finished, and yes, a few criminals who escaped registration, or who had the steel to get their records expunged."

"But we're looking at Master level casting, at least with the exsanguination spells," protested Simon. "Could a mage reach that level of skill and still escape registration?" *But you know that's possible Buckley. Forsaka is a Master Fire mage, but he's never been registered. Could the killer be an Orc with the Cabal? Forsaka claimed the Cabal had nothing to do with the neutral iron, and strangely, I believe him. The Cabal wants to keep everything the same; change is bad for their business.*

Simon realized he'd missed what Smithington had just said while he was thinking about the Cabal. "... when I was in the Academy." The firefighter went on. "He was in my class but left after the first year; had more raw talent than anyone I'd ever seen before or since. He had the talent but not the aptitude, don't you see."

"Excuse me," said Simon. "What does that mean?"

"Spell work is more than just the talent to manipulate reality," explained Smithington. "You need to be able to control it, focus it properly, and summon it at will, even when you're distracted or tired. Some never learn. This particular fellow couldn't get the control needed. Maybe the discipline was too hard, or maybe his brain just didn't work that way. Anyway, he left in the first year, went to university and became some sort of professional—advocate or healer or engineer. I don't recall. The point is, I doubt he was ever registered as a Water mage, but he could work Water magic."

CHAPTER TWENTY-FOUR

Simon took his leave of Smithington and walked back to the sled. Something the man had said about his old classmate niggled at him, but he couldn't pin it down. He was tired and sore, and his brain felt foggy with the aftereffects of his head injury.

He sat for a minute behind the steering yoke with his eyes closed trying to clear his head and focus his thoughts. The summoning tone of his mirror interrupted his efforts.

"Buckley here," he said as he swiped a hand across the mirror.

Gervis Birchfield's excited face swam into view. "LT, I just heard from Kyle Evarts. They've managed to open the images on Sommerstag's storage stick. He won't tell me what the images show. Says he wants you to see it first. How soon can you get back to the House?"

"On my way," replied Simon. "Twenty minutes depending on traffic. Ask Evarts to meet me in my office, please, Gervis."

Simon spoke the incantation and the sled rose on its cushion of air. He steered away from the curb and headed east across the square to Tanner Street. It only took fifteen minutes to reach the stables under Wycliffe House.

Evarts and Gervis were waiting in Simon's office when he arrived. Both stood as he entered. Simon nodded a greeting to Gervis and shook Evarts's hand.

"What have you got for us, Kyle?" he asked.

Evarts looked at Gervis. "This concerns the Princess. Stuff I didn't know and that I can see needs to be kept secret."

"Sergeant Birchfield has been heading the investigation from the start." Simon looked at Gervis and nodded. "I think he has a need to know what's at stake."

"Same as the neutral iron, LT?" Gervis said with a grin.

"Right," said Simon. "Under a rock unless I say otherwise. Go ahead, Kyle. Show us what you have."

Evarts still looked skeptical, but he took a small Keeper issued imager out of his pocket and set it next to Simon's larger desktop mirror. He muttered a phrase and made a passing gesture with his right hand and the spinning Peacekeeper sigil in the mirror was replaced with a still image.

The image was grainy, shot from a distance but it was still easy to recognize Liam Aster and Princess Rebeka. They were standing together appearing deep in some earnest conversation. Evarts made a gesture and the images started to scroll across the mirror. Liam stepped back and Rebeka stood with her head bowed. The next image showed her with hands raised. In the next, her hands were outstretched, and a ball of fire had formed in front of her fingertips. The final image showed a tree some distance away with scorch marks on its trunk and a few flaming branches.

"Gods above and below," breathed Gervis in a hoarse whisper. "She's a Fire mage."

"Aye, she is," said Simon.

"There's more," said Evarts.

Again the images scrolled. Flandyrs in deep conversation with the Harsaka brothers. Flandyrs and Lowell, taken from a low angle, speaking face to face in a public park. Lowell talking to Aspenwald and Kershaw in a restaurant that Simon recognized, the Old Inn in West Faring. The final set of images were of documents, letters clearly intended for Aspenwald and Kershaw from Flandyrs as well as a timetable of dates with a note directed to former Foreign Minister Alorton.

"By the Mother," said Gervis. "We have them."

"Not quite," cautioned Evarts. "I managed to pull these off the image store, but the originals were destroyed in the process. We need corroborating testimony to get these images into Court. Most were clearly taken without the consent of the people in the image. And the only person who can vouch for their validity is dead."

"We'll need to turn Lowell or Kershaw and have them testify against the others," said Simon. "My money is on Lowell. Aspenwald and Kershaw are too well protected by their family and political positions."

"But, LT," protested Gervis. "The images."

"Won't be admissible without corroborating testimony. We need to nail this down tight, Gervis. We only get one chance at it."

Gervis looked stricken but nodded assent. He turned to Evarts. "Thank you, Mr. Evarts. I assume this is tight in your own shop?"

Both Simon and Evarts smiled in amusement. "Yes, Sergeant. Close hold, my eyes only," said Evarts. He gave Simon a nod, ended the display, and handed him the image stick along with a certification of transfer of custody.

"Thank you, Kyle." Simon signed the form and handed it back to Evarts.

"Take good care of that," said Evarts to Simon. "People have been killed for less."

Simon nodded gravely. Evarts shook Birchfield's hand and left the office. Simon meanwhile locked the image stick in the wall safe behind his desk.

"Nothing about this to the team, Gervis," said Simon. "I know it's against your instincts, but close hold for now."

"Understood, LT. How do we get at Lowell?"

Simon smiled. "We wait. I'm on his hit list—he'll come to us."

"If you say so. Meanwhile, what should I do?"

"I want you and your team out by Eastport," said Simon. "We still have Giles Machemer's murder to solve, and some neutral iron weapons to account for."

"Aye, LT. I'll be in touch." He stood to leave but turned back at the door. "LT? I'd like to be there for the detentions when you move on Lowell and the rest."

"You will be, if I have any say in the matter," Simon assured him. "We may be cut out of that. This has to go through Bendict Hammersmith over at Justice. Lowell and Kershaw are in his garden, and it's up to him to weed it. If there's enough evidence to nail Alorton, we get him. He's just a private citizen now, peer or not."

Birchfield nodded. "All good."

Simon took out his mirror and summoned Hammersmith. The summoning went straight to his message scroll. He left a message. "Bendict, I have new evidence you'll need to see. Get in touch with me soonest."

He considered trying to summon Hal or Sylvie. *No, they'll reach out as soon as they can. Trying now will just make you edgier and may interrupt something critical. Calm yourself. They're both capable of handling trouble without you.*

Lessa looked into his office a few moments later and said, "Sergeant Hanks sent word that the suspect you wanted to interview is down in interrogation room three, LT."

"Thank you, Lessa."

Simon made his way down to the booking level and found Hanks waiting for him. The hallway outside the interrogation rooms was part of the stone foundations of the old fortress. The flagstone floor was worn smooth by the tramp of centuries worth of booted feet and the walls showed a slick patina of age. Glowglobes in the ceiling cast a harsh bluish light. The corridor was clean and dry but still smelled faintly of age and sweat and urine. Hanks stood easily leaning against the closed iron bound door with a large black '3' painted on it.

"I've had Pantosch stewing in there for about half an hour," said Hanks, hooking a thumb over his shoulder at the door. "How do we want to play this?"

"What have we got on him?" asked Simon.

"We know he was in town at the time of the fire and have a witness who can place him at the scene just before the alarm was called in," answered Hanks. "Witness is a delivery driver who almost ran Pantosch down as he was leaving the warehouse. The driver made a stop about two blocks on and was headed back when the Fire Brigade showed up. We found him because he was listed by the on-scene commander as a witness to the backflash."

"Right," said Simon. "You take the lead, imply that we've got an eyewitness who saw him cast the spell and we've got confirmation by aura. If he's smart, he'll deny everything, and I'll step in. If he decides to talk to you, let him run with it. Anything he says that doesn't square with what we know for sure can give us leverage to get the truth out of him."

Hanks nodded and turned to the door. It was fitted with an automatic lock, easily opened from the outside but locked from the inside as soon as the door closed. Hanks had the key on a lanyard around his neck.

The small room was a perfect eight-by-eight-foot square. Just off center in the middle of the space, a small metal table was bolted to the floor. A hard metal chair, also secured to the floor sat behind the table. Cold iron rings set in the tabletop provided shackle points for whoever sat in the metal chair. Two other padded folding chairs leaned against the wall near the door.

The chair bolted to the floor was currently occupied by a skinny long-faced Orc. His round eyes, sharp nose and slightly pointed ears confirmed Simon's thought that he was Hybarian. He looked up and sneered as Hanks entered, not noticing or at least not acknowledging Simon.

"It's about time, Bluebelly," said the Orc. His accent was mild, but definitely Hybarian. No tattoos either. This wasn't an Azeri hardboy, despite his bravado.

Hanks remained cool. He took up one of the folding chairs, opened it and set it down across the table from the Orc. He carefully extracted a notebook and stylus from his pocket and aligned them neatly with the edge of the table. Then he took a small recorder from his breast pocket, set it on the table next to the notebook and muttered the incantation to turn it on. He arranged himself comfortably in the chair. Only then did he look at the Orc who had become more and more agitated as he watched Hanks's careful preparations.

"First interview with Morningstar Pantosch. Time is 13:20. Present are Lieutenant Simon Buckley, Magic Enforcement, and Sergeant Jason Hanks, Team 3 Lead, Magic Enforcement. Mr. Pantosch, you are cautioned that anything you say in this interview may be taken down and used as evidence against you at trial. Do you understand this caution?"

"You forgot the part about an advocate," said the Orc. "You gotta tell me I have the right to an advocate, right? So, I want one."

"All in good time, Mr. Pantosch," replied Hanks smoothly. "You see, this little talk of ours is more about how you can help yourself. Once the advocates get involved, they'll tell you to shut up, to not tell us anything. By the time you do get around to telling your side, the opportunity to help yourself will have passed and you'll be looking at ten years in the Bear for conspiracy to murder."

The mention of the Bear, the infamous prison farm in the far northeast of the Commonwealth, made Pantosch's eyes widen. Still, he fell back on bluster.

"I done nothing, and you can't hold me without charging me with something. And I still want an advocate."

Hanks reached out and shut off the recorder. "Have it your way. But we've got an eyewitness who'll testify that you cast an Air spell that almost killed a squad from the Fire Brigade, including an Assistant Chief. We know you were in Cymbeline that day, and aural analysis puts you at the scene of the fire."

"Eat shit and die," said Pantosch. "You're lying. No reveal spell is good enough to record my aura."

"Not so," said Hanks. "How do you think we found you? Your aura is registered in the criminal database. You've been pinched twice before, spent some time in the City Lockup. I hear the Bear is really wet this time of year. Cold in the winter, too. Makes City look like a picnic."

Pantosch's eyes darted up to Simon and then back to Hanks. "You're bluffing. You can't prove shit, and anyway, they don't send you to the Bear for simple arson."

"Oh, but this isn't arson, Morningstar," said Hanks. "We're going to charge you with attempted murder, ten counts. One for each of the Fire Brigade team and one for the Assistant Chief you almost fried with your little backflash fire."

"I didn't set any fire. You can't hang that on me," protested the Orc, a bit too loudly.

Hanks stared him down then sighed. "Like I said, have it your way. You got anything else, LT?"

Simon nodded to Hanks. Pantosch had relaxed a bit, leaning back in his chair, anticipating an end to the interview. Simon slammed both hands onto the table, palms open and leaned forward into Pantosch's startled face.

"Listen, you piece of horseshit, your little stunt with the Air spell almost killed a whole team of firefighters. I don't give a damn who started the fire, your spell turned that warehouse into a turkey trap. That means that you're going up for attempted murder. You knew damned well what the spell would do and what would happen as soon as the doors were opened."

Pantosch tried to look defiant but withered as Simon grabbed him by his shirt and pulled him half out of the chair. "But see, I think you're too stupid to set that up on your own. Someone hired you. Who was it?"

"I didn't..."

"Shut up," roared Simon. "Someone hired you to set that trap. We know you cast the spell. You can try to lie your way out, but we know you did it." He shoved Pantosch back into the chair. "I don't see anyone else in this room, Pantosch. You're going down for this, all ten counts. No one's coming to get you out and no advocate is going to touch this case. You'll get a charity defense from a green new advocate, who won't know a writ from his own ass."

"Ain't so," said Pantosch. "I'll call the mouth who

got me off the last time. He told me he'd come if you Bluebellies tried to jam me up again."

"Forget that." Simon waved a hand in front of the Orc's face. "Unless he's stupid, he'll pass on this one. Maybe I'll just arrange for the Chief you almost fried to have five minutes alone with you. He's a Master Water mage. He'll make all the air you breathe condense in your lungs. You'll drown slowly on dry land. Or maybe he'll have some mercy and just cause all of your blood to leave your body and splatter against the wall." As Simon shouted, Pantosch's face had drained of color. He gripped the edge of the table as if holding on to the edge of a high cliff.

"Come on, Jason." Simon put as much disgust into his voice as he could. "We're done here."

Hanks started to gather up his things, but Pantosch stopped him. "Wait. What are you offering?"

Hanks looked at Simon, who nodded. "Tell us who hired you and we'll get you an advocate. We'll drop the charge to accessory to arson, City time, a year or two, but you'll avoid a trial and avoid the Bear."

"A different advocate, not the guy I had last time," said Pantosch, his voice almost pleading.

"Why not?" asked Simon. "A minute ago, you were bragging that he'd come to your rescue."

"Because he's the one who hired me," said Pantosch, now shaking with real fear. "He said I owed him for getting me out of that bad faith beef. He told me when to be at the warehouse and when to cast the Air spell. He set the fire."

"Who is he, Pantosch?" demanded Hanks. "Give us a name."

"Latham," said the Orc. "George Latham."

"Latham?" said Simon. "That makes no sense. Why would Latham want to kill?...Oh, by all the gods, no!" He turned to Hanks. "Jason, get our friend here into isolation. Individual cell, no contact with other prisoners. Only your team and the isolation guards. Understood?"

"Sure, LT," said Hanks with a puzzled look. "But why?"

"No time to explain right now. But at all costs, we need to keep Morningstar Pantosch alive and away from Latham."

"If you say so," said Hanks. "I'll take care of it."

"Thanks, Jason. I have to go. Write up this interview, get our friend here to sign a statement and then keep the whole thing under rock. Seal the paperwork and give it to Lessa. Tell her to lock it in the safe."

"All good, LT," said Hanks. "But are you certain that's really necessary?"

"Just do it," said Simon quietly. He was certain of only one thing: George Latham was a Water mage who had already killed four people. And Simon had as good as pointed him toward his next victim.

CHAPTER TWENTY-FIVE

Simon knew now what had been bothering him. Latham had been carrying a willow wood cane with a garnet set in the handle, Water magic wood and stone. He had to find Latham. Maybe more importantly, he had to find Spencer Lowell. He left the booking area and turned left toward the stables. The sled he'd checked out was still there.

Simon took out his mirror and summoned Axhart's office. Elvira Cairns answered.

"Mistress Cairns," said Simon. "I need a favor. I need to know where to find an IG Inspector named Spencer Lowell."

"And why should I know where someone from the IG's office can be found?" she asked skeptically. "And why should I tell you if I did?"

"Please, Mistress Cairns, this is a matter of life and death. Let the Captain know that Lowell is the next target for the rogue Water mage we've been looking for. I need to warn him or find him."

Her eyes narrowed. "This is square and level, Simon Buckley? None of your back tunnel foolishness?"

"As the Virgin is my witness," said Simon. "Work whatever magic you have for finding things out but let Captain Axhart know. I'm on my way out to look for the mage."

"Understood, Lieutenant. I'll summon you when I have some information. Don't try anything without backup." Her face softened. "Seriously Simon, be careful. Molly will never forgive me if anything should happen to you."

"Yes, Mistress Cairns," said Simon. He checked that his D'Stang was still in the rear compartment, then climbed in and activated the sled. Once out on Tanner he turned west, intending to start searching for Lowell at the Justice Ministry. If Lowell wasn't there, Simon could invoke Hammersmith's name and perhaps find out where he was.

He next summoned Jaime Smithington's mirror. Smithington answered immediately.

"Lieutenant Buckley, I'm surprised to hear from you so soon. Do you have news?"

"In a way, Chief," said Simon. "That young Water mage from your Academy days, the one who left in the first year; it was George Latham, true?"

"Yes." Smithington sounded surprised. "As a matter of fact, it was. How did you know?"

"I'll explain later," said Simon. "For now, don't leave your station alone and don't go near Latham."

"What? What the hells are you talking about," Smithington demanded.

"Just, please do as I say." Simon broke the connection as he pulled up in front of the Justice Ministry.

The main entrance at 10 West Tanner was cordoned off with orange crime scene rope. The Emergency Response sleds were gone, replaced by several Forensic sledges and a large portable Incident Command Center. Simon parked next to the cordon and activated the flashing orange and green lights on top of his sled. He flashed his badge at the Patrol Agent on sentry watch and signed the scene access log. Once inside the courtyard, he asked a passing clerk where he might find Hammersmith.

"Oh, his office was wrecked," said the clerk. "All of the anti-terror squad is set up in the old archives block." He pointed across the courtyard. "Over that way and down to the lower level."

The lower level looked like it had once been a dungeon. It still smelled of stale air and dust. Glowglobes strung from the low ceiling filled the long space with harsh light that did little to alleviate the feeling of gloom. People rushed to and fro, carrying files and equipment. There were no desks, only a long double row of folding tables strewn with folders and loose papers that more people seated in chairs attempted to organize.

Simon walked slowly through the chaos until he found Hammersmith propped up in his scorched office chair, plaster casts carefully arranged on the armrests, dictating to a secretary who stood nearby frantically writing notes on a pad. Hammersmith stopped abruptly when he saw Simon. The secretary, too, looked up and stopped writing.

"That will be all for now, Alfred," said Hammersmith to the earnest looking young man. "Please transcribe that and get me two copies for the files." He looked up at Simon. "I hope you haven't come to blow up this part of the building. I still can't hear anything out of my left ear."

"Nothing so drastic," said Simon, looking around. He lowered his voice. "But I do have new information that you need to hear about."

Hammersmith looked around then struggled out

of his chair and led Simon deeper into the archive. He opened a door, and they entered a tiny windowless cubicle with a small table and a couple of chairs.

"So, what have you got?" asked Hammersmith as he sat in the nearest chair. Simon remained standing, pacing as much as the tiny room allowed.

"First, Kyle Evarts, our forensics mage, managed to open the images on a storage stick found on Anika Sommerstag. It confirms connections between Flandyrs, Kershaw, Alorton, and Lowell. We'll still need corroborating testimony from one of them, or a witness to the images, but I think we can turn Lowell."

Hammersmith, to his credit, hardly blinked. He did take a deep breath before asking, "This is solid? Not fuzzy images shot from a mile away?"

"Close up images as well as documents—times, dates, and specific plans," said Simon.

"Where is Lowell and how do you plan to turn him?" asked Hammersmith.

Simon stopped pacing. "That's the second thing. I need to find him right away. His life is in danger and I'm probably responsible for that."

"What do you mean?"

"I told George Latham that Lowell probably knew about Princess Rebeka being a Fire mage," said Simon. "Latham is the Water mage who killed Sommerstag, the Harsaka brothers, and Frank Killian."

Hammersmith barked a harsh laugh but stopped when he saw the look on Simon's face. "You're serious? Latham? The King's personal advocate? Are you out of your mind?"

"I'm dead serious," said Simon. "When he came to my office to act as my advocate, he carried a willow wood cane topped with a garnet. Jaime Smithington confirmed that Latham has Water talent. He and Smithington started the mage Academy together. Latham dropped out in the first year, never completed training, and was not registered. Smithington says he had more raw talent than anyone he'd ever seen."

"So, he has talent," said Hammersmith. "That doesn't make him a killer, much less a Master mage."

"Latham is the one who pointed out to me that the only people killed by my rogue mage were those who weren't already cleared to know about the Princess," said Simon urgently. "He was part of the original group who got the Princess out of the country. He's heavily invested in keeping that a secret at all costs."

"Again, plausible but not evidence," replied Hammersmith.

"He defended an Orc named Pantosch a while back in a beef over a bad faith contract; got him off with only a few months in City lock-up," said Simon. "A couple of days ago, Smithington and a team of firefighters almost died in a backflash fire at a warehouse in the East End. The backflash was a turkey trap set to kill Smithington and the team. Someone cast an Air spell that sucked the oxygen out of the building after the fire got really hot. As soon as the team opened a door, the fresh air triggered the backflash."

"So, it was a close call for Smithington. So what?" asked Hammersmith.

"The mage who cast the Air spell was Pantosch. He'll testify that Latham hired him to do the job," said Simon. "Smithington could confirm that Latham is a Water mage. That's why he was targeted."

Hammersmith started to speak, then stopped, his head cocked in thought. He shook himself after a second. "Right," he said. "Let's say you're on to something. Latham is a highly placed, highly respected advocate. Hells, he was short listed for Justice Minister a couple of years ago. He turned it down so he could continue working as a private advocate. How do you expect to get to him, much less prove he had anything to do with the murders?"

"I don't know," admitted Simon. "My priority right now is Lowell. I need him to testify against Alorton and the others and I'm convinced he's Latham's next target. I need to find him and get him into custody."

"I may be able to help there," said Hammersmith. "He works for the IG, after all. I'll check with his office and see if they have a location."

"Thanks, Bendict." Simon extended a hand to help Hammersmith out of the chair. They made their way back to the chaos of the temporary office. While Hammersmith summoned the IG's office, Simon took out his mirror and summoned Latham's office. Latham's secretary informed him that the advocate had left for the day and was not to be disturbed. Simon broke the connection and looked toward Hammersmith.

"Thank, you Gisele," Hammersmith said and ended his own conversation. He turned to Simon. "Lowell signed out early and said he was going home. He lives up in Gilford, north of Caledonia University."

"Address?" asked Simon.

Hammersmith wrote it down on a slip of paper. He held it up for a second and looked Simon in the eyes. "You're sure you want to do this? Lowell is no friend of yours and the word around here is that the IG has doubts about why he's pushing the investigation into you and Axhart. With Lowell out of the picture, it may just go away."

"If the situation were reversed, would you let it go? Let Latham take him out?" asked Simon.

"No, I wouldn't." Hammersmith sighed and handed Simon the paper. "I'll see what kind of backup I can muster. I'd go with you, but..." he lifted his crippled arms.

"Thanks again, Bendict. I'll be all good if I can get to Lowell first."

"Good luck, Simon. I'll start drawing up warrants

for Alorton, Kershaw, and Aspenwald. Get Lowell into isolation and let me know when we're ready to move."

"Will do, but Alorton is mine, agreed?"

Hammersmith nodded his assent and Simon headed for the stairs to the Courtyard level and his sled. He took out his mirror and summoned Birchfield.

"Gervis," said Simon when the Sergeant connected the mirror. "Where are you?"

"Eastport, LT. Out near Hagadorn. What's wrong?"

"Get the rest of your team," said Simon. "Meet me in Gilford. I know who killed Anika. No time to explain right now, but Lowell is there, and we need to take him in right away." He gave Gervis the address.

"Will do, LT. It'll take an hour or so to gather the boys and get up that way. Why now?"

"No time, Gervis. Just get moving." He broke the connection. He'd reached the sled.

Crosstown traffic was heavy and although Simon used the sled's lights to clear the occasional intersection, it still took better than 30 minutes to reach the northside neighborhood known as Gilford.

Gilford had once been a village on the outskirts of the capital that housed small weaving and rope making crafters. It had long since been absorbed by the expanding city, transforming into a neighborhood of small to medium sized bungalows and homes. It was close enough to the city center to be urban, but the tree lined streets and small squares retained a village feel. It was now popular with Peacekeepers, lower-level bureaucrats, and city management workers.

Simon found the address Hammersmith had given him at the end of a narrow lane. The small bungalow stood back from the dead-end lane behind a neatly trimmed hedge. A cold iron gate breached the hedge near the far corner and a white pebbled path led from the gate to a green front door. The small home was built of yellow brick, left natural in color, and had two modest windows, also trimmed in green, flanking the front door.

A narrow drive led from the street to a detached stable just behind the house. Simon saw no sleds on the street and none in the drive. The stable door was closed, and he couldn't see through the high windows along its top.

Simon sat in the sled, suddenly reluctant to move forward. He had no hard evidence that Latham was responsible for the deaths of the Harsakas, Anika Sommerstag, and Frank Killian. What he had was circumstance, opportunity, and speculation. He was sure he was right, but if he confronted Lowell, accused Latham, and Lowell didn't believe him, he was handing the man all he needed to put him in irons. Worse, he was jeopardizing his whole team by calling them out to support his speculations. He felt like he was on very thin ice, and it was cracking beneath his feet.

He climbed out of the sled and retrieved the D'Stang bolt thrower from the rear. *In for a shilling, in for a crown.* He took a deep breath, checked the weapon's charge and magazine, both full, and brought the stock up to his shoulder as he approached the gate.

The gate swung open at a nudge from his foot. He rapidly approached the door and checked through the windows on either side but saw only an empty sitting room to the left and an equally empty dining room to the right.

Simon reached out and tried the door. The knob turned easily. He pushed the door open and brought the D'Stang up to cover the entry foyer and hallway beyond. The small house was laid out around a central hallway leading to a closed door at the back. He stepped inside sweeping first to the right and then to the left, clearing the empty rooms. A short way down the hall an opening to the left led to a small but neat kitchen while the room to the right appeared to be an office of some sort. Both were empty.

He reached the closed door at the end of the hall. He tried the knob, but it was locked. He took a step back, lowering the D'Stang slightly, then raised his right leg and kicked out with his boot, striking the door right next to the knob. The door jamb splintered but held. A second kick drove the door open to slam against the inner wall of the room. Simon leapt through, D'Stang at his shoulder, and sighted around the room. Empty.

Simon lowered his weapon and took stock of the room. A comfortable looking bed occupied the space to his left, made up with a plain but serviceable quilt. A Peacekeeper's uniform lay on the bed, neatly laid out on a hanger as if just taken out to be worn, or just removed and ready to be hung up for wear another day. Directly across from the door stood a tall chest of drawers of dark walnut, highly polished. A matching double doored wardrobe stood against the wall to the right. Simon nudged one of the doors open but saw only a uniform and a couple of business suits hanging from a wooden rod.

There was no trace of Latham or Lowell and no obvious reason for the door to be locked. Simon quickly searched the pockets of the uniform but found nothing. There was some loose change and a laundry claim ticket on top of the chest. In the top drawer he found several clean sets of hose and a Gowron bolt pistol in a clip-on holster. The other drawers contained only clothing.

He lifted the uniform from the bed and checked the bedclothes. Again, nothing special. He sat on the bed in frustration. *I don't have time for this. I can't search the whole house. Lowell was here, but he left. Where did he go?*

He shifted his position to look out the window to the back garden. The edge of the stable was just visible. Another pebbled path led from the stable, across the garden to the side of the house, presumably to the kitchen. He shifted forward to get to his feet when he noticed a side door in the stable where the path ended. It was slightly ajar.

Simon stood and made his way back to the kitchen. There was a side door between the salamander and the tall chiller. He opened it and brought the bolt thrower to his shoulder again. He followed the path around the corner of the house, checking low before stepping out into the open and approaching the stable.

He crossed the open garden quickly and put his back to the stable wall next to the door, listening carefully. At first, he heard nothing and was about to step in front of the door and open it, but then he caught the faint sound of movement, of something scraping over the concrete floor of the stable.

He crouched to lower his profile and pushed the door open. Looking around the edge of the jamb, he saw a pair of booted feet bound together by a loop of rope. They jerked in alarm as the door swung back on its hinges.

Simon stayed in a tight crouch as he entered the stable, bolt thrower up and sweeping the space for targets. A maroon Faleron four-seat sled sat in the middle of the stable. On the far side, partially concealed by the sled, a figure writhed on the floor as if attempting to worm its way to the big sliding door at the street side of the building.

Simon swept left and right as he moved deeper into the stable. On the floor on the other side of the sled he found Spencer Lowell. The IG man lay partially on his side, his wrists held behind his back in a pair of Keeper-issue manacles. A wad of cloth had been stuffed in his mouth as a gag, held in place by a short length of rope tied at the back of his neck. Similar pieces of rope secured his knees and ankles. He looked back at Simon, fear shifting to pleading in his eyes as he grunted unintelligibly against the gag.

Simon lowered the bolt thrower and pulled the utility knife from his jacket pocket. He cut the ropes around Lowell's knees and ankles, then worked the gag from his mouth.

"Thank the gods, Buckley," rasped Lowell. "Get me out of these manacles, will you. He may come back any time. He's crazy."

"Who?" asked Simon. "Latham?"

"How did you know?" Lowell looked at Simon suspiciously.

"What did he want with you, Lowell?" Simon held the D'Stang low at his side, not pointed directly at Lowell, but not pointed away from him either.

"How do I know? Get me out of these manacles and help me up. He said he'd be back."

Now Simon did point the D'Stang at Lowell. "Why? Why did he come here and what does he want with you?"

"He wants to kill me," Lowell's voice rose in panic. "He knows about the Princess. He said I wasn't supposed to know her secret, and he couldn't let anyone else live who knew."

"What about the Princess?"

Something about Simon's tone or the way he wasn't helping Lowell get free must have tipped the man off. "YOU know," he shouted. "Oh, Mother, you're in on this."

Simon pushed the D'Stang into Lowell's face. His voice was a low growl. "The question is, what do you know, and who told you?"

"Pound sand, Buckley," said Lowell. "I've got you hooked now. You're part of a criminal conspiracy to withhold evidence of arson resulting in death."

"You seem to forget, Spencer," said Simon calmly. "You're the one in manacles. I'm the one holding the bolt thrower. I can leave you here for Latham and no one will be the wiser."

"You wouldn't."

"I will if you don't start talking. Who told you about Rebeka? Was it Anika Sommerstag? Or the Harsakas?"

"Who?" Lowell shook his head. "No, Frank Killian told me. He said he'd have proof once he met with his contact from Fredonia. But he dropped out of sight before he told me where and when the meet would take place. He said you and Axhart were part of a conspiracy to hide the fact that Rebeka started that fire and he wanted you both taken down in return for the information. That's why I started the investigation."

"And that's why you paid his hotel bill," said Simon. "You didn't want any attention on Killian until you had the proof."

"How did you know about that?" Lowell asked, barely above a whisper.

"My Sergeants aren't stupid, Lowell. You and your weasel squad have been so far away from real Keeper work, you've forgotten how it's done," said Simon. "Did you do that on your own hook, or did Aspenwald order it?"

Lowell's face grew paler and his eyes widened. "Killian was my source. Aspenwald didn't know about the Princess. He was just the front man, the face."

"What was Killian to Aspenwald and Kershaw?" Lowell looked away and said nothing. Simon nudged him with the D'Stang. "I've already got enough to charge you with conspiracy to commit treason. Killian was the pick-up man for the weapons used in the attack on the King. You paid his bills. It won't take much to convince a Magistrate that you hired the Harsakas to steal some neutral iron. Your best bet to avoid the gallows is to talk to me now, before the King's Prosecutors get the case."

Lowell sighed. "Killian was the pick-up man. Aspenwald was the go-between for Kershaw and

Alorton. He contacted me and I passed the information on to Killian. The original plan got changed when the Harsakas moved early on the warehouse. Killian got wind of it and skipped on the hotel. He was there on the docks when they did the job. He helped them load the sledge. He sent me a message that the job was done and that he'd contact Aspenwald once he had the goods stored in a safe place. He never followed through, and I never heard from him again. I didn't know he was dead until you told Machemer about it."

"You killed Machemer," said Simon. "Why? Just to hang me?"

"He was getting too close to the smiths who worked the neutral iron. It wasn't my idea. Word came down from Alorton to take care of him. I didn't pull the trigger. I just put the word out to the Clans that Machemer was expendable."

"You stick with that story when you meet with the KPs," said Simon. "It may save you from the hangman." He reached down and pulled Lowell to his feet. He turned him toward the door but froze when he saw the outline of the man standing there.

"Stand aside, Simon," said George Latham from the doorway. "He can't be allowed to tell anyone else about Rebeka."

"No, Mr. Latham," said Simon respectfully. "I know you love her and will do anything to protect her, but I need him alive." He raised the D'Stang, pointing it away from Latham but clearly visible and at the ready. "Talk to Rebeka. She's willing to make a public statement in the interests of the country. She wouldn't want this death on her account."

"It's too late for that," Latham said sadly. "You saw the destruction caused by the barest hint that a noble person had killed Orcs with magic. Think how much worse that would be if it got out that the Royal Family was involved."

"If you kill Lowell, the rest of the conspirators go free. Aspenwald, Kershaw, Alorton, all free to try again. They're traitors, but without this man's testimony, we can't touch them." Simon pushed Lowell to his knees and swung the bolt thrower to bear on Latham.

"What would you have me do?" Latham's voice almost broke. "I've served the King and his Family for more than twenty-five years. I've counseled them, been a confidant to each of them, kept their secrets, shared their victories. I was there when baby Rebeka was Named before the Great Mother. I saw her first day of school, all her Name days. I can't let her be betrayed by a pack of jackals."

"And you can't stop her if she decides to tell her story to the world," answered Simon. "Think, George. We narrowly avoided a disaster that could have taken down our way of life, all because I convinced you and the King to keep Rebeka's true nature a secret. It can't stay under the rock. Someone else will figure it out. Rebeka herself is realizing that if she's to mature as a person, as a mage, because that's what she is, she has to do it in the open."

"No," cried Latham. "I can't let her do that."

"You can't stop her if it's what she decides to do," said Simon. "Killing Lowell, hells, killing all of us who know won't stop her. Do you think she'll thank you for killing Anika or the Harsakas? Killian?"

"They were going to destroy her," Latham answered. "They wanted to take down the Royal House."

"Not just them, or this idiot here. Alorton, Kershaw, Aspenwald and Flandyrs they're the real enemy. And I can get them. But I need Lowell."

Latham hung his head, staring at the floor. Lowell shifted and made as if to stand, but Simon shoved him back down. Latham didn't seem to notice. He shook his head slowly. His silver gray hair, usually so carefully combed, hung in front of his eyes. Simon lowered the bolt thrower and took half a step forward.

Suddenly Latham threw his head back with an anguished cry. He held the willow cane in both hands above his head. A brilliant ball of silver light formed between his hands, shimmering like water in the moonlight. Simon snapped the D'Stang up prepared to shoot, but Latham flexed his arms and snapped the cane in two. The shimmering ball burst like a balloon, showering them all with water.

Latham slumped, not falling but leaning back against the door frame. He dropped the pieces of the cane to the floor. Simon lowered his weapon again, slinging it under his left arm. With his right, he took a pair of manacles from his belt. Latham offered no resistance as Simon snapped them on his wrists.

"I'm sorry, George." Simon gripped the older man's shoulder. "I'll do all I can to get you a good defense."

Latham chuckled at the irony of that. He sighed. "She wanted money," he said. "Sommerstag. She contacted me two weeks ago. We met in my office, and she told me she knew about Rebeka. She had proof. She told me about the plot, about her father. She laughed about it. She wanted 500,000 Crowns for the proof. I demanded proof of the conspiracy as well. She told me about the Harsakas and about Killian. We arranged to meet on the docks by the Cut to see the exchange. I waited until Killian left. Then I cast the condensation spell on the Orcs."

He turned his head as Gervis, and the rest of the team pounded up the walkway. Simon held up a hand and Gervis mirrored the gesture stopping the rest of the team.

"What happened next?" asked Simon quietly.

Latham turned back to Simon and smiled faintly. "Sommerstag took off on her flyer before I could get to her. I followed Killian to the warehouse. He'd parked the sled inside and had just taken out his mirror when I surprised him. I surprised myself with the exsanguination spell. I didn't know I could do that. I should have paid more attention to control in my short stay at the Academy."

"And Anika?" Simon prompted.

"I caught sight of her on the roof as I came out of the warehouse. I ran to the alley and found her just coming off the ladder. She'd seen what happened to the Harsakas and was frightened, but not frightened enough to back down from her demand for money. I lost my temper, and my control, and the next thing I knew she was dead. I heard sirens coming and panicked. I left without taking her backpack."

Gervis looked from Latham to Simon, stunned. Simon handed him the D'Stang. "Your case, Gervis," he said. "You do the honors. Charge Lowell with conspiracy to commit treason and Latham with murder."

Simon brushed past Gervis as he started the ritual of reciting them their rights. The team parted for him, and he walked down the path to the street and his sled. The booking process would take several hours. He knew he'd need to be there to brief Axhart and to record a statement of Latham's confession. Still, he was in no rush to get back to Wycliffe House.

His head hurt. *Latham was the best this country had to offer. He was the face of justice and law. But if he could fall into darkness if the stakes were high enough. What hope is there for the rest of us?*

He looked around at the suburban street surrounding him, the very picture of the peace and prosperity of the modern Commonwealth. It wasn't the high rises on the King's Road or the high-priced shopping districts of the North side that were the heart of the country. It was the neighborhoods like this or Bowater or Glenharrow. Places where common folk could buy a home and a small plot of land and be as safe and comfortable and secure as the nobility of the old Magisterium. Even Orcs could aspire to own their own piece of the dream. He remembered Gripple Swampwater and his pride in ownership of ten acres of farmland.

He almost sobbed. *But they killed Gripple. They killed Ham. They killed Jack's spirit and drove Kermal into the arms of the darkness.* He dropped his head into his hands and leaned against the steering yoke. *What hope is there for the rest of us?* he thought again.

He heard Hal's voice telling him to, 'Work the case, follow the evidence, just like we always do.' He lifted his head and nodded to himself. He could do that, at least for today. He pushed the blackness down and raised the steering yoke. He spoke the incantation to activate the Air spell and the sled rose. He turned south toward Wycliffe House.

CHAPTER TWENTY-SIX

Later, he couldn't recall the drive back across town. He may have detoured, or Gervis and the team used lights and sirens, because they were already in booking by the time Simon reached the stables. He parked the sled and returned the keys to the Sergeant at the control desk.

"The Ax wants to see you, LT," said the Sergeant as he checked the sled in on his logbook. "Asked me to pass the word when I saw you."

"Thanks," Simon replied. He turned to the stairwell waving a greeting to Gervis who grinned back broadly. Simon wished he had the younger man's enthusiasm.

Elvira Cairns was still at her desk. She gave him an uncharacteristic smile. "Go in," she said. "He's expecting you. And do cheer up."

"Yes, Mistress Cairns," said Simon.

Axhart was in his shirtsleeves, his uniform jacket draped over the back of his desk chair. He sat on one of the couches that flanked the trademark green carpet and looked more relaxed than Simon had seen him in days.

He waved Simon to the opposite couch. "Sit down, Simon. First, the good news. Hal and Brookstone are being released. They should be over the border with their prisoner in an hour. I expect Hal will call in as soon as they clear the customs office."

Simon felt as if a weight had been lifted from his back. He smiled for the first time that afternoon. "Thank you, Captain."

"We'll see how you feel once that reprobate of a foster father of yours gets back to town," Axhart chuckled. "The second bit of good news is that the IG has dropped the investigation. As soon as you brought in Lowell he called with 'profound regrets for any inconvenience.' It was Lowell's project from the start anyway. Rebeka's secret is safe from that quarter."

"As to that, sir, maybe not." Simon hunched forward. "I've arrested George Latham for murder. He's the Water mage who killed Anika Sommerstag, the Harsakas, and Frank Killian."

Axhart said nothing for a few long seconds. He shook his head. "Gods above and below, Simon. The King's personal advocate? You couldn't wait and bring him in quietly on some other pretext?"

"No, sir," replied Simon quietly. "He was planning to kill Lowell. I persuaded him not to for the greater good of exposing Alorton's treason. He thought he was protecting Rebeka by taking out the people he didn't consider authorized to know the truth."

"Once he's booked, we'll clamp a lid on this. Hold him in isolation until we can control the story. Maybe persuade him to keep it quiet at trial." Axhart rubbed his eyes. "By the Mother, this thing is going to fall on us like a rockpile in a coalmine."

"If I may, sir," said Simon. "I think we need to talk to Rebeka. She is close to making a public statement as it is. If she finds out that Latham committed murder to protect her, she will do so immediately and damn the consequences." He sighed. "I think it was a mistake to try to keep this secret in the first place. It seemed the best idea at the time and maybe it was. But it can't stay buried forever, not if Rebeka is ever going to control her ability and grow into the person she's meant to be. It has to come out. Better she chooses the time and manner of the revelation herself."

"And the King? The rest of the Royal Family?" Axhart pulled at his beard. "Hells, we just went through four days of the worst rioting the country has seen since the end of the Magisterium. We barely thwarted an organized plot to kill the King. How do you think the Orcs will react if Rebeka admits she killed those gangsters?"

"I don't know, Captain," said Simon. "But you just said it yourself. They were gangsters. Rebeka commands a tremendous amount of respect down in the Hollows. Lily Ponsaka loves her like a daughter. Everywhere she goes, everyone she meets, she seems to convert to an ally. If she does it right, coordinates it with the rest of the family and says the right words, she may just convert the whole country."

Axhart looked doubtful. "And the rest of us? We'll look like we covered it up like the manipulators the political agitators accuse us of being."

Simon smiled sadly and nodded. "But the King and Rebeka will look honest, contrite, and obedient to the Accords, at great personal cost and sacrifice. Worst case, blame Latham and me as the sole conspirators. Everyone else has plausible deniability."

"Hard for the King to deny knowledge of his own daughter's real reason for abdicating," grunted Axhart.

"True, but if he makes the right statement following Rebeka's, he'll be seen as a loving father, not as a cynical politician."

Axhart again was silent for a while. Then he nodded. "I'll need to contact His Majesty right away and inform him about Latham. And we will keep that arrest under rock for now. Can you reach Rebeka?"

"Aye, sir," said Simon. "I had planned to contact Rebeka and Liam as soon as we were done here, to let them know about Latham."

"What about your contacts in the Orc community?" asked Axhart. "Can you reach out to them as well? Give them some warning?"

Simon nodded. "Lily for sure. And I may be able to reach out to the Cabal, for what it's worth. As to the Azeri Liberation Brigades and the rest of the Orc liberation radicals, who knows?"

"All good," said Axhart. "Get to it. I have some difficult conversations to have with the King and with the Prime Minister. Get out of here. Let me know if Hal gets in touch and needs anything."

Simon rose and took his leave. Outside the office, he paused and took a few deep breaths. He felt a wave of relief, both at finally knowing Hal would be home soon and surprisingly, at the prospect of Rebeka revealing her secret. He hadn't realized how much that secret had weighed on him.

He checked his timepiece. Half past seventeenth. Gervis would be tied up in booking for a while. He resolved to go back to his office and summon Rebeka and Liam from there. Then he'd go home and wait to hear from Hal. Anything else could wait until morning.

Lessa had already cleared her desk and gone home. He went through the door to his inner office and found a glass of Portalis brandy and a note on his desk.

"LT," the note read. "Mistress Cairns said you would be needing this. I know you had a hard day and am sorry I couldn't be here to help, but Mistress Cairns also said you'd rather be alone. I am proud to be working with a Peacekeeper like you.

With respect (and best wishes), Lessa Greenwater."

Tears welled up in his eyes. He carefully folded the note and placed it in the top drawer. He lifted the brandy toward the outer office in a silent toast and downed it in a single gulp.

He sat behind his desk and took out his mirror. Rebeka answered the summons immediately.

"Hello, Simon," she said. Her smile turned into a frown when she saw the expression on his face. "Gods, what's wrong? Is it Hal? Or Sylvie?"

"No, they're all good as far as I know. Hal should be across the border soon. I haven't heard from Sylvie, but she and Hamil Fairborn may be lying low until they get to West Faring." He paused. "Is Liam with you? I have news that affects both of you."

"He's here," said Rebeka. "He's in the shower. Can you wait for a few minutes?"

"Get him. I'll wait," Simon answered. Rebeka set her mirror down and he could hear her calling for Liam. Less than a minute later, both Liam and Rebeka were in the mirror, Liam in a towel with his wet hair clinging to his forehead.

"What's happened, Simon?" asked Rebeka. "Is someone hurt?"

"No, that's not it." He paused and took a deep breath. "Did you know that George Latham was a Water mage?"

Rebeka looked puzzled. Then her face changed. Her eyes were wide, but her expression was carefully neutral. Simon had seen that face before, the first time he had confronted her in Lily Ponsaka's tavern over the deaths of some Orc children.

"What are you telling me?" she asked. Liam reached out and took her hand, She gripped it tightly.

"George killed the Harsaka brothers. He killed Anika Sommerstag. He killed Frank Killian." Simon had spent much of the afternoon imagining how he would tell her this, what words he could use to soften it. In the end, he just said it, calm, matter of fact, simple.

Rebeka jerked slightly as if each statement was a physical blow. Still, she maintained rigid control over her face. She took a breath and let go of Liam's hand.

"You're sure?" It was a statement rather than a question.

"Yes," said Simon. "He told me about it himself. He thought he was protecting you."

Rebeka's control broke for an instant. "Gods damn him," she sobbed. Then her control returned. "That wasn't his place. I don't need his protection. He did enough, getting us out of the Commonwealth."

Liam put a hand on her shoulder. "We talked about this, Becky. Maybe it's time."

She looked sharply at him, then her face softened, and she touched his hand. She turned back to Simon. "Liam and I are going to make a public statement. I'm going to tell the world the real reason I abdicated and take responsibility for those deaths. I want to make my case to all the people, including the Orcs, especially the Orcs. I told you before, I could live with being thought foolish, but would not shame my family by being thought a murderer." She wiped tears from her eyes. "But trying to hide what I am has cost my family a dear friend and nearly destroyed my country. I won't let that happen. If the truth is known, it's no longer a weapon against us."

Simon nodded. "Captain Axhart is presenting the same argument to your father and the Prime Minister right now. I think if you contact your parents, they will agree and help you arrange the public statement."

Rebeka regarded him with cool eyes. "Did you also plan to try to persuade me if I hadn't brought it up?"

"You'd already said it was a consideration." Simon pointed out. "But I have too much respect for you to try to pressure you into something you don't want to do. On the other hand, I'm not surprised either. This is the right thing to do, Your Highness."

"Really, Simon," she said with a smile. "You're family. Call me Rebeka, or Becky, like Liam does."

"All right, Becky. And Sylvie and I will expect the both of you at the wedding, assuming she gets herself out of the Havens and you aren't under indictment."

Her laugh at that was warm and genuine. "Well, it's about time. Congratulations."

"Yes, congratulations, Simon," said Liam. "Is Sylvie all good? We've heard some troubling rumors from the Havens."

"I don't know, Liam," said Simon, a pang of worry surfacing in the back of his throat. *Why haven't I heard anything? What if she's been detained, or worse, just disappeared? NO! stop that. She's a warrior. She'll come back to you.* "I haven't heard from Sylvie in almost two days. She and Hamil Fairborn were going to try to cross the border near Portalis and make their way to West Faring. If all went smoothly, they should have been there by now." *Please, by the Mother, let her be safe and well.*

"Sylvie is more than capable of taking care of herself," said Liam, echoing Axhart's words. "It will be all good."

"I know you're worried, Simon," said Rebeka. "I'll keep you and Sylvie in my thoughts and say a prayer to the Mother that she will stay safe."

"Thank you, Rebeka. Send me a message or a summoning when you know the timing of your announcement." *And keep Sylvie in your prayers.*

"Aye. LT," said Liam. "Will do." With a swipe of his hand, he broke the connection.

Simon caught a ride home with a patrol team heading to their station in the North End. He walked the two blocks to his flat and unlocked the door after canceling the Warding spells. For once he found no one waiting in his front room. He managed to get out of his clothes before he tumbled into bed.

He awoke the next morning before fifth hour, still sore but not really in pain. After a hot shower he thought he'd be able to drive himself to the House. Getting into the Oxley was easy, getting out proved to be a bit more difficult.

He made it to his office before seventh hour and found that events had proceeded overnight without him. On his desk were several copies of the booking and charge reports on Lowell and Latham and a note that they would both be formally arraigned at thirteenth hour that afternoon. Lowell had engaged Faleen Handfield to be his advocate, a revealing choice. Greenleaf and Handfield represented the Commonwealth interests of a number of old Elven families from the Havens. Latham had petitioned to represent himself. To most people that might seem natural given his reputation as a formidable litigator. Simon knew better and it saddened him. He knew Latham intended to plead guilty and not reveal his reasons for killing four people.

Under the booking sheets were copies of detention warrants for Rondel Aspenwald and Lord Magnus Kershaw. There was also an original warrant with his name on it for Lord Henrik Alorton. A note was clipped to it.

"This one is yours, as promised. We move on Aspenwald and Kershaw at eleventh hour, so don't dawdle.

Regards, Bendict Hammersmith"

Simon picked up his mirror and summoned Gervis Birchfield. As soon as the Sergeant responded, Simon said, "Gervis, get your team together and meet in my office at tenth today. We have another high-profile detention warrant to serve."

"Aye, LT," said Gervis with a broad grin. "We'll be there."

"See you then." Simon broke the connection. His summoning tone sounded almost immediately. He swiped to complete the connection and Hal's face swam into view in the mirror.

"Hello, lad," said Hal. "Gelbard tells me you've been a busy boy. You couldn't wait for me? Had to take all the credit yourself?" He laughed. "Seriously, Simon, you've done well."

"Thank you, Hal. How about you and Handel? All good?"

"Oh, aye, we're none the worse for wear," said Hal. "Just sick of Ironlander 'hospitality.' Boring but no real threat. Although, Cleavestone nearly shit granite when he saw Brookstone in his best dress Keeper uniform. Thought for a second, he'd try to have us in irons until one of his retainers stepped in with a timely flagon of ale. Once he calmed down and got used to the idea, he actually seemed to take a liking to young Brookstone. They share a passion for ancient smithing techniques. Before we left, he came to the Customs House and apologized for having to detain us. Wonder of wonders."

"Is this going to sheath the blade on your old feud?" asked Simon.

"Let's not get ahead of ourselves, son," said Hal. "It might give us a place to start." Hal smiled. "A good start, truth be told. Now, what have you heard from Sylvie?"

"Nothing," sighed Simon. "I'm sick with worry. And I don't need you to remind me about how capable Sylvie is. I know all that and it doesn't help. I'm still close to breaking, Hal."

"I know, lad. I know. I won't pretend your worry isn't justified, but I also know Sylvie is strong and capable. She'll come back to you." Hal changed the subject rather than feed Simon's worry. "Handel and I are picking up our charge at the lock-up in a half hour and we'll get on the road right away. We should be home by midday tomorrow."

"All good," said Simon. "See you soon."

Lessa came in with his usual coffee and a stack of messages. "Agent Milhaven is asking to see you LT. Should I ask her to wait?"

"No, send her in," said Simon. "And Lessa, thank you for your note. And the brandy."

The young Orc woman blushed slightly but just nodded her head and bustled out of the office.

A moment later, Sonia Milhaven marched in and came to attention in front of his desk. She was the Fire mage attached to Hal's team and she looked troubled. She kept her eyes focused on the wall above Simon's head and waited for him to acknowledge her.

"At ease, Agent Milhaven," said Simon. "What can I do for you?"

Her posture eased slightly. She shifted her feet but still wouldn't meet his eye. "I want you to understand, sir, I'm no weasel. Ordinarily I'd just keep to myself and do my own job. But this is the third day and I'm worried."

"This is about Jack Ironhand, isn't it?" asked Simon.

"Yes, sir." She sounded miserable but her voice was strong. "I tried to cover for him, but..."

"I know, Sonia," said Simon. "I get the court dockets. I know Jack wasn't in court yesterday. Where is he?"

"I don't know," said Sonia, her voice almost breaking. "He's not in his flat in West Wray, Reba McPhee hasn't heard from him in a week. I checked with his sisters in the Darrowdowns, but he hasn't been there either. I even looked in a couple of taverns I know he likes. Gods, LT, I'm worried. He could have fallen in the river, or been mugged in some alley."

"How bad has the drinking been?" Simon asked quietly.

"Usually just on Weeksend, although he'd show up some mornings looking rough, like he'd passed out on his floor or something. I sent him home last Smithsday because he stank of cheap wine. He asked me to cover the day before yesterday. I haven't heard anything since." She hung her head, looking at the floor. "I'm not a weasel, sir."

"No, you're not. You're a concerned friend," said Simon. "Consider yourself acting team leader until Sergeant Stonebender returns. He's on his way and should be here by midday tomorrow. If Jack gets in touch, tell him he's on administrative leave and ask him to contact me. I've already pulled the team out of the rotation. Just work the cases you already have as best you can."

Sonia nodded and came to attention again. "Thank you, LT."

"Now go, get back to work."

"Aye, sir." She saluted, turned, and left the office.

When she was gone, Simon leaned his elbows on the desk and cradled his face in his hands. *All this, and now Jack. I should have put him on leave a month ago and insisted he get some help, sort himself out.* Simon knew Jack would turn up eventually, hopefully not in some drunk tank in another jurisdiction. But now his breakdown would become official, and his career would likely be over or at least hamstrung by a disciplinary hack that would follow him everywhere. *Sorry, Jack. It looks like I let you down too.*

He rubbed his face and cleared his eyes. The coffee was still at his elbow, at that stage where it wasn't cold, but wasn't warm enough to be drinkable. He downed it anyway. He had just finished and made a sour face when Lessa stuck her head in again.

"Was my coffee too weak?" she asked. The note in

her voice said she was teasing, something she had never done with him before.

He smiled. "No, I stupidly let it get cool. May I have another?"

"Anytime, LT." she said. "But first, Sergeant Hanks would like a word."

"Send him in," sighed Simon.

Hanks entered a moment later and he, too, stood rigidly in front of Simon's desk, not meeting his eye. *I must have been hells on a sled the last couple of days,* thought Simon. *First Sonia, now Jason.*

"At ease, Jason," said Simon. "Please, sit down."

Hanks relaxed but remained standing. "With respect, LT, have I done something wrong?"

"What? No. Please, sit down. If I've given that impression, I apologize. There's been so much going on with the riots, then the Sommerstag case that I was preoccupied. I was short with you, and I apologize. We have different styles and it will take a while for us to get each other's rhythm."

Hanks finally looked at him. He nodded and sat in the chair Simon had indicated.

"Actually," said Simon. "I wanted to update you on the Pantosch case. The information developed in that interview broke another bigger case and will lead to some high-profile arrests. That was solid investigative work, the kind that sometimes gets forgotten in this squad."

"There's a rumor that George Latham has been detained for killing Sommerstag, Killian, and a couple of Orcs. Is that why you wanted to keep a lid on the Pantosch report?" asked Hanks.

"Yes," said Simon. "Latham wanted to take out Smithington because he was one of the few people who remembered that he was a Water mage."

"You could have told me that, LT," said Hanks quietly.

"You're right. And I should have. I apologize."

Hanks nodded an acceptance and went on, "I really can do this job, LT. I don't have Hal's experience or Gervis's smarts and smooth style, but I can do this."

"I know that, Jason," said Simon. "You need to take a few chances now and then, trust your instincts. But don't change your style to try to be what you think I want. Finding Pantosch was solid work, not flashy, but exactly the right thing. The same with your work on the Hale Street arson case. Thanks to you we got a conviction there and we're close to taking down a nest of traitors here in the capital. Keep doing what you do." He paused and looked Hanks in the eye. "So what else do you have on your plate?"

Hanks smiled and began to outline the cases his team was working. It was concise and methodical, almost boring, but Simon grinned as he listened. *He'll be all good. Just a different style and pace, but he knows what's needed. He'll be all good.*

CHAPTER TWENTY-SEVEN

Gervis and his team mustered in Simon's office at ten. Simon had spent the time prior updating the information he had on Alorton. When the attacks on the King and Queen had failed, Alorton had vacated his townhouse and gone north to his family estate outside Cymbeline in the Salut Hills north of Gilford. Hammersmith had teams watching the estate day and night and confirmed that Lord Alorton was still there. He'd sent over some maps and schematics of the estate with the warning that they were several years old and might not be accurate.

Simon contacted Axhart and got authorization to mobilize a SpRT team to assist with the detention. Simon didn't know what sort of security Alorton might have, or if he'd have loyal supporters or hired muscle for protection. He wasn't taking any chances.

He quickly ran through his plan to enter the estate and take Alorton into custody. They reviewed the plans of the house and set tasks for each team member, then adjourned to the stables and the armory where they drew weapons and tactical vests before meeting up with the SpRT team and their armored sledge.

The team leader turned out to be Sergeant Burstin who shook Simon's hand warmly and greeted him in his thick Dundarian accent.

"Good to be workin' with you, LT," he said. "Does this have anything to do with that dead Elf we found in the alley some days back?"

Simon returned his grin. "Aye, that led to breaking this case and to the detention we're going to serve. Are you ready to kick down a few doors?"

"Depends on the door," said Burstin. "What are we lookin' at?" Simon told him and he gave a low whistle. "Warrant?"

"Solid," said Simon. He spread out the map of the estate and the schematics for the house and went through his plan. He detailed breaching plans for the gate, the front door, objectives for the Magic Squad, and what he wanted from the SpRT team in the way of perimeter security and fire support, if needed.

"Any questions or suggestions, Sergeant," asked Simon.

Burstin rubbed his chin. "I'd like one of my guys on overwatch as a sniper, but without onsite recon, I can't be sure of the sightlines." He punched Simon gently on the shoulder. "You've done this before, LT."

"A time or two, Sergeant. All good to go?"

"Aye, sir." Burstin turned and called to his team. "Mount up! Dorcas driving, Calloway on back door security. I'll brief the rest of you on the way."

A minute later the sledge was climbing the ramp to street level. Birchfield's team was in the sledge with the SpRT's while Gervis and Simon followed in a marked black and white Peacekeeper sled. They took Canal south to the W205 highway which formed part of the ring road circling the capital. It was faster than fighting crosstown traffic on the surface streets and the Salut Hills exit was only two miles from the Alorton estate.

The Salut Hills were an extension of the same upland that formed Glenharrow, although lower and more rolling. Their thick forests had long since been cut down for lumber and the secondary growth that now covered the area was interspersed with large homes and fenced horse pastures.

The Alorton estate clearly predated all of these new arrivals. A stand of old growth forest marked the boundary of Alorton lands, and a twelve-foot-high hedgerow lined the road. After half a mile, the hedgerow gave way to a tall cold iron fence. A short drive led to a wide iron gate marking the main entrance.

Dorcas turned the sledge into the drive and stopped in front of the gate. Simon pulled up beside him. The gate stood open and appeared unmanned and unguarded.

The Farspeaker in Simon's sled crackled, and Simon picked up the speaking stone. "What do you make of it?" Burstin asked.

"Not what I expected," said Simon into the faintly glowing stone. "But we came to do a job. Let's go in." He replaced the stone in its cradle as the sledge rose and slid forward. Gervis checked the charge on his bolt thrower and nodded to Simon. They fell in behind the sledge.

Passing through the gate, Simon felt no tingle of an activated security or alarm spell. There was no challenge, no guard. The grounds appeared deserted.

The long drive led straight to the grand old house. It was built in the faux-Elven style that had been popular in the late Magisterium period, all spires and domes in white stone and contrasting dark wood.

A wide circle fronted a tall entrance portico. The sledge stopped short of the circle and the rear clamshell door opened. The SpRT team rushed out and dispersed to form a perimeter, running at a half crouch with their high powered D'Stangs tight to their shoulders. In less than a second the door closed, and the sledge slid forward. It stopped in front of the portico and Simon slid in behind it. He and Gervis climbed out of the sled and the rest of the squad scrambled out of the sledge. They took up a breaching stack, single file with each man touching the shoulder of the man in front. Gervis took his place at the front of the stack and raised his D'Stang to his shoulder.

Simon strode forward to the double front door and the team fell in behind him. He raised his own bolt thrower and reached out to the door handle. It turned easily; the door was unlocked.

Simon raised his left hand and counted by raised fingers—1, 2, 3—then he kicked the door open and rushed in shouting "King's Agents!"

The rest of the team followed with similar shouts. Gervis and his Armorer turned right into a large dining room. Two more ascended a curving staircase to the left to search the second floor. Two others, members of the SpRt team, followed the squad in and headed down the central hall to the back of the house.

Simon turned left where the schematic showed a room labeled as the library. Two tall sliding doors closed the room off from the entry hall. Simon grasped the right-hand door and slid it back.

The room beyond was indeed set up as a library. Floor to ceiling bookshelves lined the walls and comfortable looking armchairs and couches were set out in groupings around the room. The floor was lightly stained oak covered with Azeri carpets and Dundarian rag rugs. Huge bay windows looked out over the wide front lawn.

Simon stepped into the room, sighting left and right on either side of the doors but finding no one there.

Directly in front of him he could see someone seated in a leather armchair. It faced one of the bay windows and was angled enough away from the door that he could only see the top of the person's head.

A hand lifted above the chair and waved him forward. "Do come in," said a deep sonorous voice. "There's no need for so much noise and fury. I am the only one in the house right now."

Simon kept his D'Stang at his shoulder and moved at an angle away from the door until he could clearly see the man in the chair. "King's Agent," he said. "Keep your hands where I can see them."

Henrik, Lord Alorton cocked his head at Simon and lifted his right hand. In his left he held a tumbler of dark liquid. A bottle of fine Portalis brandy and a second glass was set on a small table beside the chair.

"Of course, Lieutenant Buckley," said Alorton. "As you can see, I am only armed with this glass of very fine brandy. I'd offer you a drink, but I assume you are on duty and wouldn't indulge."

"Henrik Alorton, I am placing you under legal detention on the charge of high treason. You are cautioned that any statement you make may be taken down and used as evidence against you. You are entitled to legal counsel and if you cannot afford counsel an advocate will be appointed for your defense."

"Really, Lieutenant Buckley," said Alorton. "That's not necessary."

Simon kept the bolt thrower at the ready and approached Alorton's chair. "How do you know who I am?" he asked.

Alorton laughed. "Who else would they send? I have followed your activities since your team captured Hargash Barsaka and you killed Joby Blackpool." He gestured to Simon's weapon. "Do lower that thing. I am unarmed and offering no resistance."

"Stand up, turn around and place both hands at

the back of your neck," commanded Simon. "I have no desire to talk to you. Tell it to the hangman."

"Oh, I don't plan to ever see the hangman, Lieutenant. No, that just won't do." He raised the tumbler of brandy. "To your health, Simon Buckley."

"Stop!" Simon shouted.

"What will you do? Kill me?" asked Alorton. He raised the glass to his lips and drank the contents in a single swallow. Simon rushed forward as Alorton gave a small cough and collapsed in the chair. The glass fell from his hand and shattered on the oaken floor.

Simon lowered the D'Stang and reached down to touch Alorton's neck. There was no pulse. He raised the FS bracer on his wrist and activated it. "This is Buckley," he said. "All teams stand down. Alorton is dead. Say again, all teams stand down."

They rode back to Wycliffe House in silence. A search of Alorton's estate had been unrewarding, although ashes in the library fireplace suggested that a large number of documents had recently been burned there. Simon had called the incident in, and a crime scene team had arrived to seal the building and make a more detailed search. Simon had also informed Axhart of Alorton's suicide. The Captain had said little other than telling Simon to turn the scene over to the Crime Scene mages and return to Wycliffe.

As they turned onto Tanner Street and approached the stable, a wall of chaos confronted them. Crowds of people clogged the street. News service sleds and remote mirrorcast sledges parked near the entrance to the stables and focused their attention on the rear postern gate to the old fortress.

Simon and Gervis managed to avoid much notice as they slid down the stable ramp past the guard team in riot gear. Alorton was laid out across the back seat under a torn tarpaulin they had appropriated from a garden shed. Simon didn't want to think about how he might have explained that to an astute news team if they'd been stopped in the crowded street.

Inside the stables, the air was electric, but the activity was organized. The teams quickly learned that Aspenwald and Kershaw had been detained without incident and were now in the booking cells. Hammersmith was closeted with Axhart and Foreign Minister Helmich. They requested that Simon join them as soon as he returned.

For the first time in his career, Simon ignored a request from a superior officer. He and the team turned in their weapons and vests and Simon signed the after-action ammunition inventory, easy since they'd not discharged their bolt throwers. He met Burstin at the armorer's window.

"Thanks for your help today," Simon told him as they shook hands.

"Any time, LT. Me and the boys enjoy a little road trip, especially when there's nobody shooting at us. I'm just sorry we didn't get to bring that bastard in and watch him squirm."

Simon sighed. "Maybe for the best. I don't think I could have stood watching him walk because of some high brass jingle influence. His conviction was never a sure thing."

"Careful, LT," said Burstin. "You're sounding as cynical as old Stonebender."

"At least I come by it honestly." Simon grinned and clapped Burstin on the shoulder. "See you around, Sergeant."

Burstin stepped back and saluted. "You too, LT."

Simon watched him gather his team and lead them across the stables to their own operations area. He turned and walked down the row of personal sleds to his Oxley, climbed in, and headed for home.

CHAPTER TWENTY-EIGHT

Simon stood in front of his door with one hand on his badge and the other on his needler. The touch of his badge had told him that the Warding spells on his door were down. Again. The needler reassured him that he was armed and ready to deal with a threat if the intruder was still in the flat.

He reached out and turned the handle, pushed the door open and stepped through, rapidly bringing the needler up in a two-handed grip. He checked the entry hallway. It was empty.

Kermal's voice came from inside the flat. "I'm in the front room, Simon. Stand down."

Simon rounded the corner, needler still up and pointing at Kermal's face. "God's damn it, Kermal. Pull this stunt once more and I'm taking you in for criminal trespass. I've half a mind to stun you and stake you out naked on the King's Road."

Kermal held up his hands with a smile. "Bad day? I've got some information that might help make it better, but only if you stop pointing that needler at me."

For a second Simon tightened his grip on the needler and held it just long enough to see a flicker of concern in Kermal's eyes. Then he lowered it and returned it to the holster. He turned toward the small kitchen.

"Beer?" he asked over his shoulder.

"Wouldn't turn one down."

Simon retrieved two bottles from the chiller, opened them, and returned to the front room. He handed one to Kermal and settled into an armchair.

"What's this big news?" Simon took a long gulp from his bottle.

"I have names, images, fingerprints, and aural recordings of the Orcs who attacked Parliament and tried to kill the King." He held out a cardboard folder full of papers and Simon took it. "That's positive proof that they were all Azeri Imperial Guards, Special Operations Group. There's also a list of the people they replaced on the delegation. They intimidated most of them into cooperating by kidnapping their families, killed a couple. Our people have rescued the rest of the hostages."

"By 'our people' do you mean the Cabal, or just Wind Clan?" asked Simon.

"Does it matter?" asked Kermal. At a look from Simon, he shrugged. "Mostly Wind, but some from the other clans."

"Is Forsaka taking over the Cabal in the name of Wind Clan?"

"Gods, no," said Kermal. "He's de facto leader of the Cabal, but only because the others agree to it." Kermal paused, considering what to say. "He's trying to make reforms but is meeting a lot of resistance, especially from Serpent and Wolf clans. Wind, Ox, Fish, and Bear are solidly behind him. The rest are on the fence."

"But these dossiers are from Forsaka? He has sources in the Empire?" asked Simon.

"I don't know his sources," said Kermal holding up his hands. "But I trust the information is accurate."

"What's in it for the Cabal? How does Forsaka gain?" persisted Simon.

"The Cabal doesn't want the Empire extending its influence. Hells, even Snake and Wolf know they're better off here than they would be back in Khazurka. And they don't want backlash against Orcs here at home over these assassins. If they show that these were outside agents and their cooperation is noted by the Peacekeepers, maybe even by Justice, then they can return quietly to business as usual."

"Business being gambling, prostitution, loan leeching, and drugs," said Simon bitterly.

"Chief Forsaka is trying to change that, but it's not easy and the gangs are pushing back. These dossiers are a down payment of sorts, a plea for goodwill and breathing room. Let him try to rein in Serpent and Wolf. They account for most of the true gangsters right now. If he can cut them out, the Hollows will be a lot better for it."

Simon sipped his beer but said nothing. *What does it matter? The Cabal will never let Forsaka take control, much less make the gangs legitimate. There's too much money involved. Money can buy anything.*

Kermal seemed to sense Simon's mood. He started to stand when Simon's mirror chimed. Simon swiped it on without really checking who was on the other end. Lessa's face swam into view.

"LT?" she said urgently. "Are you at home? Captain Axhart is looking for you. What should I tell him?"

"Tell him I died. Tell him I was hurt in the raid. Tell him I'm joining Jack Ironhand on a three-day drunk," said Simon. "Hells, I don't care what you tell him. I need to be alone right now." He gave Kermal a hard look.

"All good, LT," said Lessa with a small smile. "But turn on your mirror if you're at home. The Princess is going to make a speech. I'll tell the Captain you're having problems because of your head injury." She broke the connection.

"Bloody hells," muttered Simon. "So soon?"

"You were expecting this?" Kermal asked.

"Aye, I was," said Simon. "Just not this soon." He spoke the incantation to turn on the wall mirror. "Stay. This is important for you, too."

The mirror glowed to life. Simon kept it tuned to a twenty-four hour news service and he recognized the announcer who was speaking.

"The announcement came from the Palace this morning. Since Princess Rebeka's sudden abdication almost two months ago there has been speculation as to the reason. Perhaps tonight we will learn more."

Simon retrieved another couple of beers from the chiller while various talking heads speculated on the content of the upcoming speech. He smiled. *You have no idea,* he thought. Kermal sipped the beer but stayed silent. If he suspected anything, he wasn't talking.

Finally, the mirror went blank for a second, then the coat of arms of the Royal House appeared. This was replaced by an image of Rebeka and Liam, seated side by side in plain chairs in front of a comfortable looking room. Green draperies covered the window behind the couple and a fireplace could be seen in the left background.

"My fellow citizens of the Commonwealth," said Rebeka in a clear pleasant voice. "I call you fellows because that is what you are to me now. As you all know, I have abdicated my office, surrendered my title and all the privileges it carries. I have married a good man and we are making our way in the world as common citizens.

"There has been much speculation as to my reasons for this. Many think I am a foolish, spoiled young woman who has run away impulsively. There have been less kind speculations about an unwanted pregnancy, some sort of undue influence, and even talk of love potions and black magic. I assure you now that none of those rumors are true. I truly love Liam and am proud and grateful that he has chosen to accompany me into my exile."

She reached out and took Liam's hand and gave him one of her dazzling smiles. Liam smiled back and nodded toward the audience, encouraging her to continue. She released his hand and held hers out, palm up.

"Notice I said Liam accompanied me into exile. I did not accompany him. He chose to give up his career and friends and family to come with me, and I am profoundly grateful to him.

This, then, is why I had to abdicate my office and leave the only home and country I have ever known." She stared at her own hand and muttered a few words. A small but brilliant blue flame blossomed in the air just above her palm. She lifted her hand, then closed it, snuffing the fire.

"I am a Fire mage," she said simply and clearly. "I didn't start to manifest any talent until after my twentieth birthday. Like many late-blooming mages, I was unable to fully control the Fire and was a danger to myself and those around me." She frowned and her voice broke slightly. "There were several incidents around the Palace and around Cymbeline that I deeply regret. It was Liam who taught me control. It was he who showed me that I could be the Fire's master and not its slave." She reached out and took his hand, looking into his eyes. "More importantly, he showed me love when all I could feel for myself was fear and loathing."

Liam smiled back and kissed her hand. She went on speaking. "Under the Accords that created our Commonwealth, no member of the Royal family may wield magic of any kind. These same wise laws require that I surrender my lands, my titles and any claim to the throne and forever live in exile. We, Liam and I, and my parents, had hoped to keep this a secret, not to deceive our loyal citizens, but to prevent my actions from becoming a cause for violence and discord. I see now that this was wrong. Evil men have tried to use this information to threaten my father, your King, and to foment violence and revolution in our streets."

She paused and her face set in a mask of neutrality. "I, Rebeka Aster, formerly Rebeka Fangbern, Crown Princess of Centralia, do openly and without hope of special consideration, confess to arson. Specifically, to four fires in empty warehouses that burned stockpiles of the drug known as jolt being concealed there. The fires caused considerable property damage. I also confess to arson involving the warehouse at Canal Street and the Prince Henrik Bridge in which four people were killed. Those people were Farsk Kronska and his close associates, all part of the Canal Street Scalpers, a drug gang. That is no excuse for my actions, although, in my own defense, I did not know at the time that these men were in the warehouse. That said, I stand ready to return to the Commonwealth if the King's Prosecutor summons me. There is no formal extradition treaty with the Free States, but I will not use that to escape trial if Justice so demands one."

The mirror stayed on Rebeka's face for a long second, then cut to the Royal Coat of Arms again. Simon shut the mirror off, having no desire to hear the newsies spin what the Princess had just said.

"What do you think, Kermal?" He drained the last of his beer and set the bottle on a side table.

"I think that was about the bravest thing I have ever seen," said Kermal softly. "I hope Liam realizes he'll have to earn the love of a woman like that every day of his life."

"I think he knows," said Simon with a wry smile. "He may not have known what he was getting into, but he has no illusions now. No, I meant, what do you think this will mean to your people, to Orcs down in the Hollows."

"Oh, I think it will be all good," said Kermal. "Rebeka was already popular from her work with Lily Ponsaka and the throwaway children. No one misses Farsk Kronska. And even those Orcs who have no love for the Royal Family, hate the Azeri Empire even more. Forsaka and the Clans are already spreading the word about the assassins. Once you and Justice go public with the proof, I don't think there will be any more trouble than usual."

"I hope you're right. The riots combined with a successful assassination of the King or Queen might well have destroyed the country, or at least plunged it into civil war. We got lucky."

"Aye," said Kermal, finishing his beer and standing up. "But a wise man once said that luck is what happens when fortune meets preparation. You were the one who was prepared to push the investigation when it might have gotten lost in the background of the riots. The luck is of your making."

Simon did not rise to see him out. He just shrugged. "Maybe. But all it achieved was a return to the status quo. We haven't made any progress."

"Sometimes, that's the best you can hope for." He made his way to the hallway and the door. He turned back. "As long as there are people like you and Rebeka, there's hope."

Simon didn't respond. He heard the door slam as Kermal left the flat, but still didn't move from the chair. He was still sitting there an hour later when his mirror chimed. He answered it.

"Buckley," he said dully.

"Simon, are you all good?" It was Hal, his rough face concerned. "We looked for you at the House. Lessa said you were home feeling poorly. What the hells is going on?"

"I'm fine, Hal. I just needed some time alone. You heard about Alorton?"

Hal nodded. "The bastard escaped Justice, or Justice was done. Depends on your point of view."

"NO," said Simon, his voice nearly a shout. "He was our link to Flandyrs. He was the center of the plot here. Now Lowell and Aspenwald and Kershaw can plead guilty to lesser charges and avoid being hanged for treason. We've accomplished nothing."

"You stopped the assassination of the King," said Hal sternly. "You solved four murders. You took Aspenwald and Kershaw out of public office forever. If the KP knows what he's doing, he'll lay on enough charges that they'll never breathe free air again. That's not nothing, lad."

"And still Flandyrs mocks us from his safe sanctuary in Tintagel, the Cabal wants business as usual, the secret of undetectable weapons is out, and Sylvie hasn't checked in yet." Simon rubbed his eyes. "Sorry, I'm tired and in a foul mood. Actually, I have information that Axhart and Hammersmith need to see. Are they still there?"

"Don't know," said Hal. "It's after seventeenth. Whatever you have will keep, at least until tomorrow, maybe until after Weeksend. Get some sleep. Check with the duty cadre tomorrow. If Gelbard is in, I'm sure he'll see you. But you're expected at home tomorrow evening for dinner. Usual time."

"Yes, Hal. Love to Molly. I'll see you both tomorrow." It was easier to acquiesce than to argue. He was tired and his head still hurt. Hal was right. The dossiers would keep for another day or two now that the assassins were dead and Lowell and company were in custody. He tossed the empty bottles in the trash and went to bed.

Sleep eluded him. *I know she's alive. I can feel her.* He rubbed his chest. *In here. But why hasn't she contacted us? This shared* ghiras *stuff is all well and good, but it's not helping me find her.*

Sometime between midnight and third hour his eyes closed and he slept.

CHAPTER TWENTY-NINE

Simon rose late, showered, and dressed carefully in a clean uniform. He buckled on his saber and hung his badge lanyard from the strap at his jacket shoulder. Tucking the folder of dossiers under his arm he left the flat.

It was Weeksend, so traffic was light. The stables under Wycliffe House were nearly empty. Only the duty crews were on and many of them came and went during the day. Simon parked the Oxley and climbed the stairs to the first level. The desk Sergeant told him that Axhart was in his office and offered to call ahead and announce him. Simon told him not to bother.

He climbed the stairs to the command level and walked the long hallway to Axhart's office. The door to the outer office was open, Elvira Cairns's desk neat and empty. The inner office door was closed. Simon reached out and knocked.

"Come in, Simon," Axhart called.

Simon stepped through the door and approached

Axhart's desk. He stood stiffly and did not sit.

"The desk Sergeant told me you were coming," said Axhart genially. "Sit."

"I'd rather stand, sir," said Simon. He held out the folder. "These are dossiers and documents that prove that the assassins who attacked the King and Queen were Azeri agents, Imperial Guards. They should help with the case against the Empire and my source in the Hollows thinks making them public, along with the Princess's speech last night will keep things calm down there. A sort of return to status quo."

Axhart took the folder and flipped through it briefly. "Excellent. I'll get these to Minister Helmich. He'll put them to good use. And yes, I agree they should be made public. Even the gangs hate the Empire more than they hate us. Good work."

Simon came to attention. "Thank you, sir."

"What else, Simon?" asked Axhart. "You have something else to say, so out with it."

"I'd like to request a leave of absence, sir," said Simon. "Personal issues."

Axhart didn't say anything for several seconds. He replaced the dossiers carefully in the folder and placed it at the corner of his desk. He leaned back and folded his arms.

"Why," he asked. "The real reason, not some platitude about 'finding yourself.'"

"I have failed my teams. Jack Ironhand has been missing for three days. I didn't give him the support he needed. I judged Jason Hanks based on my own standards, not on his merits. I was ready to dismiss him. He's a solid Keeper. I should have supported him." Axhart waved a dismissive hand, but Simon pressed on. "I allowed Alorton to commit suicide right in front of me. As a result, we lost our evidence that Flandyrs was behind the attacks on the King. We stopped the plot but lost the war. The Orcs are still under the thumb of the Cabal; the Opposition, who would have rejoiced at the death of the King, are still respected in Parliament; nothing on the streets has changed. I feel all used up. My heart isn't in it anymore. And Sylvie is still missing. I need to find her, and I can't do that wearing this badge."

Axhart again remained silent for a long time. When he spoke, his voice was both soft and sad. "You once asked me how to hold the wolf by the tail and not get bitten. Well, lad, the wolf has bitten. You can get through this. The bite can heal, and the scar can make you tougher. Go home to Glenharrow. Have dinner with the family like always, but talk to Hal. Sleep on it. If you still want to put your career on hold, maybe cripple it, I won't stop you. And I hope your Lady is all good. I understand your worry."

"Thank you, sir," Simon said stiffly.

"Get out of here," said Axhart. "I'll see to the dossiers. Give my regards to Molly."

Simon turned on his heel and left the office. He made his way to his own office and sat behind the desk. Looking around, he realized that other than the battered old couch and a few books, he had nothing personal that he wished to take with him. Even the couch wasn't something that had meaning outside of Wycliffe House. What he would miss were people, not things. Lessa and their daily routine of coffee and messages, the team Sergeants and their reports, even the paperwork headaches. He'd take the day Axhart had offered him and talk things over with Hal and Molly. Who knew? Maybe he'd change his mind.

He drove out of the stables and followed Tanner Street to All Gods Square. He wasn't religious, but he stopped and lit a candle in the Temple of the Mother. She had been his mother's patron, and although he had only hazy memories of her, he felt the connection. He prayed for Sylvie's safe return, but only half believed it would help.

He drove on into Westport, the main shipping and dock district along the Finnigan. He parked his sled near King Olaf Warf and walked down to the quayside. He spent a long time watching the big ships move slowly along the estuary pushed by tugs and guided by river pilots. He had been born down here near these docks, had spent the first ten years of his life roaming the district. It still felt like home. It was where he came when he was troubled. It was his roots. The summoning tone on his mirror sounded several times. He ignored it.

He drove aimlessly through the narrow streets of Westport, finally crossing the bridge and continuing on to Glenharrow. He reached Stonebender Hall just after sixteenth hour. Dinner was usually at half past seventeenth, so he figured he had time. He was wrong. Before he could even open the heavy oak door, Hal threw it back.

"Where have you been, lad?" he asked. "Get in here. We need to talk."

"Westport," Simon said.

"Ah," Hal replied. He knew that Simon went to Westport when he was confused or conflicted. "Go on in. Molly is waiting and we have news."

Simon followed Hal through the entry hall and down the corridor to the kitchen. Molly was there, sitting at the table rather than bustling about as usual. She was talking on a hand mirror. She looked up as Simon entered.

"Simon is here now," she said. "Tell him." She handed Simon the mirror.

"Simon, it's good to see you again," said Hamil Fairborn.

"Hamil, where are you?" asked Simon. "Where's Sylvie?"

"I'm in West Faring," the Elf answered. "Simon,

Sylvie's been taken. They hit us in the marshes south of Portalis two days ago. We separated. I made it across the border yesterday. Sylvie was captured. I saw them take her away. She's being held in the Graystorm compound in Tintagel."

"You separated? You left her?"

"It was her idea," said Fairborn. "She knew she was the real target. Her father wanted her taken back to Tintagel as an example of traditional family fealty. She wanted me to get to the Commonwealth, to tell you what had happened."

"She's a prisoner?" asked Simon.

"Yes," said Fairborn. "They'll make an example of her, but she's more valuable to them as a symbol of the superiority of tradition. She's still a Graystorm, even in what they'll sell as disgrace."

Simon closed his eyes. *She's alive.* He knew that. He could feel her presence in his core. *She's alive.* "Are you all good?"

"I'm fine. A little tired is all."

"Get to the Peacekeeper station by the north gate in the Old Wall," said Simon. "Ask for Sergeant Utzler. Tell him I sent you, he'll arrange transport to Wycliffe House."

"Aye," said Fairborn. "Will do. See you soon. And Simon, there was nothing I could have done. I promise you, I'll do whatever it takes to get her back."

"I know you will." Simon swiped the mirror off.

Molly stood and put her arms around Simon's waist. She guided him to a chair, and he sat down. Molly stroked his hair the way she had done when he was ten and mourning his father. Hal came over and put a hand on his shoulder.

Simon looked at him. "I've put in for a leave of absence, Hal. At first it was because I thought I'd failed the team. Axhart told me to take a day to reconsider. I don't need a day. I have to get her out. I can't do that and still wear the badge."

"We're with you, lad," said Hal. He turned to Molly. "Call the family, love. We have work to do."

ACKNOWLEDGMENTS:

Many thanks to Sharon Skinner for her advice, editorial acumen, and friendship. Having a writing colleague whom you admire and respect pushing you to do better, to write more, to respect your readers and to create new worlds is a gift that I don't take lightly. Thanks also to Bob Nelson of Brick Cave Media for his support and belief in me as an author and member of his team.

Thanks also to my readers, especially those who have followed this series and waited patiently for this next installment. It's because of you that the world in these books lives and breathes.

As always, thanks to my wife Michele for her support, understanding, and tolerance of my obsession with both of my crafts.

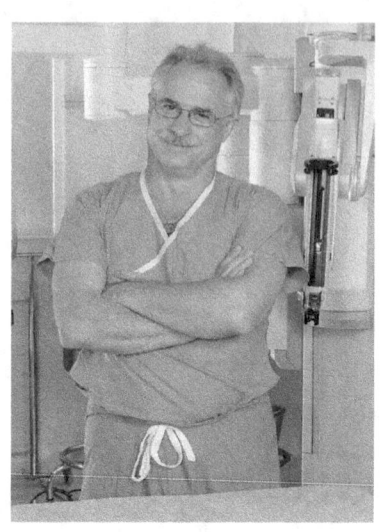

ABOUT THE AUTHOR:

Bruce Davis is a writer of Science Fiction and Fantasy. His current books, published by Brick Cave Media, include the Magic Law series of which Silver Magic is the third installment. It, along with Platinum Magic and Gold Magic are a mash-up of High Fantasy and Police Procedural set in a modern world. Also published by Brick Cave are his Profit Logbook series of SF novels about Zach Mbele, former Martian special forces commando and captain of the fast freighter, the Profit.

In his day job, he is a Trauma and Critical Care surgeon at a Phoenix area Level 1 Trauma Center. His independently published non-fiction memoir Dancing in the Operating Room is a glimpse into the life and training of a Trauma Surgeon.

He lives in Mesa, AZ with his wife who tolerates his passions for writing, science fiction conventions, kayaking, and collecting functional swords and custom knives.